GRO... IN GOR... ...N GLEN

KELLIE HAILES

Copyright © 2025 by Kellie Hailes

All rights reserved.

No part of this book may be reproduced in any form or by any electronic or mechanical means, including information storage and retrieval systems, without written permission from the author, except for the use of brief quotations in a book review. No AI training.

This book is a work of fiction. All names, characters and incidents depicted are a work of the author's imagination. Any resemblance to actual persons (living or dead), places, spaces, and buildings is completely coincidental.

ONE

Nodding her thanks to the bus driver, Natalia adjusted her heaving rucksack and took in the village she was to call home for a month. A simple lane greeted her, with a few shops on either side in the form of a grocer, a charity shop that also housed a community library, a café, pub, and an empty shop next to that.

Francesca, the farmer who'd offered her the job in Gordon Glen – a woman with a voice that was as raspy as her laugh was raucous – had told her it was a great place for young people to spend a summer, but the exuberant words on the phone didn't match the eerily quiet lane, bar for a couple of parked cars and a stray dog sniffing about the door of the closed café.

'River's great for swimming in. Nightlife is good. Or so I've heard. The shops aren't the worst. Or so I've heard. And the café's got the best food around.'

Natalia didn't need to be a mind reader for what came next.

'Or so I've heard.'

A quick web search of Gordon Glen hadn't added believability to the farmer's review...

Two stars – fine for a stop off in between going anywhere else.

Three stars – okay if you don't have your hopes all that high.

One star – there were women reading tarot cards in the pub and they looked at me weird. Since then, my cat has passed away, I lost my job, and my husband might be having an affair with our neighbour. If I could give zero stars, I would.

But having just quit her job – if you could call it quitting after being strongly advised that you were unsuited to your role as a retail assistant in a major clothing chain store due to being too honest with the customers – 'okay if you don't have your hopes all that high' was good enough for Natalia, because at this point in her twenty-five years on earth, her hopes were no longer all that high. Many jobs, no career, and two parents who disapproved of her every move had that effect on a girl.

With another doomed attempt at finding her place in the world under her belt, and the prospect of going to university to study something serious enough in order to please her parents in the offing, a trip down to Cornwall to take care of sunflowers for a month, described by the farmer as 'babysitting them', and later selling them to the public, had seemed like a good way to spend her time while figuring out what she was meant to do with her life.

But first, she had to find Gordon Farm.

Pulling her mobile phone out from her bag, Natalia brought up the maps app and tried to make sense of the directions Francesca had given her. Squinting at the screen, she followed the arrow that told her to walk down the lane towards another lane on the right.

Seconds later, the arrow went haywire, twisting her around, sending her back in the direction she'd just come from. With a huff of exasperation, Natalia did as she was told.

'Hey, watch where you're going.'

Startled by the terse remark, Natalia came to a halt, then noticed a dark-haired man, wearing tan cargo shorts and a black T-shirt, crouched a few feet in front of her, tomatoes in shades of yellow and black scattered around him.

'Oh, shit. Sorry. Did I do that?' Dropping her bag, Natalia ducked down and began helping him gather up the tomatoes.

The man glanced up, the thundercloud shrouding his expression morphing into one of surprise as he took Natalia in. A quick shake of his head saw the surprise disappear.

'Not your mistake. I thought I saw a field mouse and did some odd hoppity skippity jump thing to avoid it and ended up tripping over my feet.' He scanned the empty lane. 'I guess it scarpered away safely.' A smile softened his eyes, revealing the hint of a dimple in his right cheek. 'I just didn't want you tripping over me or squashing the tomatoes.'

'Kind of you.' Natalia returned the smile, then picked up a tomato, noticing it wasn't just black but more of an aubergine colour. 'What kind of tomatoes are these?'

'Indigo Rose. One of the many kinds of tomatoes that are grown by my Aunty Francesca. She had a mad Gordon woman whim to only grow heirloom fruit and veges, which turned out to not be so mad after all. Anyway, there's been a run on heirloom tomatoes at the shop and my sister said they needed a fresh lot immediately. Although these are done for. Unsaleable. I'll have to do another pick.'

'Aunty Francesca...' Natalia angled her head, trying to recall if the farmer with the same name had mentioned anything about farming fruit or vegetables. 'As in the owner of Gordon Farm?'

'The one and only.' Understanding dawned on the man's face, somehow brightening his brown eyes, giving them the look of a Tiger's Eye crystal Natalia had once bought from a market stall, only to be chastised by her father for buying something so superfluous. 'You're heading to Gordon Farm? You're the sunflower babysitter. Natalie was it? And did you know you were walking in the wrong direction?'

Natalia glared at her phone mutinously, then held her hand out. 'Natalia, actually. Natalia Hawthorne. And my mobile's map app was on the blink. Clearly. And you are?'

'Jeremy. Jeremy Gordon. Assistant manager of Gordon Farm.'

Jeremy reached out, and they shook hands.

'Oh.' Natalia withdrew her hand as a sharp bolt hit her palm. 'Sorry. Static electricity. Weird.' *And also weird that Jeremy's aunt had never once mentioned his existence, considering they'd be working on the same plot of land.*

'You say that now,' Jeremy murmured. 'But you'll get used to strange things happening in this village.'

Natalia cast her gaze over the lane once more, not seeing anything strange about it. 'It all looks quite normal to me. Albeit quiet.'

'Appearances can be deceiving.' Jeremy gathered up the last of the tomatoes, then pushed himself up. 'Now, since I'm going back there anyway, how about I escort you to Gordon Farm and show you around? You won't have to worry about taking care of the vegetables or fruit, that's all on me, but it's good to know the place's boundaries.'

'As in where it starts and where it ends?'

'As in where you don't want to walk if you don't want to be shot at by my aunt's superstitious gun-toting neighbour.'

'"A superstitious gun-toting neighbour"? Maybe this place is as strange as you say it is.' Natalia grinned, then went to pick up her rucksack but was beaten to it by Jeremy, who lifted it over his shoulder like it was as light as a small bag of apples.

'Oh, that's just the beginning of it.' Jeremy let out a

light snort. 'I think after being here a little while, you'll wonder if you've gone half-mad, or if the rest of the people here are.'

'Time will tell.' Natalia reached for her rucksack. 'And you don't have to take that. I'm more than capable.'

Jeremy's gaze went from the top of her five-foot eleven-inch auburn-haired head, down to the bottom of her red-sneakered toes. 'I'm sure you are, but I'm also not the type to let a lady do all the hard work when I'm also more than capable.'

Goose bumps raced over Natalia's skin at his words, and she shivered involuntarily. Was that a double entendre wrapped in a gentlemanly attitude, or had she just imagined it?

'But if you want to carry the tomatoes, I wouldn't say no.'

Natalia tucked her mobile back into the side pocket of her bag, then picked up the box. 'Deal.'

With a flourish of hand, Jeremy indicated it was time to get a move on, then started off down the lane.

'Morning, Mabel.' Jeremy nodded to a woman wearing a flippy yellow sundress. 'Good day for it.'

'That depends on what "it" is.' Mabel waggled her perfectly groomed brows up and down, then headed towards the charity shop.

Jeremy grinned. 'Mabel's had three husbands. Says she has to trade them in when they run out of steam. Keeps telling me I'm next.'

'Well, she's an attractive woman. You could do worse.'

'And it would sure make my sisters happy.' Fresh thunderclouds closed in around Jeremy's face and his shoulders bunched up for a moment, before he shook whatever had irritated him off. 'Anyway, enough about my sisters. Or Mabel. I've no interest in her, and no interest in pleasing someone if it does not also please myself. Life's too short. So, tell me Natalia Hawthorne, what brought you here? I would've thought being a sunflower babysitter would suit a young university student more than a grown woman?'

Natalia didn't know whether to agree with or feel irritated by Jeremy's assessment of the situation. Either way, she didn't know him well enough to be honest with him, just as he didn't know her well enough to divulge why his sisters were such a thorn in his side.

'Let's call it good timing.' She flashed him what she hoped was an easy-going, breezy smile. 'I finished up at a job and figured sunflower babysitting would be an enjoyable way to spend some time while I looked for a new one.' Natalia took in the rolling green hills that flanked either side of Glen Gordon, like two sentries, or two paths one could take. 'And I wasn't wrong. I mean, look at this place. It's beautiful. Peaceful. Although how it got the name "glen" when it's just a couple of hills rather than a valley and all the way down in Cornwall rather than up in Scotland, I do not know.'

'That would be another whimsical Gordon woman

moment.' Jeremy shifted the rucksack to his other shoulder. 'One I'm sure you'll hear the tale of should you meet the rest of my family. Or should I say *when*.'

'You make it sound like they'll be at my door pounding on it the second I get settled in.'

'Or half a second before you have.' Jeremy's chest rose then fell as he exhaled deeply. 'They're what you might call... a lot.'

'Oh.' Natalia followed Jeremy as he took the right turn she'd initially thought she was meant to take before her app had sent her almost literally straight into him. 'That sounds...'

'Like something you'd rather avoid? If you want, I can tell them you're more of a keep to yourself type and that they need to leave you alone.'

Natalia angled her head, surprised that a stranger could sum her up so perfectly. For as long as she could remember, she'd kept herself at a distance from people, preferring to keep relationships light and easy, knowing that letting a person in could lead to them hurting you with their expectations, their words. Both. 'How can you tell? Or was it just a guess?'

'Perhaps a simple case of takes one to know one. Although in my case I don't get a lot of opportunity to enjoy the alone part of being a loner.'

Natalia waited for Jeremy to fill in the blank space left by his silence, but no words came, which was understandable. He was hardly going to spill his feelings within ten minutes of meeting her. Just as she had no intention of rattling on about how she did not know what to do next with her life that didn't end up with her wandering into another dead-end job or being stuck at school studying something parent approved like law, accountancy, or, their personal favourite – medicine, given that was where they'd chosen to put their energy; her mother being a general practitioner, and her father, a surgeon.

Jeremy's chin dipped, his brows raising. 'Here we are. Home sweet home.'

They came to a stop in front of a stone and slate cottage. Its garden a glorious riot of colour, with pink and purple hydrangea bushes intermingling with soft yellow roses and showy dahlias in crimson red and creamy white. The only hint of order being the lavender that lined either side of the path that led to the front door.

It's like a witch's cottage. The thought sent a fresh wave of goose bumps spilling over Natalia, despite the heat of the early afternoon sun.

'I'm just warning you, the inside is as busy as the out.' Jeremy reached down and pulled a key out from under a welcome mat, which featured a barely there version of the word itself. The 'welcome' rubbed away from years, if not decades, of people coming and going.

Opening the door, he stepped aside. 'Welcome to your new abode.'

The gesture was so sweet, so sincere, Natalia could almost feel the concrete wall she kept around her heart soften.

Stepping inside, she quickly discovered Jeremy

hadn't been lying. She wouldn't be staying so much in an abode as an art gallery, with pieces displayed on every wall. A giant canvas featuring the main lane of Gordon Glen lined the entrance; a perfect rendition, albeit with a butcher where the empty shop now lay. In the painting's corner, a kitten played with a feathery dandelion. On closer inspection, you could see the dandelion seeds knocked off by the kitten's paw dancing in an invisible wind.

'Amazing,' she breathed.

'You've not seen anything yet.'

Jeremy led Natalia to the sitting room, where more art adorned the walls, along with sculptures of hares sitting in chairs having silent conversations on the mantlepiece. Their ears flip flopping this way and that, somehow expressing their emotions: amusement, astonishment and derision.

'This is amazing. All of it. Francesca never mentioned that she was an artist.'

Jeremy came to stand behind her, and Natalia caught the hint of an earthy, salty scent that spoke of a morning working at the farm. Underneath there was a touch of pine, perhaps from the soap he used to wash his hands or the foam he used to shave with. Either way, if you were the kind of person looking to be entranced by another's smell, Jeremy's was nothing short of intoxicating. But Natalia had no desire to be intoxicated. No matter how pleasant the man standing behind her appeared to be.

'That's because she's not. This is my mother's

work. The two grew up here with my uncle and my grandparents. As did the Gordons before them, and before them, and before them, right back to when the first Gordon settled here in sixteen sixty-one.' Jeremy touched the top of one hare's head, his lips pressing together as if he wanted to say more, but knew better than to do so.

'That's some family history.' Natalia noticed a large navy sweater strewn over the back of the worn, chestnut-coloured leather couch. Her pulse picked up as the potential meaning of its existence came to her. 'Jeremy, being that I didn't know about you when I applied for the job, and being that you work here, and being that this is a family home...'

'I don't live here.' Jeremy set Natalia's rucksack on the floor. 'You're not sharing this space with me. Or anyone else, for that matter. My place is on the other side of the village. It's the only way I can get any peace from my family.' He rolled his eyes, but there was a tightness at the corner of his lips, which reminded her of the way his demeanour had turned stormy when he'd mentioned his sisters.

'Good to know. I've not lived with anyone for many years and, if I were to be honest, I'm not in a hurry to do so again.'

'Roger that.' Jeremy brought two fingers up to his temple and saluted her. A series of beeps emitted from his cargo short's pocket. Pulling out his mobile, he swiped it open, then gave a sigh. 'According to my sister, the shop doesn't need tomatoes anymore.

Honestly, sometimes I feel like she sends me on these errands for her own amusement.'

Natalia shrugged. 'Can't say I have a sister, or any sibling, to know what that would feel like. Maybe, if you were to give her the benefit of the doubt, it was simply a case of the shop going quiet, which meant the tomato rush ended?'

'You're giving Tilly so much credit right now, it's not funny.' Sliding his mobile back in his pocket, Jeremy pointed towards the rear of the cottage. 'Kitchen, bathroom, two bedrooms. Upstairs is just storage. Nothing to see there, unless you like cobwebs. If you're heading out to investigate the land, the area as far as the sunflowers go, right to the edge where the river runs is yours to roam. If you see a stretch of land bordered by apple trees, turn around immediately, unless you want to risk your life.'

Natalia's heart twinged at the matter-of-fact instructions. Jeremy had mentioned showing her around, and some part of her had looked forward to his company, which was more than a touch unusual. Perhaps she'd allowed herself to get a little too lonely.

Refusing to show how his turnaround had affected her, Natalia gave Jeremy her brightest smile. 'Okay, thanks for that. So, I guess I'll be seeing you sooner rather than later?'

'Indeed, you will. The produce won't look after itself.' Jeremy screwed his nose up. 'Well, technically, they do most of the time.' He rolled his eyes in self-deprecation.

'But they still need someone to pick them, to take them to the shop, and maybe even to talk to them.'

Jeremy's brows arrowed together. 'Talk to them?'

Natalia shrugged. 'I've read that plants like being spoken to. Maybe I should read Shakespeare to the sunflowers?'

Jeremy widened his eyes, then grimaced. 'Makes me almost want to read a horror story to the courgettes to see if they shrivel up from fear.'

Natalia let out a huff of laughter. 'Perhaps. Or maybe they'll flourish out of fear of getting the chop?'

'Now I'm very tempted to give it a go just to see whose theory is correct.' Jeremy grinned. 'Well, I'd better get going. I was due at my family home thirty minutes ago, and the last thing I need is for that gaggle to be gasbagging about my whereabouts.'

Despite the eye roll and the moments of stormy expressions, Natalia could see that Jeremy had a world of love for those who might gasbag, even if they drove him a touch mad.

'Well, I won't keep you. I guess you know where the door is?'

'Only been going in and out of it for twenty-eight odd years.' Jeremy's smile widened. 'If you need anything, give me a call. My number's in the falling apart notebook by the phone in the hallway.' He went to turn, then paused. 'Oh, and if you find yourself at a loose end, feel free to come over to my family's home. We're just eating dinner, and probably drinking too much wine.'

'As well as gasbagging,' Natalia added.

'Exactly. It's nothing serious or pompous. Just a bunch of people shooting their mouths off and having a laugh. It's not much of a trek, either. If you go back the way we came, keep going up the lane, then take the next road left. The family home is down there. You'll hear us before you see us, but if you don't, look for the cottage with the thatched roof and sunshine yellow door. And before you brush off the invitation, you'll be more than welcome. It'd be good to see you. And it'll save you being interrupted and intruded on by that lot coming around here first.'

'Good. Glad. Grateful, even. And thank you. I'll think about it.' Natalia smiled then waved him off, not realising her own shoulders were hitched higher than usual until she heard the click of the front door closing.

Sighing a breath not of relief but of quiet exhaustion, Natalia collapsed on the couch, then pulled her legs up and cuddled them as she looked around the place she was to call home for the next month. A quartet of pigs danced in a circle on the coffee table before her. A duck appeared to howl at the sun in a painting on the wall opposite. And her palm still itched after the unexpected electric shock that came with meeting Jeremy and shaking his hand.

He was right. This place was a bit weird. Even more weirdly, for the first time in a long time – perhaps ever – she felt right at home.

TWO

'Here us before you see us. Waffle. Waffle. Waffle. Sunshine yellow door. Waffle. Waffle. Waffle. It'd be good to see you.'

Jeremy cringed into his glass of pinot gris as he replayed for possibly the gazillionth time in the last two hours, his interaction with Natalia. What a blathering idiot. Could he have spoken faster? Thrown more words at her? Appeared even more desperate to see her again even though he was likely to see her the next day when he went to work?

All these years of keeping women at a distance, except for when they consented to be kept at very much not a distance for one night only, and all it took was a tall woman with a cascade of hair the colour of Aunty Francesca's sofa and a pair of lips that matched her hair in lushness, and he morphed into a hormonal teenage boy with a harvest moon-sized crush. That, and his stomach had tugged in the oddest way when he first laid eyes on her, like some part of him recognised her. A thought he'd shrugged off, hating how woowoo it sounded; like something his sisters would babble on about. A sign of true love. Of curse-breaking love.

Except curses weren't real, and he wasn't about to fall in love just to make his sisters happy.

He pressed the thought into his brain and wished he could transfer it to an area lower so that it too could get the message that Natalia was off limits. Yes, she was only here for a short time, which in Jeremy's book equalled the perfect amount of time, but he was going to be working with her and seeing her regularly, which broke his well worked out rules of intimacy. Add to that the strange sense of knowing her already and the way his heart had turned into a trampoline that was being jumped on by a couple of medal winning trampolinists whenever he dared look at her for longer than five seconds, and Natalia was danger with a capital D. Also, a capital, A, N, G, E and R.

'Can you believe Aunty Francesca's actually left Gordon Glen to go on a cruise?' Tilly, his twin sister, shook her head, her mop of dark curls bouncing on her shoulders. 'I thought that woman was super glued to the farm. Do you think she's met someone online? Having a secret rendezvous with some lucky lady or gent?'

'The way she smells?' Gemma, the eldest of the Gordon family, waved her hand in front of her nose. 'I think you'd be hard-pressed to find someone who loves the scent of armpit odour and manure.'

Clare, the youngest of the siblings, circled her wine glass lazily, turning the liquid in it into a lazy whirlpool. 'Well, there's someone for everyone. Or so they say.'

'Not that we'd know.' Tilly mumbled, then shook her fist in the air while looking up at the ceiling. 'Show us the love, Cupid. We're ready. Our ovaries aren't getting any younger and I'm keen to make a baby or four. Better yet, show our bloody brother the love. If we're going to find it, he needs to find it first. Stupid Gordon curse,' she grumbled to herself, then took a good glug of wine.

'Love schmove. Some of us just want some action.' Gemma sighed. 'Honestly, we need to breathe some life into this place. I haven't seen a head turner in forever.'

'Well, that's not a shallow sentiment at all.' Jeremy smirked, letting out an 'ooph' as a cushion sailed through the air, catching him on the side of the head.

'Glass houses. Stones.' Gemma stuck her tongue out at Jeremy. 'If you were any shallower, you'd resemble a puddle with a thimble of water in it.'

'You say shallow. I say discerning.' Jeremy shrugged.

'And I say strumpet.' Tilly grinned, earning herself a high five from Clare.

'Well, at least I'm attractive to the opposite sex. Unlike you lot.' Jeremy repressed another grin as the faces around him darkened in mutiny.

His sisters were far too easy to wind up, and

despite being supposedly too mature to do so, he couldn't help himself. It was too fun watching them explode.

'You are an absolute bell end.'

'I'm telling Mum.'

'I hope your scrotum drops off.'

'Leave my son's scrotum alone.'

Jeremy attempted to duck as his mother swanned into the sitting room in a cloud of patchouli perfume and a jangle of jewellery, but her practiced hand mussed his hair before he could evade it.

'Never forget, girls, that Jeremy here is the only hope I have for grandchildren, and I won't have you cursing the bits that'll help with that.' Sinking into the sofa opposite Jeremy and Tilly, his mother smoothed her voluminous silk dress and eyed the bottle of wine. 'Glass. Wine. Now. Go.'

Clare scurried off to the kitchen, returning promptly with the glass, before pouring the wine and passing it to her mother.

'You're a dear.' His mother took a sip, then let out a long sigh. 'Oh, I needed that. My latest portrait is giving me all sorts of grief. I just can't get the nose quite right. It either looks like Old Woman McGinnity is about to sneeze or like she's smelled Francesca's underarms.'

'Which is why Aunty Francesca is not having a romantic rendezvous on the cruise.' Tilly raised her wine glass in triumph. 'Like I said.'

The family collapsed in laughter as she went to

take a sip but was too busy gloating to notice she'd missed her lips, the wine spilling down the front of her grey T-shirt.

'Shut up, the lot of you.' Tilly grumped, pulling the damp material away from her chest. 'I hope you all come down with the pox.'

Fresh howls of laughter rose at Tilly's indignation; the family falling about in various states of rocking and stomach clutching.

'Er, hello?'

The sound of a husky, but most definitely feminine voice that he'd not expected to hear, despite his invitation, snapped Jeremy back to reality.

'Natalia. Hi.' He stood up, unconsciously smoothing the bottle green polo shirt he'd changed into before heading to the family home. 'You found us.'

'You weren't wrong about the laughing.' Natalia remained in the doorway that led to the hall, her gaze going between each of the people in the sitting room. 'And if this is an imposition, if I'm one, I can leave. In fact, I should. This was a ridiculous idea.'

'What? No. You just got here.' Darting around the couch, Jeremy took Natalia by the elbow and ushered her to his spot on the couch. 'Tilly was just making a fool of herself. Tilly, Gemma, Clare, Mum, this is Natalia. Natalia, this is Tilly, Gemma, Clare and Mum.'

'You can call me Agnes, darling.' His mother extended a hand, and Natalia gave it the same brief shake she'd given Jeremy earlier.

Efficient, to the point, and so brief it made Jeremy wonder if Natalia hated touching people, or being touched by them.

'Nice to meet you, Agnes. Nice to meet all of you.' Natalia nodded, remaining in an upright position rather than sinking into the sofa's plush cushions.

The woman needed a wine. Stat.

Wasting no time in case she up and left, Jeremy raced to the kitchen, grabbed another glass, as well as a tea towel for Tilly, and hoofed it back to the sitting room. 'Tilly, catch.'

Tilly caught the towel with a nod of thanks, leaving Jeremy to fill the wine glass.

'Natalia, for you.' He held the glass in her direction. 'Sorry, I assumed you didn't mind a drink. Would you rather something else? Water? Something fizzy? Juice?'

'This'll do just fine. More than fine.' Taking the glass, Natalia took a fortifying sip, her spine curving ever so slightly into the cushion behind her. 'Sorry. I wouldn't usually barge into the home of people I don't know, especially when I've only known Jeremy here for all of twenty minutes. This is all very... odd of me.'

'Well, you're not the only person behaving oddly,' Gemma murmured into her glass, casting Jeremy a sly look.

Jeremy slid his hands into his shorts' pockets, afraid that if he didn't, he'd facepalm himself for waffling again. It was like Natalia had some bizarre effect on his tongue that caused it to go into high speed verbal diarrhea. Usually, he was the model of calm and collected around women. Knowing that he had no intentions of taking anything further than one night of mutual enjoyment meant there was nothing to lose, so there was no reason to get flustered.

'Are you saying that Tilly doesn't normally miss when it comes to drinking wine?' Natalia looked over at Tilly, who'd given up dabbing her T-shirt dry and had decided the tea towel was better stuffed down her chest as a barrier between the wet cloth and her bare skin.

'You're not wrong.' Tilly refilled her glass. 'That was a first. I think Gemma's referring to Je-'

'We need more wine.' Jeremy interrupted before Tilly could betray him by making it known that Natalia's presence was turning him into a babbling weirdo. 'Is there more, Mum?'

'Is there more wine? Does Gordon Glen need more single youths so that I might see you lot married and out of my hair? Of course there's more wine.' His mother raised her brows, then relaxed, smiling over at Natalia. 'I say that I want my littlest loves out of my hair, but I suspect if I ever finally marry them off they'll just end up coming here as often as ever, but with a plus one, or plus many if they end up making me grandbabies.'

Jeremy backed away, grateful to escape the sitting room for the quiet of the kitchen. He'd spent his adult life hearing his family go on about how he needed to find love so the curse could be broken and they could find love. The last thing he needed was to hear yet another repeat of the story, which surely was where the conversation was heading. Rarely did it head anywhere else, especially as the candles on their birthday cakes became more numerous and his lack of long-term love life became more obvious.

Finding a fresh bottle of pinot gris in the fridge's vegetable bin, he pressed it against his forehead and ordered his mind and body to pull itself together. Natalia was a new co-worker, someone who was helping out at the farm and then heading off for good. There was no reason to get antsy around her, or to think she differed from any other woman he'd met before.

Feeling his heart rate return to normal, he made his way back to the lounge.

'You know what we could do…' Clare tapped her chin, her eyes bright. 'Create an event for singles. Like a picnic or something. We could do it somewhere special. Somewhere romantic. Somewhere that'll look great in social media posts, so even if you walk away without finding the love of your life, or the like for now, you'll have fond memories.'

Jeremy groaned internally at the conversation he'd returned to. If they weren't rehashing the family curse, of course they'd be wahing on about love and dating and romance. They thought about nothing else. Slowly, he inched his way back towards the kitchen, hoping he could escape out the backdoor before anyone noticed he'd been gone for too long.

'Somewhere like the sunflower patch.' Gemma tipped back the rest of her wine. 'Even though it's not in full bloom, it would be a brilliant spot for people to meet the potential loves of their lives. Genius. Hell, we could do a whole sunflower season of events. I mean, Aunty Francesca was always going to open it to the public at the end for them to pick and buy the sunflowers, right? Why not take the opportunity to do more? To inject a bit more life into the old place. Natalia, what do you think?'

By the look on Natalia's face, which had become disturbingly ashen as Clare and Gemma had spouted their ideas in her direction, Natalia didn't think much of the idea at all. So much so, Jeremy abandoned his plan to take off. He couldn't leave Natalia alone with his love-mad sisters. Not when he'd been the one to suggest she come over. Whether he liked it or not, he was going to have to do the bigger thing and come to her rescue.

'Oh my god, you two.' Jeremy rolled his eyes as he sat the wine on the coffee table. 'Natalia's just got here. Literally. Actually. Whatever-it-is-illy. Give her a couple of days to settle in and find her feet before she's forced to deal with your overwhelming need to meet your better halves.'

'Well, someone has to do something around here if we're going to meet someone. More to the point, if *you're* going to meet someone.' Gemma clapped her hands together in the irritating older sister way she had that meant everything was sorted and no more correspondence was to be entered into. 'Anyway, it's decided. We're holding a singles picnic in the sunflowers to try to make that happen. And Natalia doesn't have to do it all by herself. Jeremy, you can help set up a social media page. Clare can put up flyers in the café and pub promoting it, as well as do the same in the pubs and cafes the villages and towns over. And Tilly can help with anything else when she's not working at the shop.'

'And what will you be doing?' Jeremy stared as pointedly as possible at his older sister, knowing the answer.

'I'll be the host on the day. That way I can get a good look at the talent, but not have to deal with those who clearly aren't suitable.'

'Natalia?' Jeremy turned to face her. 'What do you have to say? Are you okay with this? Because "no" is a perfectly acceptable answer.'

'Er,' Natalia grimaced. 'It's not exactly what I signed up for when I agreed to work for your aunt.'

'That's a yes, then?' Gemma nodded, gifting Natalia her most winning smile. 'Of course it's a yes. It'll be a great way for you to get to know the community while you're here. To integrate yourself. The last thing you want is to spend a month making like a hermit. You'll end up like Aunty Francesca.'

'Living her best life on a month-long cruise?' Tilly's smile was as saccharine sweet as Gemma's had been encouraging yet determined.

'Alone. Rattling around in a cobwebbed, cluttered

cottage. Talking to the field mice that like to wander inside for fun.'

'There's field mice?' Natalia's brows rose as her eyes widened. 'I didn't think about that.'

'You'll be fine. They'll only come out if they sense you desperately need friendship. So best you keep yourself busy.' Gemma raised her wine glass. 'To Picnicking in the Sunflowers.' Her eyebrows arrowed together. 'We should probably find a better name. Tilly, that can be your first job.'

Jeremy glanced around at his family as they followed suit, clinking glasses, leaving him and Natalia alone in their uncertainty that Gemma's plan was a good one.

Pulling out her phone, Natalia glanced at the screen, then stood up. 'I'm so sorry, I just realised it was getting on for dinner. I should leave.'

'No, no. Shan't hear of it.' His mother shook her head. 'You'll stay.'

Natalia made a show of stretching her arms above her head, her mouth opening wide in a yawn. 'So kind of you to offer, but the bus ride here has left me ready for an early night.'

Jeremy, knowing a getaway plan when he saw one, winked at Natalia. His heart doing a little jump as her lips quirked to the side, before she covered them in the faux throw of a fresh yawn.

'A rain check it will have to be.' His mother nodded. 'Have a safe walk home. Don't worry about the field mice. They're too busy gossiping about the latest arrival to bother her tonight.'

Natalia shot him a quizzical look at his mother's words, but Jeremy could only shrug. To understand his family, you had to be a part of it, and it would take more than a few words to explain their history, and therefore their future.

Following Natalia to the front door, he held it open for her. 'Thanks for coming. Sorry about all this.'

'Sorry? It's the happiest I've seen a family in years. Perhaps ever.' Her lips turned down for a split second before lifting once more. 'I won't avoid the rain check.'

'And they'll adore you for that.'

Silence descended between them, and Jeremy found himself caught between the strange sensation of wanting to kiss Natalia goodnight on the cheek and slapping her on the back with a hearty 'see you tomorrow'.

'Well. Good night.' Natalia flashed him the thumbs up.

Returning the gesture while feeling foolish for doing so, Jeremy shut the door and returned to the sitting room.

'Oh my god. Look at you. Look at your face. It's gone all pink.' Tilly's mouth curved into a long oval. 'You like her. Jeremy has caught a case of the fancies. I never thought I'd see the day. The women of the world are going to hold a national day of mourning when they discover you're off the market.'

'Even better. The curse will finally be broken.'

Clare's shoulders slumped as she exhaled a sigh of pure relief. 'Finally.'

'Mum, does he have to get married for it to break?'

'Is meeting Natalia enough?'

'Can they just date before we can find true love?''

'Or hook up a few times but in a way that leaves an indelible mark on his soul?'

'Or does it really have to be old-fashioned ring on finger, living in holy matrimony kind of thing?'

Defensiveness kicked in as his sisters began to plot the rest of his life, and Jeremy set his glass down, causing the remaining liquid to tsunami up and down its sides. 'You all need to settle down. I was embarrassed. That was why my cheeks were pink. I invited a new friend around and you ambushed her with one of your ridiculous plans.'

Tilly's low lip fell into a pout. 'No need to be mean.'

'Yeah,' Clare agreed. 'We're just excited, and we like her.'

'And you two look... right.' Gemma concluded. 'Something I think you know but don't want to admit.'

Jeremy looked to his mother for help, but her gaze was on the liquid she was swirling in her glass, her eyes distant. Probably scrying, as she was wont to do. Which meant she would be of no help to him.

'We'll have to get the cards out.'

'They'll tell us what's what.'

'And you won't be able to deny what future's

showing in those, Jeremy Gordon.' Gemma's imperious oldest sister voice was back.

Sighing, Jeremy went to the kitchen, hoping his lack of presence would see their chatter cease. Opening the pantry, he surveyed the food, not hungry, but unwilling to go back into the sitting room any time soon.

He wondered what Natalia would eat that night and hoped that Aunty Francesca had stocked the shelves before leaving. That she would not be left eating frozen fish fingers and chips, or stale honey sandwiches. Pushing the ponderances away, he shut the door a little too loudly, then leaned his head against the cool timber.

He loved his family. He did. They weren't bad people. But the more his sisters were determined to break the curse on his behalf, the more determined he was to ensure it remained. Even if that meant keeping the one woman he'd ever felt something for at arm's length.

THREE

Considering she'd slept the best she had in months, perhaps even years, Natalia found it hard to peel her eyes open. It was as if the field mice she'd been so wary of had scuttled into the bedroom and attached miniature magnets to her upper and lower lashes, causing them to stick together, rendering them unable to be opened without great effort.

Get up. Things to do. Promises to fulfil. A field to tend. Sunflowers to babysit.

Natalia managed to open her eyes a sliver and took in the watery rays of light filtering through the threadbare curtains. At least it wasn't too late. She could start her day in good stead and, all going well, continue it that way. Her ears perked up as from outside came the purr of a car engine. Natalia waited for it to continue down the lane, but it grew louder, before cutting out outside the bedroom window.

Francesca hadn't mentioned early morning visitors,

but then perhaps that was how people rolled in a small village. Early birds getting the worm and all that. Maybe it was a delivery, or a neighbour dropping off something they'd borrowed, not realising Francesca was away. Either way, it wouldn't do to greet them with sleep crusting her eyes and her hair looking like something the field mice might like to nest in.

Swinging her legs over the side of the bed, Natalia pushed herself into a sitting position, raked her hands through her hair, then reached over to her toilet bag and rifled around until she found a hair tie. Bending over, she twisted the still-tangled mane into a topknot, while appreciating the rush of blood to her head. Not as effective as a hit of icy cold water to the face, but it went some way to making her feel half-alive rather than like the walking dead.

The careful click of a car door shutting saw her grab the light cotton robe she packed and put it on, tying the belt tightly so as not to scandalise whoever was approaching the door with the sight of her skimpy shorty pyjamas.

Ducking down, Natalia checked her reflection in the small mirror Francesca kept on her one set of drawers. Bloodshot eyes, mice nest hair, dull complexion. Beautiful. Poking her tongue out at herself, she raced to the front door, intending to deal to the visitor as quickly as possible so she could get on with the rest of her day.

Plastering a smile upon her face, she pulled open the door. 'Good morning.'

The doorway was empty.

Not wanting to submit her feet to the cool pavers that made their way from the road frontage to the farmhouse, Natalia leaned over, searching for her mysterious guest. 'Hello?'

There wasn't a soul in sight. A car, for sure. But apparently it'd been driven by a ghost. Or perhaps a burglar. Which made a lot more sense when she stopped to think about it. Everything she'd ever seen on the tele or read about in books told her that small villages knew everything about everyone. So if the residents of Gordon Glen knew Francesca was away, then perhaps one of them had taken it upon themselves to relieve Francesca of her worldly belongings, not knowing that she'd hired a house and sunflower sitter.

Except now they'd heard her calling out, which meant they'd know she was there, and that she'd seen their car and was therefore an accessory to their act of thievery.

Shit.

Closing the door quietly, Natalia backed up, looking for something to use as a weapon should the thief come looking for her. Noticing an umbrella stand to the side of the front door, she grabbed the longest, largest umbrella, with the pointiest tip. It wouldn't kill, but it'd certainly maim if she swung or jabbed it hard enough.

Weapon in hand, she went into a crouch and crept down the hallway to the small kitchen, assuming the burglar would've gone around the back to check out the contents of the sheds that lined the boundary between the backyard and the farm's fields. As slowly as she could so as not to attract attention, Natalia pushed herself up and tried to see through the ruffled net curtain that hung in the kitchen window. No one was to be seen or heard. Was the pilferer, realising Natalia was onto them, preparing to sneak up on her and tie her up before they did their dastardly deed?

Natalia wished for nothing more than to squeeze her eyes shut against the fear and hide until everything was better, but doing that could lead to her own demise, or to having to explain to Francesca why her hard-earned tools were stolen under Natalia's watch. There was only one thing for it – she was going to have to go outside and confront the would-be criminal.

Ducking down once more, Natalia inhaled deeply, then exhaled.

You've got this. Rush out. Yell. Make a scene. Stab. Stab. Stab. Watch them scurry away. Job done.

Her eyes flew open as the click of a lock being opened met her ears. Jumping up, she swivelled around and ran for the door, pushing the umbrella out in front of her, ready to fight back whoever was about to come through.

'Get out of here, you arse bucket delinquent dickhead!'

Not thinking twice, worried that doing so would see her lose the advantage of surprise, Natalia heaved the umbrella forward, whooping in satisfaction as it connected with surprisingly firm flesh, pushing whoever was on the receiving end backwards and, from the 'ooph' that followed, onto their backside.

Rushing out, she lifted the umbrella high above the head, stopping as she was met with raised arms, an untucked t-shirt that had risen to reveal an extremely toned, with a hint of abs, stomach, and the pleading eyes of Jeremy.

'Oh. Shit.' Natalia lowered the umbrella, then let it drop to the ground. 'Jeremy. Oh. Shit. I thought you were a burglar. Oh. Sh-'

'Yes, I get it. "Oh shit".' Jeremy collapsed back on the ground. 'Are you going to say sorry instead of "shit" at any point? It might go some way to helping me feel a bit better about this situation.' Groaning, he rubbed his stomach where the umbrella had struck.

'Yes. Of course. Sorry.' Natalia settled onto her knees and brought her hands together. 'So sorry. Very sorry. Had I known you were coming this early I'd have not attacked you with an umbrella.'

'And here I was thinking that all this...' Jeremy's hand flicked up and down the length of Natalia's body. 'Was for my benefit.'

Natalia glanced down. *Oh, shit.* In the melee, her robe had opened, exposing her nightwear, which was most definitely not visitor-friendly. And especially not Jeremy-friendly. He was her colleague. Hell, he was pretty much her employer, being that he was the farm assistant. For him to see her in such a state was not only embarrassing, but inappropriate.

'Not for your benefit. Not for anyone's. Well,

except for my own' Standing up, Natalia re-tied her robe, making sure to double knot it, then reached out her hand. 'Here, let me help you up. I'll make you a cup of tea to say a proper sorry.'

Jeremy's lips quirked to the side, and for a moment Natalia was sure he was about to make a crude joke, indicating there were other ways to say a proper sorry. As quickly as the quirk appeared, it disappeared, and Jeremy took her hand.

'Thank you. A cool pack might be good, too. Pretty sure Aunty Francesca keeps one in the fridge where the cheese should be.'

Despite the cool morning air, Jeremy's skin felt electric against hers. As if the cells in their palms, when pressed together, connected, creating a heat source that felt uncomfortable, unnatural. Or perhaps too natural.

Unsettled by the feeling, Natalia dropped Jeremy's hand the moment he'd found his footing.

'So. Tea. And ice pack.' Turning around, Natalia strode back into the house, doing her best impression of a woman in control, a woman who knew what was what. A woman who'd not just accidentally all but flashed someone she barely knew, and whose hand was still burning from a feeling she couldn't quite explain. She peaked out the window to see Jeremy staring at his hand like it was foreign to him. It would seem she wasn't the only one.

Putting the strangeness of the situation to the side, Natalia opened the fridge and bathed in its chilly air.

Only stopping when she realised said air was causing her nipples to shrivel and make themselves known. Stupid thin fabric. It may have been the height of summer, but she'd been remiss not to bring her thickest, cosiest, most nipple-concealing bathrobe.

Finding the ice pack, she shut the fridge door and twisted around just enough to make throwing the ice pack through the backdoor to Jeremy possible without revealing her latest bodily faux pas.

'There you go. Pop that under your shirt.' Side-shuffling to the kitchen bench, Natalia flicked down the switch on the half-full kettle and began opening then shutting kitchen doors in an effort to find tea bags and sugar.

'How about you sit, I'll make the tea. I know this place like the back of my hand.'

Natalia jerked as Jeremy touched her hip ever so lightly, indicating he needed her to move to the side.

'Sorry. Didn't mean to frighten you.' He flashed an apologetic smile.

'No. It's nothing.' *If nothing's being zapped by weird, tingly sparks whenever you touch me.* 'Sorry. I'm just used to being on my own. Not used to people randomly touching me.'

'Oh.' Jeremy nodded as he opened the cupboard to the right of the kitchen bench and pulled out the tea bags and sugar, then went to the fridge and grabbed the milk. 'No boyfriend back from wherever you usually live then? Which is where exactly?'

'London. Born and bred.' Natalia pulled out one of

the small square dining table's chairs and sank into it, grateful to be on easy territory. So long as Jeremy didn't want to explore her existential crisis, she could talk love and life. Or lack of love and the basics of life. Anything deeper and she'd find an excuse to be anywhere else. 'And no boyfriend. Not for some time.'

'Last one did some damage?' Jeremy dropped tea bags into the mugs, which he'd pulled from a bottom cupboard to the left of the sink. 'Made a dent in the old ticker?'

'Er, no.' Natalia tried not to show her surprise that Jeremy would go down that lane. Not all romances ended in heartbreak, some simply ended. Lack of interest. Lack of commonality. General boredom with each other. 'More that the chemistry just sort of died after a couple of months. That's usually what happens, isn't it?'

Jeremy shrugged. 'I wouldn't know. I'm not a relationship kind of guy. I'd have thought you'd have figured that out by the way my sisters were going on last night.'

Despite his facing away from her, Natalia caught a hint of bitterness in Jeremy' tone. From his inability to be in a lasting relationship, or because he didn't like the way his sisters hassled him about it.

'Are you telling me you've never had a long-term relationship?'

'Not one. It's just not my kind of thing.' Pouring hot water into the mugs, Jeremy held up the sugar jar. 'You want?'

'No. Just a dash of milk's all I need. Thanks.'

'Same. I guess that means we're sweet enough already.' Turning around, his expression revealed no hint of the sourness Natalia had detected. If anything, with the golden morning light that was coming in the window edging his face and the warm smile lifting the corners of his lips, he looked every inch the charming man without a romantic or family-related care in the world, now or ever. 'So, you've not moved around a lot. Is that why you came down here? I mean, surely you could've found a filler job in London easily enough.'

It was Natalia's turn not to betray the truth. 'I like to keep things moving. Try new things. Stagnancy is death and all that.'

Jeremy's smile faltered. 'You really believe that?'

'Of course.' Natalia tipped her head to the side, unsure what it was she'd said that had seen Jeremy's lips curl downwards at the corners. 'You don't?'

'Well, yes. No. I mean...' Jeremy turned around and dashed the tea with milk, removed the bags and set them in the sink, then brought the mugs to the table. 'I guess there are different stagnancies that aren't really stagnant. Like, don't you have to be uncomfortable where you are to be stagnant? So if you're happy doing the same thing every day, you're not stagnant, you're satisfied.'

'Maybe.' Natalia swivelled her mug to the left, then back around to the right. 'But can you be satisfied if you're not actively pursuing anything new? Not striving to better yourself?'

'But why do you need to do that? Why create strife if everything's going okay as it is?' Jeremy picked up his mug, blew on the tea, then took a sip, the action pushing his upper lip out a little.

Natalia noticed that the colour of his lips were almost the exact shade of cherry blossoms. A colour that ought to be feminine, but on Jeremy only enhanced his inherent masculinity. Meanwhile, his words grew the picture she was building of a man who didn't like to try too hard in life. Who took the simple route rather than pushing himself to be more. Or maybe he was lucky enough to know who he was and what he wanted, unlike Natalia, who was still trying to figure it out. There was only one thing she knew for sure... it was too early in the day and in their burgeoning working relationship to be getting this deep and meaningful.

'But why is "okay" good enough? Isn't "okay" boring? Shouldn't we want more? Isn't that the human condition?' Natalia mentally rolled her eyes at herself. *So much for not getting deep and meaningful.* She waved her hand. 'What am I on about? It's too early for talks like this. These sorts of talks ought to be reserved for the best of friends, or strangers on a drunken night out. Not for two people who've known each other for less than twenty-four hours and whose paths keep crossing somewhat unexpectedly.'

'Or joining when one pops into the other's family home to say hi,' Jeremy grinned.

'That too.' Natalia wrinkled her nose at the memory. What she'd been thinking walking into a stranger's house, she didn't know. It wasn't something she'd ever done before, but as she'd sat in Francesca's strange living room, staring at a strange vista, feeling all very... strange, she'd decided to distract herself with a walk, half-wondering if she truly could hear Jeremy's family laughing before seeing the house he'd described. She'd believed his words to carry a touch of hyperbole until she'd heard the hooting and hollering, and its warmth had drawn her in. 'Thanks for the invite, by the way. I hadn't been quite prepared for how alone I'd feel here. I mean, I'm good with being alone. Spend a lot of time that way. But here, for some reason, it felt different.'

'Don't you mean lonely, rather than "alone". Just you in a little old cottage in the middle of nowhere trying to find your bearings?'

Natalia shuddered at the term 'lonely'. Lonely felt like a weakness. Like you couldn't handle your own company. Like you needed people. Something she most definitely did not require. People were fine, in small enough doses, but they weren't a necessity. Or at least she hadn't thought so until yesterday.

'I guess I'm used to the hustle and bustle of the city.' She wrapped her hands around the teacup, embracing its comforting heat. 'Which means I've learned something new about myself.'

'That you were stagnant in your own way? By never venturing out of the city?' Jeremy winked, letting her know he wasn't using her words against her, just gently teasing.

'That it was possible for me to feel truly lonely. It'll give me something else to work on. A bit of self-improvement, because stagnation's not just about being on the physical move And I don't mean that in an inappropriate way.' Natalia wrinkled her nose at Jeremy, who snort-chortled in return. 'So, why are you here so early? And how's the stomach feeling? Is the cool pack working?'

'It's fine.' Jeremy removed the cool pack and set it on the table. 'I'm made of strong stuff. And I'm always here this early in summer. It's a good time to harvest the vegetables for the shop, as well as the restaurants and cafes we supply. Means I can get the produce to them nice and early. Then, after I do the rest of my jobs, I can go home and do my own thing.'

Natalia leaned forward, sensing there was more to Jeremy's "own thing" than he was letting on. 'Which is?'

'Which is what?' His expression was as blank as his tone.

Natalia nudged his foot. 'Don't be glib. What's your own thing?'

'Nothing much. I just like to draw buildings. Come up with design ideas. That sort of thing.'

'For fun?' Natalia dipped her chin and raised her brows. 'Because that sounds more like an architect's job than a hobby.'

'Well, that'd be because I studied to become one. Then didn't.'

Jeremy's tone was measured, like he was walking a tightrope that he didn't want to fall off in case he revealed more than was comfortable.

'I see. That's impressive.' Natalia left it at that, sensing pressing Jeremy would see him make his excuses and head out to the fields; because that's what she'd do if she found herself in his shoes.

Jeremy pushed the tea away, a sure sign he was getting ready to make his escape if necessary. 'Are you sure you see? Because you're inspecting me like I'm a petri dish under a microscope.'

Natalia shrugged, keeping her demeanour easy. 'I guess I didn't see you as an architect.'

'That's because you saw me as a model who's on his way to ageing out, right?' He angled his arm and placed the palm of his hand on the nape of his neck, turning his head to the side, staring into the mid-distance for a few seconds before dropping his arm and turning back to Natalia. 'It's an easy mistake to make. Many have. I've spent half my life batting away agents.'

'Agents in Gordon Glen?' Natalia couldn't help but smile at the silliness being performed before her, even though she knew it was a distraction. 'Somehow I don't think a village this small is attracting modelling agents like moths to a lamp.'

'Nice of you to say I'm a lamp. Shiny. Bright. Something that gets turned on.'

Natalia groaned and covered her face with her

hands. 'I can't believe you just said that. That was terrible.'

'It was. I'm sorry. Habit.'

Cracking two of her fingers apart, Natalia eyeballed Jeremy. 'Do you say cheesy lines with a hint – or a lot – of sexual innuendo in front of women all the time?'

'Well, not all the time. Only when the mood strikes. And only if the mood is obviously reciprocal. And when it is, my personal brand of cheesy charm works.' He shrugged like it was no big deal, which, if Natalia thought it through without judgement, it really wasn't.

If women liked his pickup lines and no one was taking advantage of anyone, then Jeremy was well within his rights to acknowledge that he could charm a woman. Not that she'd ever be said woman. In her book, pickup lines held the same allure as thunderstorms. Fun for some, but for her, better neither seen nor heard.

'Well, you can keep your cheesy charm. I think I prefer the version of you that was kind enough to invite me over to your family's home and not make me feel awkward when I actually did the unthinkable and came.'

Jeremy waved away the compliment. 'It's just the way I was raised. I know my take on relationships isn't thought fondly of by some people – mainly my sisters. But I do try to not be a dick to people.'

'I can get on board with that. And for what few

thoughts that have entered my mind that have featured you, I can see through your actions that you're not a dick.' Natalia pushed her seat back and picked up her mug. 'And speaking of actions. It sounds like you've a job to do.'

Jeremy looked up at the clock above the kitchen sink. 'That I do.' Standing, he made his way to the back door. 'Thanks for the tea, and for the reminder that I need to work on my ab muscles so that the next time I'm stabbed by a half-naked lady holding an umbrella, it won't hurt quite so much.'

'Happy to test your progress when you're ready.' Natalia tried to make light of the situation while willing the flush she felt rising at being described as "half-naked" to dissipate.

'I'd love to say I'd take you up on that, but I'd hate for you to think I was treating you like any other woman by offering another way you could test the progress while being all cheeky and charming about it.' Jeremy waggled his brows and opened the door. 'That being said, if you can bear to be parted from your pyjamas, I wouldn't hate having a hand out there. It gets a bit quiet in the fields. It'd be nice to have someone to chat to.'

Natalia picked up the mugs and walked them to the sink. 'You know, I think I'll take you up on that. It'll be nice to get my hands dirty.' She paused, knowing it was too late to take the words back. 'No double entendre intended.'

Jeremy laughed. 'Of course not. See you out there.'

With a nod he was gone, leaving Natalia to wash the mugs and wonder what would happen if she dropped a double entendre that was very much intended. Placing the mugs on the drying rack, she snorted at the absurdity of the idea. Weird touching tingles and decent conversations aside, there was as much chance of her changing Jeremy's mind about relationships as there was her figuring out a way to please her parents. And some things weren't worth the time or effort.

FOUR

Picking up the wheelbarrow, Jeremy rolled it to the next row over, where plump yellow courgettes nestled amongst their beds of leafy green. Setting it down, he eyed the freshly harvested goods inside. Lettuces, sweetcorn and carrots nestled together, ready for delivery, with the courgettes, beans and tomatoes to come, along with the increasingly popular elephant garlic that his aunty had taken to growing in the last few years.

When she'd announced she was swapping the farm's produce from the tried-and-true types of vegetables to heirloom varieties, the locals had thought she'd finally gone full mad and that she'd go broke within a couple of years. But word quickly spread of the different varieties and the quality, and now she was making more money than she'd ever dreamed of.

Except that Aunty Francesca being Aunty

Francesca – Aunty Francesca being a Gordon woman – would tell anyone who'd listened that she wasn't some savvy business woman but that she'd had a vision about the farm producing heirloom products, which is why she'd done it.

'One must follow the muse, my dear,' she'd told him on more than one occasion.

Apparently, his muse had gone missing. That's if Jeremy ever had one to start with. Muses seemed to give the Gordon men a miss. Perhaps that's why they were surrounded by bossy, interfering, well-meaning women.

Bending down, he pulled out his trusty knife and got to work harvesting the courgettes, while trying not to let the image of light blue cotton shorty pyjamas edged in lace of the same colour that revealed long lengths of strong looking limbs and silky-smooth skin distract him. He was here to work, not wonder.

Although it was hard not to.

Everything about Natalia was attractive to him. Which was a problem. Physically, she was like an eighty's supermodel. Muscular, firm, curvaceous, nearly as tall as he was, with hair that gleamed with health, even when up in a bun first thing in the morning when most women he knew were apologising about bed head, if not full on rats' nests. Then there was her glowing skin, her eyes that danced not with only good humour but also intelligence and a shrewdness that told him she would not allow herself to be messed with.

All of which made her the absolute worst choice of woman. She'd made it clear she wasn't interested in his snappy one liners or tongue-in-cheek humour. What she preferred was his kindness, his thoughtfulness, his friendship. And Jeremy knew better than to mix friendship with pleasure.

The only trait that made Natalia right for right now? Her moveability. It didn't take a genius or hours spent in deep conversation to figure out Natalia didn't know what she wanted, or where she wanted it. Her admittance of having multiple jobs was proof of that, as was the fact that she was willing to travel all the way to the-middle-of-nowhere Cornwall to spend a month tending sunflowers.

If only he didn't already like her so much. If only she didn't set off all sorts of odd tugs at his solar plexus and sparks over his skin whenever she was near. It was like her presence set off an internal warning system that wooing her would lead to no good.

'Why don't you just snap them off their stems?'

Jeremy focused on the work at hand, hating that even Natalia's voice was attractive. Lower in register, husky, but with a sweetness. Not unlike dark chocolate. His other great weakness.

'If I snap them off, it could hurt the main plant. Cutting them at the stem's the best way to do it.'

'And how do you know when they're ready to pull?'

'Not pull. Cut.' Jeremy looked up and immediately wished he hadn't.

If the shorty pyjamas had him tongue tied and hot and flustered, then Natalia's current get up was going to give him a heart attack.

Calm down, lad. It's not the first time you've seen a woman in a pair of denim shorts and a white tank top.

Except those women didn't have shapely calves that led up to the kind of firm thighs that his sisters would bleat over whenever they saw them in a fitness magazine, complaining that it was unrealistic for women to have thighs like that, that they could only be painted on with body makeup. And while the tank top covered more than the shorty pyjamas had, it curved over Natalia's firm-looking stomach and breasts, emphasising what lay underneath.

Which you are not *to think about.*

Natalia squatted beside him, bringing with her the scent of honeydew. Sweet, with a touch of musk. Would her skin taste of it? Her lips? Her...

Would you stop paying attention to the woman and get back to work? You're acting like a lovestruck teen.

Except he wasn't a teen, and he wasn't in love. Nor did he ever intend to be.

'And why's this one so big?' Natalia lifted a leaf to reveal a courgette that had morphed into a marrow.

'Because I didn't pay good enough attention the last few picks.' Jeremy shuffled over to the offending vegetable and sliced it off the plant. 'Here, pop it in the wheelbarrow. It's still sellable, but not ideal.'

'It's still a courgette, right? Wouldn't you want it bigger?'

God, could she stop talking about big things and wanting things that were bigger? It was hard enough to keep his own courgette from growing bigger than Jeremy wanted whenever Natalia got too close, looked too sweet, or fixed him with a knowing eye and called him on his b.s.

Jeremy looked up at Natalia. 'It's a marrow.'

'But it's on the courgette plant.'

'Courgette vines.' Jeremy gently corrected Natalia, wishing that her lack of botanical knowledge could magically make her less attractive. 'When they get too large, we call them marrows.'

'And you can still eat them? But they're not as popular? Even though they're cheaper.' Natalia's brows drew closer together with every question, creating a line between them that Jeremy wanted to reach out and massage away.

'They're not as nice in texture, nor as flavoursome in taste. But they're good in stews. You can also make them into a bake, or even a cake. That wasn't meant to rhyme.'

'Of course not.' Natalia placed the marrow down next to the purple potatoes and gave it a loving pat. 'A marrow in a barrow. Like a courgette but not as narrow.'

'Is the rest of our conversation going to sound like a nursery rhyme book, because if so I think I'll send you to the sunflower field earlier than I'd planned.'

'You had more plans for me?' Natalia picked up the

wheelbarrow by its handles and followed Jeremy to the garlic row.

'Well, I figured I could get you to help me pack the vegetables into the car, then I could take you into town, show you the shop, buy you a coffee at the café afterwards to say thanks.' Jeremy's face flushed as the words came out. 'Which sounds like…'

'Not a date, a thank you. Don't worry. I know I'm not your type. You'd have to see me too often, for one.'

'Exactly.' Jeremy nodded and made a show of fanning his face, banishing the last of his embarrassment. 'Thanks for not making that awkward. I made the mistake of asking one of my sisters' friends out for coffee one day after they'd helped me carry a particularly big order into the pub and she took it to mean that I'd finally noticed her, wanted a full-fledged relationship, and that the coffee was going to lead to commitment.'

Natalia grimaced. 'Awkward, indeed.'

'More so when she started turning up at family dinners and trying to hold my hand in front of my siblings. They were having absolute kittens, thinking their loveless brother had finally met his match.' Jeremy grabbed the hand trowel from the wheelbarrow and squatted down, loosening the soil around half a dozen bulbs, then lifted them out, shaking the dirt off the fleshy bulbs as he went. 'So, I had to have a chat with them, and her, and nobody spoke to me for a week. Actually, their friend never spoke to me again, but it wouldn't have been fair to mislead her.'

'Well, for one it would've hindered your pullability.' Natalia took the bulbs from him and set them next to the marrow. 'And you couldn't have that.'

'Well, no.' Jeremy placed the trowel in the tool bucket, picked up the wheelbarrow and began the walk around the farmhouse to the car. 'It's hard to explain that you're actually single when there's a woman hanging off your arm.' Setting the wheelbarrow down, he opened the boot of his old, beat-up sedan.

'Funny, I didn't picture you being the kind of person to have a sensible car.' Natalia began placing the vegetables into the boxes Jeremy has prepared. 'Kind of how I wouldn't have ever thought of you as studying to be an architect.'

'You've done an awful lot of thinking about me in the last wee bit.' Jeremy nudged Natalia's side with his elbow. 'Do I have a case of my sisters' friend part deux on my hands?'

'Ha. No.' Natalia shut the sedan's boot. 'More like the tidbits you've shared about yourself have been surprising. It's nice to be surprised.'

Jeremy picked up the wheelbarrow and pushed it back to the shed, then locked it away. 'Well, that's all there is, I'm afraid. Jeremy Gordon – failed architect cum farmer, brother to three love-mad sisters, and chronically, determinedly single. No more surprises for you.'

'Hmmm,' Natalia crossed her arms. 'I'm not so sure about that.'

Jeremy shrugged. 'Think what you like, but I'm a

simple man. Anyway, how about you lock up the cottage and meet me in the car?'

'Sounds good. I'll be back in two ticks.'

Jeremy settled into the front seat and exhaled. Thank god Natalia was here for a month and no longer. Her inability to see him as everyone else did – easy going, unbothered, so chill he could happily live in a freezer – could be dangerous. Thankfully, she was only in Gordon Glen for a month. Any longer and he suspected she'd eventually pry the truth from him that no one else in the village had even considered might be there – that underneath the relaxed veneer was a person with walls high and boundaries fortified, all because he was sick and tired of the pressures placed upon him by his family. The expectation from them to do as they wanted so grand he could only fight back by keeping his self to himself.

The car shifted as Natalia settled into the passenger seat, fanning herself with an old folded up newspaper.

'Is it always this hot this early? I'm going to need one of those battery-powered miniature fans if I'm going to survive the next month.'

Jeremy flapped his hands in her direction, noting the fine beading of sweat upon her chest and forehead. 'Not usually. I mean, we have heat waves like anyone else, but usually it's fairly temperate.'

'Temperate.' Natalia chuckled. Husky and low, like they'd shared an intimate moment, it sent goose bumps scurrying over Jeremy's skin. 'That's an old man's word if ever I heard of one. Can't say I've ever heard anyone say it in real life.'

'You weren't hanging out with old men in London?'

'Not unless they were paying me good money.' Natalia's top teeth dug into her lower lip for a moment. 'That sounded…'

'Like you were a sugar baby?'

'Is that what they're called? Although, I suppose if you're a sugar baby, that means you have a sugar daddy… or would that make you a sugar daughter?' Natalia screwed up her nose, then gagged. 'Nope. Not that. That's really wrong. Super wrong. The wrongest of wrong. And definitive proof I was never a sugar anything.'

'Agreed.' Starting the car, Jeremy began the two-minute drive to the shops. 'So, who did you hang out with in London, if not old men who paid you good money?'

'For the record, it was to make them coffee. I worked in a café close to a retirement village.' Natalia's grin disappeared and her teeth met her bottom lip again, almost as if she subconsciously didn't want to answer. That opening up about her life would start a wave of openness that she would struggle to stop.

Or maybe Jeremy was projecting. Knowing that if anyone had bothered to ask him about his university days, more than how his marks were and what he got up to on the weekend, he too would clam up. Knowing that for two years his life had opened up. That he'd seen a different way of living. One he'd embraced until the pull to return had become too much. The guilt at leaving his family in flux having overwhelmed him. Leaving him angry, resentful, and more determined than ever to stand apart from the Gordon family. As much as they would let him.

Natalia released her lip and gave Jeremy a weak smile. 'As for who I spent time with, it was workmates, mostly. I'm not close with my parents and I'm an only child, so I kind of had to create my own family, except...' She gave a small shrug. 'I'm not really great at that.'

'Only child syndrome type thing?' Jeremy asked with a wink. 'Don't like to share your toys? Used to getting your own way?'

'I'm going to decide that you're teasing.' Natalia tugged at a frayed thread on her jean shorts.

'Good. Because I am. Truth be told, I can't imagine what it's like to grow up with no one but yourself.' Jeremy turned into the village lane, then pulled into a park outside the shop. The lane was its usual weekday quiet; Gordon Glen only filling up with visitors on the weekends as they travelled from one place to another. The area wasn't struggling, but nor was it thriving. Maybe his sisters' madcap singles idea might help fill some of the human void. If anything, it might provide a welcome distraction from the woman sitting next to him.

'Your sisters must've kept you on your toes.' Natalia opened her door and went to the back of the car, opening the boot and taking a box in arm without being asked. 'Or were you coddled being the only boy?'

Jeremy took the other box with a snort, then shut the boot. 'The idea of being coddled by that lot is as likely as me being picked to join the English cricket team any time soon.'

Striding ahead of Natalia, he opened the door for her, then stepped aside to give her space to enter. With a nod of thanks, she stepped over the threshold; her warm, melon scent enveloping Jeremy in a way that would've been enticing, if it didn't set off the internal warning bell in his heart that had only turned up after his first interaction with Natalia.

'I guess that's why you've had such success being a ladies' man. You might be in it for a short time, not a long time, but living with three sisters and, from what I saw, a dominant-type mother, you've had no choice but to mind your manners and treat women with respect.'

'And that'll be why I've never found myself on the wrong end of an accusing finger.' Jeremy sat his box of vegetables down on the farm stall counter and waited for Natalia to follow suit. 'Well, apart from that one time.'

'But we don't talk about that.' Natalia began loading the tomatoes into the empty basket labelled with the name of said fruit.

Jeremy added 'great initiative' to the list of Natalia's attributes that he was most certainly not allowed to dwell on. 'Well, we try not to. And once, for the first time in ever, is more than enough.'

'Agreed. It sounded deeply uncomfortable.'

With a grimace, Natalia focused on stacking the fruit, not saying another word until she had carefully placed every piece of produce in its basket.

Placing the courgettes in place, Jeremy dusted off his hands and picked up his boxes, Natalia following suit. 'Thanks for that. Last time I asked Tilly to help, I pretty much had to do everything for her. Apparently stacking produce at her place of work was too weird for words.'

'Has she always worked here?'

Jeremy nodded. 'Since school. Went full time after she left. Seems happy enough, but sometimes I wonder if she's stuck in a rut that she doesn't know how to get out of.'

'Or maybe she's waiting for Prince Charming to ride in on his late model electric vehicle and whisk her away?'

'More like waiting for Prince Charming to ride in on his late model electric vehicle, fall in love with the area, decide to settle down so the only thing she'll have to change is the bed she sleeps in. That's if she doesn't convince him to stay at mum and dad's.'

'Your sister still lives at home? At her age?' Natalia's jaw dropped, and Jeremy resisted the urge to tuck her perfectly rounded chin under his finger before bringing her lush lips together once more. 'On purpose?'

'If you had a mother who doted on her children, who loved cooking for them, picking up after them, helping them out, wouldn't you want to stay at home rather than fly the coop?'

'Sounds idyllic.' Natalia tweaked a tomato. 'So, what made you leave?'

'Well, bringing a woman home to mum when the intention is a one night only, no strings attached thing, can send the wrong signal. Especially in my family.'

'Is young Jeremy here bragging about his conquests?'

A raspy voice, rich with bemusement, interrupted their conversation. Jeremy rolled his eyes at Natalia, glad that he had his back to the shop's owner, Finnius, because if he'd caught the eye roll, Jeremy would have his ear clipped in two seconds flat. Finnius may be in his nineties, but he was as quick with a physical and verbal retort.

Natalia smiled as Finnius came to stand between them. 'No, not at all. Jeremy was simply explaining that he'd rather not bring home a woman to his mother unless it was serious.'

Finnius snorted. 'Serious? The lad barely knows the meaning of the word. Only thing he's serious about is his work, but he's only a bloody farmer. Not even a real one. Had his job given to him when he returned without a degree from university. Good bloody waste of money, that was.'

Natalia's smile remained in place, but the rising of

her cheekbones suggested tension. 'Now, now, sir. I'm sorry, what's your name?'

'Finnius. Finnius McKee.' Finnius thrust his hand out, and Natalia shook it in the efficient manner that Jeremy had grown accustomed to seeing.

'Finnius, not everyone finds their place in the world easily. Some people have to try different things. And with that comes acceptance.'

'Acceptance?' FInnius snorted again. 'How so?'

'Well, if you learn to accept that not everyone lives life the way you think they ought to, you save yourself a lot of unnecessary stress. And you don't look like a pillock when you voice an unwanted or unasked for opinion.'

Finnius stroked the grey scrag that peppered his jawline. 'Can't say I've thought of it like that.'

'Few do.' Natalia's cheekbones lowered. 'Which is why you ought to apologise to Jeremy for being so rude just now.'

Much as Natalia's jaw had dropped moments before, Finnius' dropped so hard that Jeremy was surprised it didn't smash through the wooden floorboards. No one spoke to Finnius like that. No one dared. Until now.

Despite knowing better, admiration added to the attraction he felt for Natalia. He'd never met another woman like her. Not even his own sisters or mother would dare take on Finnius. He'd been known to bar people from buying food at the shop when they'd tried.

'Er, well...' Finnius's gaze went to his beaten-up

leather loafers. 'I guess, ah, sorry is in order, young Jeremy. I'll think before I speak next time.'

'Thank you, Finnius. Much appreciated.' Jeremy nodded in Finnius' direction, then found himself being manhandled toward the door.

'Well, we must be off. Jeremy promised me a coffee at the café. Happy selling, Finnius.' With a wave and an even broader smile, Natalia opened the shop's door and dragged Jeremy out into the sunshine. 'How rude was he?'

'He was being Finnius.' Jeremy didn't know why he was all but apologising for the man, but considering Finnius was doing the community a service by stocking his aunt's vegetables, he felt somewhat obliged to defend him. 'He's ninety-three, he gets to be that way.'

'I don't think age excuses bad behaviour.' Natalia glanced down, then tugged away her hand, which was still lying upon Jeremy's forearm, sending off so much heat that Jeremy was surprised his skin wasn't imprinted with a scorch mark.

'I'll remind you of that when you're his age.' Jeremy nodded to the café. 'Shall we?'

Natalia gently nudged him. 'You think we'll still know each other when we're in our nineties?'

Her tone was good humoured, but the words sent a gymnast flick-flacking through Jeremy's lower stomach. When was the last time he'd said anything to a woman that might indicate longevity in a relationship?

He immediately knew the answer: never.

'Probably not. You don't strike me as a small village kind of person.'

Jeremy opened the door to the café, ignoring the flash of hurt that bolted through Natalia's eyes. He'd hit a nerve, and he didn't know why. What he did know was that he had to pretend not to care. His independence depended on it.

FIVE

'Look at what the cat dragged in.'

Natalia followed the sound of the voice to a table filled with Jeremy's sisters, whose gazes were laser-beamed on the two of them, their eyes sparkling with interest, their lips quirked to the side. The family resemblance more obvious than ever.

What would that feel like? To have someone who looked like you, who cackled like you, who was so similar to you, but not you? To share a history that started from the moment you were born? To squabble and make up, to cuddle and love, to simply be with a person who knew you as well as you knew yourself – if not better?

'You three,' Jeremy retorted. 'That's what the cat dragged in.' Ignoring his sisters, he turned to Natalia. 'Do you want to find a seat? Preferably one that's as far away from this lot as possible? I'll order coffees and a bite to eat. Is there anything you're allergic to, straight up hate, or would prefer to eat over something else?'

Natalia took in the food cabinet, her stomach gurgling at the sight of freshly made scones, muffins, sweet and savoury brioches, wraps and filled bagels, not to mention quiches, sausage rolls and pies. 'That all looks amazing. I'll leave it up to you to choose, but I'll take a cappuccino for my coffee.'

'Consider it done.' With a curt nod, Jeremy turned his back to her, leaving Natalia to source the seats.

'Natalia, get those long legs over here,' Tilly called out, as her sisters pulled over another table and placed the chairs around the new seating arrangement. 'We've got big things to discuss. This sunflower festival is going to be amazing.'

Sunflower festival? When had one picnic for singles along with an end-of-season pick-your-own day, become an entire festival?

Seeing no other option that wouldn't insult Jeremy's family, especially when they'd made every effort to make her feel welcome on the two occasions she'd met them, Natalia took a seat and sent a mental 'sorry' to Jeremy who was engaged in conversation with the café owner. An attractive woman, who looked to be around Natalia's age, but on the short side with a halo of golden curls framing her pretty face, despite her hair being pulled back into a ballerina bun.

'Oh, that's Sarah. You don't have to worry about her.' Clare patted Natalia on the forearm. 'She goes out with Jeremy's best friend, Chris. They live together and everything. On the marriage track, if you ask me.'

'That's nice for them.' Natalia smiled politely, her gut clenching at the idea that the girls thought she had any interest in their brother. 'And I wasn't worried about her. There's nothing going on between Jeremy and me. This isn't a date. Just a thank you for helping Jeremy stock the shop this morning.'

'If you say so.' Clare's eyes twinkled. 'But it's okay if you change your mind. More than okay. We'd be thrilled.'

Not wanting to protest too much or to give the girls hope, Natalia smiled and decided it was time to change the topic. 'So, what's this about a festival? Last time I heard there was a picnic being proposed, but no mention of a festival. And I'm not sure how your aunt would feel about people traipsing up and down her sunflower field willy nilly. Wouldn't you need to check with her first?'

'It's just you two look so good together.' Tilly continued, ignoring Natalia's question. 'And it's high time he gave up his bachelor ways. The rest of us aren't getting any younger.'

Natalia got the distinct impression she was missing something. 'Er, what has Jeremy's relationship status got to do with you? You're making it sound like there's some family rule that means you can't date until he dates.'

'You mean Jeremy hasn't told you?' Gemma's brows rose so high they nearly hit her hairline.

'Jeremy hasn't told Natalia what?' Jeremy sank into the chair next to Natalia.

'About the curse.' Tilly dipped her chin, her voice deep with meaning.

'Oh god, we're not going on about that, are we?' Jeremy rubbed the back of his neck. 'Natalia doesn't need to find out just how odd this family is.'

'It's not odd. It's history. It's a fact. And it's important.' Gemma turned to Clare. 'Clare, you should tell it.'

'Uh, uh,' Clare replied, shaking her head. 'Not me. I always get it a little mixed up.'

'And I always end up angry at Jeremy.' Gemma frowned at her brother. 'He's really letting down the team.'

'And I like hearing it rather than saying it.' Tilly relaxed back in her seat. 'Jeremy should be the one to tell it.'

'Tilly, no.' Jeremy mimed zipping his lips shut.

'Come on, darling brother. It's technically centred around you, you know.' Tilly gave an encouraging nod. 'And you've never once told it.'

Jeremy unzipped his lips. 'Because it's a silly tale and I don't believe in it, and it has nothing to do with me.' He re-zipped and sat back, refusing to do his sisters' bidding.

Natalia watched the interaction, half feeling sorry for Jeremy being bossed around, half interested to see who'd win and tell the tale that she was becoming increasingly interested in hearing.

'If that's true, and it has nothing to do with you,' Gemma's brows bunched together in a frown. 'Then why is it that generation after generation of Gordon women haven't been able to fall happily in love until the first male born does? Why is it that whenever we girls, or the girls who've gone before us, meet a person we like, it's doomed to fail until the penised one gives his heart to another? Why is it – and this might be the worst part of all, depending on what your goals or dreams are – we can't leave Gordon Glen for any decent length of time without something bad happening to us until you're all loved up with hearts in your eyes and a dearly beloved on your arm?'

'Stupid curse,' Clare chuntered. 'Sometimes I wish Rhona had just allowed herself to be captured, then tried and found guilty as a witch. Then at least none of this would be happening.'

'If that happened, oh brainless one,' sarcasm dripped off Gemma's tongue. 'Then none of us would be here.'

'What Gemma said.' Tilly rolled her eyes, then let out a huff. 'Well, if Jeremy won't tell the tale, then I guess it's on me. We can't leave poor Natalia hanging.'

Natalia held her hands up. 'I'm not hanging. I'm fine not to know.'

'You are and you need to know.' Gemma raised her brows. 'So let Tilly talk. Tilly, go.'

Sitting up straighter, an air of importance shrouding her, Tilly waited until all eyes were on her, then began. 'Back in the days of the Scottish witch trials, Rhona Gordon was accused of witchcraft. Apparently, talking to birds and knowing how to heal people with plants was a no-no. Rhona's lover got wind of what was to come and helped Rhona escape, but had to stay behind to look after his own family.'

'Scum,' Clare sneered.

'Dirty rotten cheater,' Gemma screwed her nose up.

'Some might say an affair goes both ways.' Jeremy piped up, then shrank as his sisters glared at him.

'So, Rhona made her way down to Cornwall,' Tilly raised her voice, silencing the trio. 'Tired, hungry and sure she was safe from harm, she stumbled into an area with a river, flanked by hills – albeit little ones – and a magical aura that reminded her of home. So, she settled into the area, using what money her lover had given her to have the cottage you're staying in Natalia built. At least a little bit of it. There were extensions over the years. Plumbing. Electricity. All that good stuff.'

'Apart from the affair, that all sounds well and good.' Natalia shook her head. 'So, what caused the curse?'

'She was pregnant.' Tilly paused dramatically. 'With her lover's babies. Twins. A boy and a girl. Nursing a broken heart, while determined to keep the one reminder...'

'Two reminders,' Gemma interrupted.

'Whatever.' Tilly rolled her eyes. 'Determined to keep the *two* reminders of her long-lost beau safe and to never be alone herself ever again, Rhona imbued the Glen with a force that meant her family could not leave the Glen for any decent period until the firstborn son found true love.'

'That all sounds rather controlling.' Natalia couldn't help but think, based on the interactions of the Gordon women with their brother, that the apples hadn't fallen far from the tree.

'Oh, that's not all there is.' Tilly grimaced. 'Over time, many a Gordon woman tried to sidestep the curse only to fall foul of it, such as trying to leave the area for more than a short amount of time, or marrying a man before the first-born son fell in love, only for the union to fall apart, leaving the woman heartbroken for life. Thankfully, those affected recorded their failings, leaving us with a decent road map of what not to do.'

'For example.' Gemma lifted her thumb up. 'We must carry on the Gordon name. We can't take our future beloved's last name, they must take ours. Rhona apparently believed there was strength in the Gordon name, and that by taking a man's surname our strength would falter.'

'And how does that work?' Natalia kept her burgeoning smile to herself. As mad as the story was, she didn't want to insult the Gordon girls, as it was clearly important to them.

'Well, one ancestor's husband had a heart attack and died after she took his name, and another's husband went mad and threw himself into the river. Both events left the poor women shells of themselves. Anyway, enough of that maudlin talk. There's more.' Gemma's index finger rose. 'One of us must stay in the

Glen permanently. Another ancestor who tested this rule tried to make her way back up to Scotland, made it as far as Newcastle, caught some sort of virus and made it home again just in time to pass away.' Gemma raised her middle finger. 'And we can't take flight on holiday all at once. One of the Gordon spawn must remain behind at all times. There's no reason to think anything might go wrong if all went on holiday at the same time, but I think you can agree it's not worth the risk. Essentially, Rhona made it so that we're...' Gemma flapped her hands for a few seconds in a terrible impression of a bird, then pinned them to her sides. 'Stuck. Whether we like it or not.'

Jeremy made a show of freeing his zipped-up lips once and for all. 'And that's all there is to it. Not too convoluted – or completely insane. Thoughts, Natalia?'

Natalia squinted and steepled her hands in front of her, trying to take the story seriously while struggling to do exactly that. 'So, just to make sure that I've understood what I've heard... The male of the family has to find love before the women can. And every single person is stuck in Gordon Glen until that happens. But even if the male falls in love, freeing up the women to find their other half, then someone has to stay here in order to keep the family line going in the Glen.'

'Exactly. Except it's every single *woman* who must stay here until Jeremy sorts himself out.' Tilly picked up her glass of water and necked it as if she wished it were something stronger. 'It's utterly depressing, isn't it?'

Natalia nodded her thanks to Sarah as she set the cappuccino down in front of her. 'It's certainly not something I'd wish on anyone. Assuming it's true. Assuming you're not pulling my leg.'

'We're not pulling your leg,' sighed Clare. 'We wish. Unfortunately, the curse is a fact, which is why we need Jeremy to stop being so difficult about falling in love so we can get on with the rest of our lives.'

Natalia glanced at Jeremy, noting the thunderclouds had formed. 'That's a lot of pressure for one person – in this case, for Jeremy – to be under. It all seems a bit unfair, to be honest.'

'Well,' Tilly sighed. 'It is what it is.'

'And so, it's always been.' Clare's bottom lip fell into a pout. 'Grounded and loveless, thanks to our stubbornly single brother.'

'So, bringing everything back to the here and now.' Natalia leaned forward. 'Why are you all so obsessed with this singles sunflower festival idea if it's not going to bring you love since it sounds like that could end in certain death?'

'Nowhere in the history books does it say we can't have fun.' Gemma stretched her arms above her head, then released them. 'Attraction doesn't have to equal happily ever after. And since we've all but given up on Jeremy giving up his bachelor ways, we'll just have to make do with a good time not equaling a long time.'

'Speak for yourself.' Tilly stuck her tongue out at

Gemma. 'I still have hope that my darling twin will lose his head over a woman.'

Natalia didn't miss the way Tilly's gaze flicked between herself and Jeremy, but chose not to bring attention to it. It would only add pressure to Jeremy, and it seemed like he had more than enough on his plate when it came to his family's expectations.

'Well, I guess there's only one way to help Jeremy find the love of his life...' Under the table, Natalia ankle tapped Jeremy, letting him know she wasn't buying into his sisters' beliefs, but simply moving the conversation along. 'And that's to do this festival idea of yours. Though not too big, I have my charges to think of.' She turned to Gemma. 'So, Gemma, what's the plan?'

'Well, there's the picnic. We could get people to bring their blankets and picnic baskets, play some music, have them relax by the river so as not to disturb the sunflowers too much. It could be fun. Make it light-hearted, perhaps have half the people bring a cheese and the other half a condiment and if they find a match, they can eat together.'

'Or maybe we could let adults choose who they want to spend time with,' Jeremy deadpanned. 'I could have a lovely fig jam and see a ripe piece of Camembert, but if the person supplying it doesn't spin my wheels, then I'm not going to sit down and have a conversation. It'd be getting their hopes up for more, and that's not fair.'

'Ah, our brother,' Clare sighed. 'Always the

gentlemen and, dare I say it, correct. Letting love happen organically is the only way.'

'Fine.' Gemma threw her hands up. 'Whatever. It was just an idea.'

'A good idea,' Natalia agreed, knowing she would not be taking part in any way, shape or form, other than acting as guardian of the sunflowers.

'Then, after that, we could do a singles silent dance party.' Tilly waggled her fingers in the air and shimmied her shoulders to music only she could hear.

'A silent dance party?' Natalia angled her head to the side, intrigued. 'How does that work?'

'No idea. Saw it on some video online and thought it looked like a bit of fun.'

'Tilly, you're not seriously suggesting hosting an event you know nothing about?' Jeremy exhaled long and loud while shaking his head.

'Well, how hard can it be? You make a playlist, transmit the music, make sure everyone knows to have Bluetooth headphones?' Tilly rolled her eyes at her brother. 'It doesn't take a genius to figure it out.'

'Which is good, because you're anything but.'

Tilly glared mutinously at her brother. Seconds later, Jeremy yelped in pain, bent down and began rubbing his shin.

'Uncalled for,' he groused.

'Yes, your comment was.' Tilly stared pointedly before returning her gaze to Natalia. 'So, what do you think?'

'I think it could be okay. But why does it have to be

silent?' Natalia saw the farm in her mind's eye. Aside from the gun-toting neighbour, there weren't a lot of other people living around it, and she couldn't imagine the eels or fish in the river complaining at the noise.

'Aunty Francesca always says that the wrong music can interfere with a plant's growth, and I don't want to risk her ire if she comes home to find a crop's gone bust because I felt the need to pull some shapes to pop music.'

'Which is why at the picnic we'll play some classical stuff.' Gemma screwed her nose up in distaste. 'Apparently, the plants love it.'

'Okay.' Natalia nodded, not wanting to question her employer's growing methods. 'Anything else being cooked up that I ought to know about?'

'Well, maybe we could do a speed dating type thing, too?' Tilly's cheeks pinked up. 'It might be a way for those who have their eye on someone who's also single to get to know them better. You know, they could invite them along and then take advantage of the situation.'

'Tilly and Benjamin up a tree...' Clare sang under her breath, earning herself an elbow to the rib cage from Gemma.

'Do you want half your hair pulled out in a chunk again?' Gemma hissed. 'Will you ever learn, woman? The middle one gets feral when you push her on the topic of Benjamin.'

Clare shrugged unapologetically as she massaged her side. 'It's not my fault she's been mooning over him forever and has done nothing about it because she's afraid of the curse and doesn't want her crush back-firing before it's had a chance to be anything more.'

'There's that...' Tilly picked up a napkin and wiped muffin crumbs and a splodge of blueberry from the corner of her mouth. 'And that he's hardly in town, so there's not even the opportunity for a fling, let alone the chance to invite him to the festival.'

'What does he do that sees him travel so much?' Natalia took a sip of her cappuccino, then let out a soft, unexpected moan of appreciation.

'Good, right?' Jeremy picked up his own cup and took a drink, then sat it down with a satisfied smile. 'Sarah's a whiz on the coffee machine.'

'And in the kitchen.' Natalia picked up the last of the caramel and white chocolate brioche and popped it in her mouth before any of the Gordon girls scooped it up for themselves. 'Speaking of sweet things. Tilly, you were saying?'

'So,' Tilly paused, pride brightening her eyes and lifting her cheekbones. 'Benjamin works in television.'

'But what does he do on television, Tils?' Clare wrinkled her nose at her sister. 'No need to be obtuse.'

'Just host one of the world's most popular dating shows.' Tilly's grin widened.

Natalia nodded politely, not being one to watch dating shows and not really knowing anything about them.

'As in...' Gemma gave a nod of encouragement. 'You know you want to say it.'

'As in "Romance in the Tropics".'

Natalia clapped her hand over her mouth, realising she was in danger of spraying crumbs all over the table. Tilly was in love with Benjamin Jambon? Bloody hell. Even she'd heard of that television host, even if she'd never watched his show. He was as famous for being on tele as he was for dating a slew of beautiful women, and his face was on all the covers of the weekly magazines almost all the time. As politely as she could, she hurried the eating process and swallowed the mouthful of food.

'I know, right?' Clare's head was bobbing back and forth in glee. 'If my sister's going to set herself up for failure, she's going to do it in the best way possible.'

Natalia didn't know whether Clare was being cruel or kind, but she did know she wasn't wrong. If you were going to have a crush on someone ungettable for the average person living in a blink-and-you'll-miss-it village, then Benjamin Jambon was as good as you could get.

'I'm not setting myself up for failure,' Tilly huffed. 'We're friends. We know each other. We're on a first name basis. And I'm sure I saw him giving me the glad eye at the pub last time he was home.'

'Home? Gordon Glen is Benjamin Jambon's home?' Natalia blinked, unsure how she'd never heard that snippet of information. Lord knows she'd read enough papers and magazines cover-to-cover during slow periods at a kiosk she'd worked in for a time back in London that she knew more than she should about most famous people, if not the shows they worked on. 'Is this common knowledge?'

'Not really.' Tilly pulled the saucer holding Natalie's drink closer, then picked up the cup and took a sip. 'He usually just says he's from a small town in Cornwall in interviews, and usually interviewers are more interested in behind-the-scenes capers and his latest girlfriend than his idyllic childhood.'

'And during that idyllic childhood, was there any indication that you two might have a thing for each other?'

Tilly set the cup down. 'No. But what would be the point? So long as Jeremy's single, I'm destined to be single, which is why I've decided to shoot my shot with Benjamin the next time he's in town. I'm going to follow my darling brother's ways and have a little fun.'

'And then we'll pick up the pieces once he leaves.' Clare clucked her tongue disapprovingly. 'Your plan is a recipe for disaster.'

'At the moment it is.' Tilly cast her brother a sidelong look. 'But I still have hope that Jeremy's going to do a turnaround that'll see everything come right.'

Jeremy snorted. 'Keep dreaming, Tils. If you want this so-called curse broken, you'll have to figure out another way to make it happen. And with that,' Jeremy scooted his chair back, then stood up. 'I'm heading back to the farm. Natalia? Do you want to wander back with me, or would you rather sit with this lot and hear them prattle on about their lack of love lives?'

As if connected mentally, all three Gordon girls poked their tongues out in perfect synchronisation.

'I can't wait for you to eat your words, little brother.' Gemma followed her tongue poke up with the two-finger salute.

'And I can't wait for you all to come to your senses and see that the only curse in this village is the one you are creating by believing in the tale.'

'Pfft.' Clare dismissed her brother with a flick of her hand. 'Go play with your vegetables. Natalia, thanks for being cool about our sunflower festival idea. Thanks for being cool, full stop. All things crossed that your coolness will rub off on our brother and he'll stop being such a stick in the mud.'

Jeremy's nostrils flared. Time to evacuate, Natalia decided. Even an only child could sense when a storm was brewing between siblings.

'I'll do my best, Clare.' Gathering her bag, Natalia stood and headed for the door. 'Good to see you all. Until next time.'

Grabbing Jeremy as she walked past, she dragged him outside, then down the village lane.

'They're insufferable,' he grumped, his footsteps kicking up plumes of dirt. 'Also, they're insane. There's no such thing as a curse. There's only such a thing as people creating their futures by doggedly believing in it.'

'And do you think some people might create their futures by being so anti-curse that they doggedly avoid love?'

Jeremy's nostrils flared again. Natalia knew she was walking on thin ice by flipping his assessment of the situation, but she couldn't help but feel like she was missing a piece of the puzzle. Jeremy was kind, friendly, funny and – if you weren't working with and for him – very attractive on the eye. And it wasn't like he didn't like women, he just didn't want to settle down with one. But could that be because of the pressure put on him by his family? Or was there another reason? Had he been hurt badly at some point and was protecting his heart, much as she protected hers?

'I hear what you're saying and it's not the case. I'm not doggedly avoiding love. I'm just not interested in being tied down. Not when I'm alr-' He paused, then shook his head in annoyance. 'Not when I'm already busy enough with family and work. Between the demands of those, a woman would come off third best, and that wouldn't be fair.'

'I can respect that.' *But I don't have to believe it.* Jeremy's tone was off. Weary. Flat. Like he'd found an excuse rather than the truth.

Reaching the car, Jeremy opened her door and waited for Natalia to get in before closing it behind her. Kind, friendly, funny, attractive, and a gentleman. Some lucky woman was missing out. Maybe the sunflower festival might bring her to Jeremy, and love would bloom.

SIX

Jeremy drove the spade into the ground, pressing the sole of his boot down onto its edge with all his might. Taking his frustration out on the compacted dirt beneath.

Of all the families he could've been born into, why did it have to be the one family that insisted he was the key to their happiness? Who took every opportunity they had to remind him of it. Who had decided that their destinies were dependent on him fulfilling the rules of a curse. Absurdity. All of it.

Feeling the dirt give, he turned it over, then raised his leg, ready to drive it down on the spade again.

'Isn't there a machine that can do that?'

Jeremy gritted his teeth at the bright tone in Natalia's voice. After dealing with his sisters at the café, he was in no mood to talk to anyone, even the one person who didn't hassle him about his so-called birthright.

'I'm sure I saw one in the shed when I had a poke round before. I can bring it out for you, if you like?'

He shook his head, bringing his leg down, proving the point that he was fine as he was. He didn't need to be told what to do, or helped, or given a hand. Whether it be in love, life, or work.

'Is everything okay? Have I said something? Done something?'

Jeremy looked up from digging, his annoyance blooming as he caught the hurt in Natalia's eyes. Annoyance at himself. She didn't deserve to be ignored, or spoken to curtly; not when she was only trying to be helpful. The problem was, everyone around him was always trying to do exactly that, when all he needed was to be left alone to come to his own decisions in his own time.

'You're fine. And,' he made a show of checking his watch. 'I'm done for the day. I'll see you tomorrow.'

Not waiting for Natalia's reply, he took off down the field towards the sheds, dragging the spade behind him, cursing his sisters for ruining his mood. Again. Had it just been him and Natalia, the conversation would've been light, friendly. Easy.

Instead, he'd been dragged into yet another bloody conversation about the bloody curse, with the added 'bonus' of a singles festival set in the sunflowers.

Jeremy tried to recall the last time he'd gone a day without hearing about his bachelor ways, or his need to settle down, or how he was letting the family down by not falling in love. Years. Perhaps even a decade ago, back in his university days, where he'd felt free for the first time to be who he wanted to be. No one knowing about his family's unconventional ways, the history that led them to Gordon Glen, or the beliefs that kept them stuck in time and space until the first-born male freed them by falling head over heels in love. Giving what little control they had away to yet another woman.

At least, that's how it looked to him.

A flash of iridescent blue against the faded green of the summer grass caught his eye.

'Shit.' Giving a hop, skip and jump, he avoided the small butterfly who'd made its home in a most dangerous spot. 'Sorry, little one. That was a close call.' Crouching down, he picked it up, smiling as its legs ticked his finger as it crawled its way up towards the tip.

Lifting the butterfly up, he placed it on a pink flower of the rhododendron tree his aunt had planted years ago. It should've stopped blooming months ago, but – much like the Gordon women – it had a mind of its own and lasted through the summer months, even if the blooms weren't as plentiful as during spring.

'Go well, my friend.'

The butterfly's antennae wiggled in his direction as if to say thank you, lightening the clouds that hovered heavily around Jeremy's heart and mind. Time alone would see the mood shift. It always did.

Dampening a rag at the garden tap, he wiped the spade down, then returned it to the shed, purposefully not looking at the tiller Natalia had mentioned. He felt badly enough as it was, seeing the machine would only emphasise how awfully he'd behaved.

I'll apologise tomorrow, he promised himself as he got behind the wheel of his car and headed towards the village, intent on getting dinner supplies, then spending the rest of the night on the couch, phone off, watching whatever was on the box.

The idea of a night of freedom at hand, Jeremy pulled up to the shop, his mood already ten times better.

Grabbing his reusable bag from the back, he sauntered into the shop. Instant noodles, beer and eggs for the next day's breakfast on his mental grocery list. His verging on good mood evaporating when he noticed who was behind the counter.

'It's meant to be your day off.' Jeremy didn't even bother hiding his freshly resurfaced irritation. 'What are you doing here?'

'That's a nice way to greet your friendly shop assistant.' Tilly screwed her face up in displeasure at Jeremy's tone. 'Finnius felt ill, so I offered to help him out. It's called being nice. You might want to look it up in a dictionary.'

'Whatever.' Jeremy rolled his eyes and made his way to the fridge. Opening the door, he paused in front of it, relishing the cold air, while making himself promise he would not lose his head at his sister in public. They didn't need to be fodder for the gossipers of the village, and getting into a fight would not fix the problem of being a Gordon. He just needed to pay, leave, and continue with his plan to spend the evening in his own presence.

Grabbing the beer, he picked up the eggs and instant noodles and brought them to the counter. 'Just these, thanks.'

'"Just these thanks",' Tilly mimicked. 'No hot date tonight, then? Haven't managed to wheedle your way into Natalia's affections?'

'I'm having a quiet one.' Jeremy kept his voice even, despite his rising ire. 'And Natalia's working with me. It would be inappropriate for me to do anything other than treat her with the respect she deserves.'

Ringing up his purchase, Tilly let out a small snort. 'Never thought I'd see the day that you'd respect a woman.'

'I respect all women. You know that.' Jeremy pulled out his money card, intent on getting out of the shop before his sister could make a bad day worse.

'Not enough to treat them as anything more than one, done, and just a bit of fun.' Tilly bagged up his groceries and shoved them in his direction. 'Or maybe there's something special about Natalia that's making you hold back? Maybe you know that if you went for a one-and-done you'd want more and you're too afraid of rejection or getting hurt to even try. For all any of us know, she could be the one that sets us free and you're too cowardly to even try to find out. I mean, Clare and Gemma think you two look good together, and we're seeing signs of coupledom all over the place. Even the next-door neighbours' cats were nose kissing this morning, and usually they spit and hiss at each other before taking a swipe.'

'Oh for...' Jeremy buttoned his lips before the expletive that lingered on his tongue could explode out. 'Look, just for once, can you let this go? It was embarrassing enough with you all going on about our mad family's stupid beliefs this morning. I don't want Natalia dragged into it. I don't think she deserves to be.'

'Well, we think she deserves to know. I mean, she's working on the family farm. She's comfortable enough popping into our house without knocking first – and how many people can you say that about? Most of the town's afraid of us, some are even scared of us. It's just a few that think we're okay, though only in small doses. You can't blame us for embracing Natalia. She's one of the few people who'll sit with us in public.'

'That's because she doesn't know you all well enough to run the other way.'

'Mean.' Tilly's face fell. 'We're not that bad. We are who we are, we come from who we come from, and we can't change. It's not always easy being a Gordon woman, even though we do our best to make it look that way. You should know that.'

Jeremy closed his eyes to his sister's pain. It always came back to them. To how his sisters felt, how they were inconvenienced, how their life was dictated by his actions. Or inaction. No one ever stopped to think that maybe the hardest place to hold in the Gordon family was that of the first-born male. The expectation, the demands, the pleading to fall in love was enough to make a person run the other way. And lord knows he'd tried that by going off to university, but even Falmouth hadn't been far away enough to keep his family's incessant bleating at bay, or away.

'Don't you think we wish we were born into any old family that weren't tied to the land, who could fall in love whenever they wanted, who could walk down the lane without people moving to the side a little more than necessary in case you cast a spell on them. I mean, we don't even cast spells. We're not even witches. We're just a bit witchy. There's a difference. And it's not like we can get away from that either, it's expectation. Gordon women read the cards, pay attention to the energies, notice nature. Those are the rules. Hell, it's more than "the rules", it's in our DNA.'

Tiring of Tilly's pity party, Jeremy opened his eyes and prepared to pull her back to reality. 'And if you could get away from the expectations of being a Gordon woman, would you? Would you quit reading cards and noticing signs? Could you let go of the infamy?'

Tilly quirked her lips to the side and dropped her gaze, as Jeremy knew she would. For all their complaining, the women in his family prided themselves on upholding the ways of Rhona. Of honouring her sacrifice by living the life she'd had to run from in fear of death.

'No. I guess not,' Tilly sighed, then looked up at Jeremy, her golden-brown eyes darkening as her expression turned serious. 'But I really would like it if you could just break the curse for our generation and finally fall in love. We all would.'

Grabbing the bag, tiring of the conversation, sick of the whole day, Jeremy shook his head. 'Well, that's not going to happen. I've no interest in love. From my perspective, all it's done for our family has caused a whole lot of pain.'

'Selfish,' Tilly muttered, as he walked out.

And perhaps he was. But it wasn't up to him to break the Gordon curse. Because there wasn't one. It was just a story. And if the girls wanted a happy ending, they were going to have to create it themselves.

SEVEN

Natalia reached out, brushing the closest sunflower stalk, admiring its resilience – prickly, strong, capable of holding itself up without support. It reminded her of herself, or perhaps of how her family life had forged her.

Unlike the hustle and bustle, the laughter and light that she'd seen in the Gordon household, the Hawthorne home had been all about peace, quiet, structure. Like a church, but with beds and food on the table at precisely seven in the morning, six at night, and midday during the weekends. Difficult questions or feelings shut down with 'not now, Natalia', or 'don't be dramatic, Natalia'. Tears quickly hidden with a wipe of sleeve or turn of back.

At least the cold upbringing had taught her to get used to being kept at arm's length by others. Something that had made her first full day on the job easier to deal with as Jeremy had become more and more monosyllabic on the car ride back from the café, then all but disappeared. Not joining her for lunch in the farmhouse, or even saying goodbye when he left.

Dropping her hand, Natalia repressed a sigh. She had no idea what she'd done wrong, but if they were going to work together, or at least in the same vicinity, then she was going to have to find out.

'You look like a girl who's got the weight of the world on her shoulders, not a lass who lucked out with a cruisy gig babysitting sunflowers for a month.'

Natalia turned to find Tilly standing a few metres away, hands on her hips, head tilted to one side, brows raised.

'I'm fine. Honest.' Natalia attempted an unbothered shrug.

'You're fine, *or* you've had the joy of dealing with my brother, who, let me guess...' Tilly raised a finger. 'Went all quiet on you, disappeared into his work, and did whatever the equivalent is of ghosting when you're not in a romantic relationship with the person.'

'I'm pretty sure you can ghost someone you're not dating.' Natalia grinned.

'Probably. Not that I'd know. No point dating when it can't go anywhere.'

In no mood to hear anything more about the Gordon curse, Natalia chose not to respond.

'You must think we're mad with all our talk of curses. And maybe we are. But it's all that we know.' Tilly bent over and plucked a weed from the ground. 'You like gardening?'

Natalia bit down on her lip and contemplated telling Tilly what she'd told Francesca: a lie.

'You don't.' Tilly snort laughed. 'People who like gardening are quick to go into raptures about it the moment you give them an opening. So, you fibbed to Aunty Francesca in order to get the job?'

'Will you tell on me if I tell you the truth?'

Tilly placed her hand over her heart. 'Promise I won't.'

'I did.' Natalia shoved her hands into the back pockets of her denim shorts, then walked towards the sound of rippling water. 'I'd been stuck in London so long I needed to get out for a bit.'

'Needed to dry out? Get away from all the drugs?'

Tilly's words were said so innocently, Natalia couldn't be sure if she was having her on or simply thought that was a possibility.

'Heart break?' Tilly offered. 'Is that why you're immune to my brother's charms?'

Natalia shook her head, charmed more by Jeremy's sister's innocence. Tilly appeared untouched by the harsher realities of life, leading her to believe that a person ran away from home due to what she saw as the harshest realities, like addiction and relationship breakdowns.

'No, not heartbreak. Not addiction issues either. I simply needed a change of scenery. I'd been in the same place too long and wanted to breathe a different kind of air.' Natalia stepped between two sunflowers and found herself at the bank of the river.

Lush swathes of grass swayed in the light breeze, the sun glinted off the river like someone had showered it with diamonds, and the hills opposite hovered over them, not ominously but protectively, as if they would come alive and hurt anyone who tried to hurt those who lived in Gordon Glen. Natalia could see why Rhona would have chosen the area to settle down in.

'So, you're no different from me, then?' Tilly plonked herself down on the grass, then extended her legs out front, anchoring her hands behind her. 'Immune to my brother's charms and known to be stuck in a place for too long that it starts to feel unhealthy.'

Natalia sunk down beside Tilly and pulled her legs up to her chest, hugging them to her. 'You're stuck here? I got the impression you wouldn't want to be anywhere else.'

Tilly's jaw jutted out in thought. 'You're right. Wrong choice of word on my part. I'm not stuck, more that I wouldn't know where else to go even if the curse didn't have me anchored here, apart from being allowed the odd getaway here and there. Which I never take. I mean, you should have a reason for going somewhere, right? Like, you came here in order to get a new perspective, a change of air.' Tilly made a point of inhaling deeply, then exhaled with a long sigh of appreciation. 'And good air it is.'

Natalia followed suit, realising she'd not paid any attention to the scent of Gordon Glen. Breathing in, she caught the aroma of sweet grass, a hint of earthiness from the dirt lining the boundary between field and river bank, the refreshing, crisp scent of the river, and a slightly dusky smell from the parts of the river that lived in perpetual dampness.

Exhaling, she turned to Tilly. 'That scent is a world away from London. No vehicle exhaust, no wafts of rubbish, or hints of pee from where a late-night partier had run out of bladder room and felt the need to do their business in whatever corner was closest.'

'Really?' Tilly's nose screwed up, and not in the adorable way it did when she was bemused or being amusing. 'That's how it smells? Remind me not to visit.'

'It's not that bad. It's actually quite beautiful. Lovely parks, interesting people, there's always something to do. I guess when you live anywhere long enough, you forget the good points.'

'Only if the bad points get too much.' Tilly eyed Natalia speculatively. 'Which'd be why you made your way here. Bad points got too much.'

Natalia returned Tilly's look with impassivity. Better to say nothing than to admit the bad point had been herself. That the weight of being an eternal disappointment to her mother and father had become too much, and she needed a fresh start to help her figure out the rest of her life. To find a way to make her parents accept her. Even if that meant no longer accepting herself for who she was, warts and lack of ambition and all.

'God,' Tilly let out a pah of irritation. 'You're as

bad as Jeremy. Whenever I ask him anything remotely deep and meaningful, he just stares at me until I give up on hoping for an answer.'

'Maybe that's why I'm not going all gaga over him.' Natalia lifted her brows and forced a smile to curl the edges of her lips. 'We're too similar.'

'Well, he's not one for drugs, or booze, or heartbreak.' Tilly picked a blade of grass and began twisting it back and forth between her thumb and forefinger. 'At least that's what he lets on.'

'Are you intimating that he's got some secret issue?' Natalia angled her head to the side and tried to imagine Jeremy sneaking shots of vodka from a hip flask between tending the rows of vegetables. Impossible. He was too... straight. Even in his lady loving ways, he was a gentleman, or so everyone – Jeremy included – had said. 'I can't imagine him being into drinks or drugs in a major way.'

'That's because I meant heartbreak.' Tilly stared into the middle distance, her eyes narrowing. 'I shouldn't say it. I've never mentioned it to Jeremy. Or the girls. Especially not the girls...'

Tilly gave Natalia a meaningful look, silently explaining that her sisters, as much as she loved them, could not be trusted with the knowledge Tilly held. But she felt Natalia could be.

'But not long after Jeremy came back from university, I found him on the laptop that we all shared back in the old days because mum refused to have more than one device in the house, and he was staring at the screen with the weirdest look on his face. Soon as he caught wind of me being there, he slammed it shut, then told me off for being too quiet. Now, I don't know about you, Natalia, but the only time I behave like that is when I've been caught doing something I know I shouldn't be doing.'

Natalia dipped her chin, acknowledging the truth of Tilly's statement.

'So, after he stalked off to bed in a huff, which, for the record, had become the norm after his return home – something we all put down to shrinking pains, being that he'd gone out into the world and had new experiences and was now trying to get back into the routine of Gordon Glen and its quiet village ways – I opened up the laptop and had a quick squiz at the internet history.'

Tilly went still, her demeanour becoming eerily calm. Natalia found the word 'and' burning the tip of her tongue.

'Go on. Say it. "And..."' Tilly elbowed Natalia gently in her side. 'You know you want to hear what happened next.'

'Won't.' Natalia shook her head. 'You're telling the story and I'm not a gossip.'

'Pfft.' Tilly rolled her eyes. 'Look at yourself, you're almost on a ninety-degree angle in anticipation.'

Natalia glanced down, then let out a huff. Ninety degrees? More like she was all but hanging off Tilly's shoulder.

'The body never lies,' Tilly sang. Her off-key tune

causing a duck somewhere on the other side of the river bank to squawk in annoyance. 'Though who can blame you for wanting to know? My sisters would have me tied up to a chair and shone a lamp in my eyes if I did this to them.'

Natalia straightened up. 'Well, I'm not the type to wrestle anyone into a chair for information, and I'm not going to beg. So, you can either tell me this secret you've been holding onto for years, or you can continue keeping it. And don't blame me if you end up exploding from the need to spill the beans.'

'Whatever.' Tilly waved the comment away. 'I've been able to keep quiet this long. I could do it longer.'

'But could you?' Natalia grinned, suspecting she knew the answer. 'Are you sure? Because there's always that moment when you come so close to doing something you've always wanted to do that backing off becomes impossible.'

'Like in the movies when a heroine's about to kiss the boy she likes and they've been flirting with the idea of it forever, and their lips are millimetres apart, and barring someone storming in on them – which won't happen, because it's already happened twice – the only option is for them to go in for the snog.' Tilly closed her eyes and sighed, the bliss of the idea lifting her cheeks and lips. 'Best part of any romance. Even better than the post-kiss fight, followed by the makeup scene at the end.'

'If you say so.' Natalia watched a duck waddle down to the river and plop itself in, a drake following not long after. Did ducks have first kisses? Or fights? She huffed with laughter at the idea of their two beaks clacking together, or their wings at odd angles as they told each other off.

'What?' Tilly's eyes flew open, a line appearing between her brows. 'Do you think I'm ridiculous for loving romances?'

'Of course not.' Natalia nodded to the birds. 'I was just wondering if ducks kiss.'

'As if.' Tilly pulled out her mobile and began tapping the screen. 'Oh my god. No. I take it back. They do. Except it's more of a nuzzle situation.' Tilly tapped and swiped at her mobile again, then thrust it under Natalia's nose. 'Here. This is what I'm talking about.'

Natalia blinked, expecting to see a video of ducks kissing, instead a woman with long, wavy blonde hair that wouldn't have gone amiss on a mermaid, sparkling blue eyes and a freckle just below her right eye that took her from modelesque unattainable to welcoming girl next door.

'That's what – or who – he'd been looking at.' Tilly's cheeks reddened. 'Well, a younger version of that. I might've been keeping a slight eye on her just in case she ever turned up in Gordon Glen hoping to lure Jeremy in, before breaking his heart all over again. Her name's Camille. Jeremy brought her home one summer, said they were just friends, but who moons over pictures of "just friends"?'

For a split second, Natalia wrestled with the idea

of giving the phone back to Tilly or scrolling down to see who this 'just friend' was and what she did for a living.

'Oh, go on. You know you want to.' Tilly's shoulder nudged Natalia's. 'This is the woman that turned my brother from marriage material to a confirmed bachelor. That makes her special. In a wretched way. Who wouldn't want to know everything in the world about her?'

'I can understand you doing that – you've known Jeremy literally since the day you were born. But I'm new. A fly by nighter, at that. It's not my business.' Natalia went to hand the mobile back, but Tilly pushed it back in her direction.

'Fine. I take your point. But now that I've started sharing, you've got to let me finish. I have been literally keeping in this piece of information for a decade.'

'And it's safe to show me because I won't be hanging around, therefore it won't get back to your brother that you know his big secret?'

'More like, I want you to know what you're getting into. I want you to see that Jeremy wasn't always the way he was.'

Natalia didn't know what to make of Tilly's cryptic words. Jeremy, whether in past or present form, wasn't much, if any, of her business. And while she liked him well enough – when he wasn't putting her on silent – there was no way she was 'getting into' anything with him. But that didn't mean that curiosity wasn't killing her inner cat.

'Fine.' Natalia held up her hands in defeat. 'Spill.'

'I like that you know when to see sense. It's a most excellent trait. Especially when it means I get my way.' Tilly nodded her approval, then took the mobile back, her fingers flying over the screen. 'I ended up doing a bit more digging, just to be sure I wasn't barking up the wrong tree, and found a picture of them with their arms wrapped around each other at some university function. "Just friends" my arse.'

Tilly held up the mobile, revealing the picture. Slightly grainy, she could make out Jeremy, wearing a navy sweater and jeans, and glued to his hip was a younger version of the woman she'd seen earlier, wearing skinny jeans and a nautical stripe top. As Tilly had described, their arms were wrapped around each other in a way that made them definitely look more like a couple than a couple of mates.

Natalia's stomach tightened uncomfortably. Probably because she'd never felt that close to anyone. So close that their absence hurt her indefinitely. What she was most definitely not experiencing was jealousy. That would be beyond ridiculous. Ludicrous, even.

Moving Tilly's hand away, glad to be rid of the sight, Natalia tipped her head to the cornflower blue sky and took a deep, centring breath. 'Tilly, if you ever wanted to give up working at the shop to be a detective, I think there'd be work out there for you.'

'Yeah, I know. I'm pretty good at internet sleuthing. Need anyone looked up?'

Natalia shook her head. 'Nope. Not a soul. I don't like life to get messy.'

'Then you'd better not fall for my brother.' Tilly widened her eyes to emphasise her advice. 'He does his best. He means well, but he's left his fair share of unhappy women in his wake.'

'Really?' Natalia forced herself to stay put, to not straighten up, or look more interested than she was. 'He's made quite the point of telling me he makes his intentions clear, that he's not the settling down type, that he doesn't spend time with women who aren't on the same page.'

'He mentioned the debacle with our friend Lucy?'

'He did. It sounded awkward, and only intensified his need to be clear in his expectations.' Natalia focused on the river, knowing Tilly would fill in the quiet sooner rather than later.

'What if I were to tell you that's the story he tells women to ensure they know they don't stand a chance of anything more than one night? It puts a boundary up no one can traverse. And they accept it, too. Probably because he's a good person. Safe. The thing is,' Tilly nudged Natalia. 'It's easier to do the "poor me, my actions were confused and I never want to hurt anyone again" act than it is to say "I can't do more than a one-night thing because I fell in love at university and then the woman left me to become a famous Hollywood costume designer and my heart is eternally broken".'

'Except you don't know that his heart is broken. Maybe Jeremy truly isn't interested in settling down.'

Tilly face-palmed herself and groaned in exasperation. 'You didn't see him when he returned, Natalia. He was grumpy and snappy. Secretive. Then he never went near a woman for more than one night ever again. You don't do that for no good reason. You don't get all uptight and twisted about love for a crush. Or a short-term fling.' Tilly's hands landed heavily on the grass as she turned to Natalia. 'Are you being this difficult on purpose?'

Natalia laughed, breaking the tension. 'Of course not. I just wouldn't want to jump to conclusions.' *Or think too much about the fact your brother told me about the friend debacle, which might have meant he was setting me up in order to knock me down... into bed.*

'Well, if it walks like a duck and talks like a duck...' Tilly shrugged.

From across the way, a duck quacked as if to confirm Tilly's point.

'Maybe it's a duck,' Natalia agreed. 'And Jeremy's secret is safe with me. As is your snooping.'

'Thanks.' Tilly pushed herself up and offered Natalia her hand. 'It's nice to have a friend around these parts. I love my sisters, but friends and sisters are different beasties, and it's good to have both.'

Never having had either, Natalia simply nodded, then took Tilly's hand and allowed herself to be helped up.

'Just be gentle with my brother, okay?' Tilly was

facing forward, making it hard for Natalia to read her thoughts, but she could hear the emotion in her words. Tilly cared deeply for Jeremy, and knew his heart was tender, despite his actions. 'He's more sensitive than he looks.'

'And he's just a friend. Like you.' Natalia linked her arm through the crook of Tilly's. 'I wouldn't do anything to upset either of you.'

Especially now that she knew Jeremy wasn't as bulletproof as he made out. Which made the two of them.

EIGHT

Jeremy pulled his pillow over his head and groaned at the loud rumble that had woken him up. He'd smashed his instant noodles back, then cooked up eggs on toast. There was no way his stomach could or should be so hungry in the middle of the night.

Rolling over, determined to ignore his tummy's grumbles, he attempted to settle back into sleep, only for the rumbling to start all over again. Louder this time, and not coming from his stomach as his sleep-addled state had first suggested, but from outside.

Shit.

If there was one thing his aunt did not like, it was a thunderstorm. A massive, unexpected storm years ago, complete with hail the size of golf balls, had all but wiped out the winter crop, sending the local cafes and restaurants into a scramble, while killing off a good percentage of the farm's profits.

Jeremy had checked the weather forecast before

going to bed, as he always did in case he needed to go back to the farm and prepare the crops for a storm, but there'd been no mention of bad weather.

Another rumble cracked the stillness of the night, spurring him into action. Sleep could wait, but saving all his hard work could not.

Swinging his legs out of bed, Jeremy grabbed his shorts from where he'd left them on the floor the night before and pulled them over his pants, then grabbed the t-shirt puddled next to the shorts and yanked it over his head. Running to the front of the cottage, he toed his sneakers on, grabbed his car keys and raced to the car, not bothering to lock the front door, doubting anyone dodgy would be out and about in a thunderstorm – especially in Gordon Glen, where crime usually came in the form of a kid stealing sweets from the shop or a drunk local taking a pint glass home from the pub.

Grateful for the quiet roads, Jeremy made it to the farm in minutes. The farmhouse sat in darkness, as he'd expected it to be in the witching hours of the night, and he turned his headlights off as he rolled into the drive so as not to wake up Natalia. After giving her the silent treatment earlier, he didn't need to throw himself further into her bad books.

Bringing the car to a rolling stop, Jeremy turned on his mobile's torch, then leaped out and ran around to the shed where his aunt kept tarps and stakes. Out of the corner of his eye, the sky lit up as lightning flickered in the distance, and he began counting to gauge how far away the storm was.

One one-thousand.
Two one-thousand.
Three one-thousand.

Twenty seconds later, the thunder crashed. The storm was close enough that he wouldn't have time to cover all the beds, but so long as a wind didn't pick up too soon, making the job even harder, he could cover the majority.

'Oy, you. What're you doing there?' Natalia's hushed, sleepy voice floated over the warm night air. 'Don't make a move. I'm armed and dangerous.'

Jeremy turned the light toward the sound, scanning the ground until it found a pair of slippered feet. Raising the torch slowly, it revealed a threadbare but body-covering bathrobe – his aunt's, he presumed – followed by wide, smiling lips. A quick side-to-side swipe of the torch showed a lack of weapon.

'Joking. No umbrella. Not this time. I heard the storm, then the car's engine cut out close to the cottage, and figured it must have been you come to do something about it. Need a hand?'

Wanting to apologise for his behaviour, but knowing there wasn't time, Jeremy promised he'd make it up to Natalia later.

'Please. That's kind of you.' He cocked his head as another flash, followed by a rumble fifteen seconds later, rippled over the sky. 'We just need to unfold the tarps, place them over the vegetables that aren't underground, and then stake them down.'

'So, now's not the time for you to remind me which vegetables grow underground?' Natalia turned on her mobile's torch and placed it in the front pocket of her denim shorts so that it lit the ground before her.

Jeremy didn't bother replying, knowing Natalia was teasing. 'Now's the time to get moving. We'll do the courgettes, the cucumbers, lettuces, beans and peas, and try to do something with the tomatoes. There are longer stakes we could drive into the ground and cover with frost cloth.'

'Because the tarps are too heavy for the stakes when they're that high.' Natalia picked up an armload of plastic. 'Got it.'

Together they worked in silence, getting the equipment to the vegetable plots, the wind picking up with every trip back and forth. Glancing up at the sky, across which clouds scuttled, revealing flashes of stars in between their haste to move on, Jeremy prayed to the weather gods that the storm would go around rather than go over.

A flash of lightning followed by a too close for comfort roll of thunder, and he had his answer.

'I hate storms,' Natalia muttered under her breath. 'Dreadful things. So angry.' A fresh bolt of lightning illuminated the sky, and a longer, rowdier roll of thunder bellowed not far behind, causing her to jump.

Jeremy noted how still Natalia became after the

fright, how her face grew so pale he might well have seen it in the dark even without the light of the mobile.

'Natalia. Grab the two ends of the tarp, stand at the top of the row, I'll roll it out, then come around with the hammer and knock the stakes in.'

With a small nod, she did as asked, leaving Jeremy to roll out the plastic as fat drops of rain began to fall. Working as quickly as possible, they went from row to row. The wind picked up, sending the plants' leaves into a flurry. The rain pelted down. And lightning flashed every ten seconds or so, with thunder coming soon after.

'We're done.' Jeremy grabbed the last of the tarps and stakes, then passed the hammer to Natalia. 'Let's get to the cottage.'

'But the lettuces.' Natalia's eyes widened in panic. 'They're not covered.'

'They'll live.' Jeremy crossed his fingers, grateful they were hidden by the dark. Then immediately felt guilty for telling a fib. 'And if they don't, they'll flourish soon enough. Lettuces are good like that. We've got the most important vegetables covered.' Another bolt of lightning and roar of thunder saw Natalia's saucer-sized eyes widen further. 'Now quick. Let's get inside.'

Not needing to be told again, Natalia rushed for the house, each step sending mud flying. Stumbling into the farmhouse, Jeremy dropped the tarps and stakes, slammed the door behind them, then leaned against it, his chest heaving as he tried to catch his breath. Glancing down, his jaw dropping at the state of his legs. They weren't so much spattered with mud as they were caked in it.

'We're a mess.' Natalia echoed his thoughts. 'We look like two tourists who wanted to have a mud bath at some fancy spa but forgot to take off our clothing.'

'Or like two people who just saved a bunch of vegetables from certain death.' Jeremy shook his head, sending droplets flying, causing Natalia to squeal as they landed on her. The squeal becoming a yelp as a lightning strike and thunder roll occurred almost simultaneously.

'God, Natalia, you're terrified.' Jeremy took a step towards her and caught the sound of chattering teeth. 'Let's get you to the sitting room.'

Taking Natalia by the shoulders, he guided her in the direction, then settled her down on the couch. Heading to his aunt's bedroom, he grabbed a woollen blanket from the chest that sat at the end of the bed, then took it back to Natalia and wrapped it around her.

'Better?'

She nodded, but her face remained as stark as the full moon on a cloudless night, and her teeth continued clacking together.

'Liar.' He shook his head. 'I'm lighting the fire.'

Before she could protest, he strode to the fireplace and began assembling a mixture of kindling, paper and fire starters, while sending a silent thank you to his aunt for always keeping a stock of wood inside, even during the summer.

Grabbing the matches from the wooden ornamental box on the mantelpiece, he squatted down and lit the fire with a satisfying flare of flame.

'Won't be long now.' Jeremy remained crouched in front of the fire, making sure it caught and stayed that way. 'Good. Now,' he turned to face Natalia, whose cheeks had gained a little colour. 'Let's get you out of those wet clothes.'

'Look at the man. Can't help himself,' she whispered. 'Sees an opportunity to get a woman naked and takes it.'

'Oh, ye of little faith. Or too much faith.' Jeremy grinned and tapped his finger against his chin, guiding his gaze to the ceiling in mock thought. 'Ye of little faith would mean you always figured I would get you naked eventually, and ye of too much faith would mean you hoped I'd have done it sooner.'

Natalia fixed him with an unimpressed stare. 'Or maybe you're going doolally from the cold. I'm not the only one who's drenched, remember? Maybe the blood's run from your brain into other areas in order to warm you up.'

'That'll be it.' Jeremy rubbed his hands together. 'Don't move. I'll be back.'

'So long as that storm's raging...' The thunder roared as if to emphasise Natalia's point. 'I'm not going anywhere.'

Racing back to his aunt's room, Jeremy rifled through the wooden drawers and found a pair of his aunt's jeans, a t-shirt with almost more holes than fabric, and a bright orange sweater that his mother had knitted her brother for Christmas, and had clearly never been worn by the lack of pulls or bobbling on the fabric. Grateful they were of similar size, he placed the clothes on top of the drawers, then turned to Natalia's rucksack, which was stashed in the corner, a mixture of clothing and shoes sprouting from the top of it.

Jeremy paused, unsure whether going through Natalia's worldly goods was the right thing to do. Who knew what he'd find? His sisters had once spent a good half hour cackling over a story about a woman's vibrator being discovered in handheld luggage, saying that only an idiot would put one there, and that it was better to store it in your checked bag. That his sisters knew to do that had revolted him so much he'd scarpered from the room, but no matter how hard he tried to put it from his mind, the conversation had stayed with him. Perhaps so one day in the future he knew to be respectful of Natalia's belongings, because finding such an instrument would add yet another layer of attraction to the woman he was trying to keep friend-zoned.

His sisters pleasuring themselves? Worst thought ever.

Natalia lying back, finding the spot that made her sigh. Made her moan? Made her...

He squeezed his eyes shut and clenched his fists hard enough for his clipped nails to dig into his skin. Natalia was not a willing partner. Natalia was not a one-night stand. Natalia was simply a person who was funny and intelligent and hardworking, and exactly his type in every single way.

A flash of lightning brightened the room, and another rumble followed. Still too close for comfort. A squeak from the living room hurried Jeremy up. He had to focus on what he needed, not what he desired.

Bending down, keeping his gaze on clothes and clothes only, he grabbed a pair of sweatpants, a hoodie and a pair of socks, then raced back to the living room to find Natalia still on the couch, but with the blanket pulled over her head.

'Here.' He thrust the clothing under the blanket. 'Cosy clothes. Is it okay if I use your room to change? Or I could use the bathroom?'

Thunder ripped through the sky, and the blanket before him shook. This wasn't just the fear Natalia was dealing with. This was terror.

Jeremy's heart went out to her. Abandoning his plan to get changed, he sat down beside her, lifted the blanket, then pulled it over his head, shrouding them both in darkness. Beside him, Natalia continued to shake, but he could feel her emotions ebb.

'Have you always been this scared of a storm?' He kept his voice low, his tone non-judgemental, caring. Letting her know he was a safe space.

'No. But yes. Since I was little.' The words came haltingly as fear kept a tight grip on her vocal cords.

'Can I take your hand?' Jeremy recalled her previous comment about him being unable to help himself when it came to hitting on women with a fling in mind. Though said in jest, it had come from a place of truth. He made no bones about his relationship preferences, so it was natural for Natalia to not expect him to simply be there for her without some sort of strings attached. But right now, right here, seeing her so trapped in anxiety, so vulnerable, he was in freefall. All strings cut. 'As a friend. As comfort. Nothing more. I promise.'

Her cold hand made its way into his and he wrapped his other hand around it, hoping it would help to warm her faster, soothe her more efficiently.

'Want to talk about it?'

He let the question hang there. Not pressing. Not pushing. If Natalia wanted to open up, it had to be on her terms.

A quick intake of breath followed, then he felt her relax a touch as she exhaled.

'Promise not to think me silly?'

'I promise.'

'Thank you.'

A longer silence followed, then Natalia's other hand wheedled its way between Jeremy's, and he felt her body angle in his direction.

'When I was little, there was a big storm at my house. Bigger than this.'

Tension bloomed between them, and Jeremy could almost feel Natalia being transported back in time. The flight or fight within her going into effect.

'Breathe, Natalia. It's okay. You're safe. In the

farmhouse. With me. Under a blanket. Nothing can get you here.'

A fresh exhale followed. 'Thank you. I needed that. To be anchored.'

Jeremy sensed a weight to her last words, but kept his tongue still.

'There was a storm, and I woke up. So scared. The tree outside my window had a branch that tapped in a breeze, and it thumped over and over. The lightning made it look like an ogre was trying to get in. The thunder. Continuous. Loud. Scary. And no one came.' Natalia bit back a sob, and Jeremy squeezed her hands once more, letting her know he was there, that she wasn't alone. 'I huddled under my covers, waiting for my parents to come. They didn't. I screamed their names. They didn't hear. Or chose not to.' Her tone became stilted. Bitter. Tinged with anger.

Jeremy tried to imagine his parents not coming to his room in the event of a massive storm. Couldn't. Whenever the sky had a tantrum, his mother, with his father in tow, would round their family up and turn it into an event. Dragging mattresses into the living room, pushing back furniture to make space for them. From there, they'd wait the storm out with storytelling, complete with roasting marshmallows in the fireplace. Sometimes they'd even do a dance to make the storm stop. Storms were magical events in the Gordon family, not miserable ones.

'I didn't even have a toy to hold. Wasn't allowed one. Toys were for babies. I was four.'

Natalia's body jerked as thunder rolled, then settled as he reached out and cupped her cheek, wet with tears. He stroked them away with the pad of his thumb and wished they were friends enough that he could bring her in for a hug. Make her feel as safe as he'd felt as a child.

'It felt like hours passed. Probably was minutes. But I found the courage to run to their room. They were awake. Reading. And they told me to grow up. To go back to bed. To not be silly. It was just a storm.'

Just a storm to them. To grownups. But to a little girl, it was a monster coming in the night to hurt her. How could they be so callous? How could they be so cruel?

'Natalia, I'm so sorry.'

'Don't be,' she whispered, the angry edge back. 'I got used to it.'

'You shouldn't have had to.'

Natalia didn't reply, but a fresh tear reached his thumb, telling him everything he needed to know.

Helplessness swamped Jeremy. He was used to tears; living in a household of women whose hormones had synced up, resulting in raging fights or days of being down in the dumps, meant he'd seen his fair share. But they'd always passed, and they'd never been caused by anything so traumatic. Usually it was a stolen piece of clothing or someone eating the last of the ice cream that set his sisters, and sometimes his mother, off. He'd learned to do as his father advised and just lie low and leave them to it. But this was different. This was a woman sharing a piece of her past that had hurt deeply. Perhaps even damaged her. And not just any woman. Natalia. Someone he found himself inexplicably drawn to. Someone he wanted to get to know better. Someone who he suspected he could come to care for.

Too late, a small voice deep inside whispered. *You already do.*

Jeremy tried to tamp the voice down, to deny what it was saying, but was unable. It was a fact: he did care. He felt it in his bones. In his heart. And while allowing himself to give his heart to Natalia was not an option, not when he'd promised to keep love at bay until his sister's stopped being held over a barrel by a family tale, there was no reason why he couldn't treat her like he would any other friend that he cared about.

'You know what we need to do?' He tugged at the blanket, letting it slip off slowly so that Natalia could stop its path and scurry under it again should she feel the need. 'We need to dance the storm away.'

Natalia gave him a weak smile as she palmed away the streaks on her cheeks left by her tears. 'I don't think the meteorologists would say that's a thing.'

'It's a thing. I've seen it work.'

Natalia shook her head. 'You're mad.'

'Perhaps I am, but you won't know for sure until you try.' Jeremy stood and offered Natalia his hand.

She eyed it sceptically, then looked up at him, a twinkle in her eye. 'Prove that you're mad or prove that storm dances work?'

'Perhaps both.' Jeremy tried not to show the shock that hit him as Natalia's hand found his. Her touch sending a jolt of electricity that rivalled the storm outside up his arm.

'So, how does one dance a storm away?'

Jeremy took Natalia's other hand, then stepped back, ensuring there was a respectful amount of distance between them. 'First, we step from side to side, like this.' He moved one foot to its twin, touched it, then moved it back, the second foot following suit immediately after.

'We're going to look like a couple of tweens at their first dance. Terrifying. That'll frighten the thunder away.'

Jeremy's heart lightened as he saw the fear that had held Natalia captive fall away as she fell into step with him, a look of 'what the heck am I doing, no idea, but I'm doing it anyway' disbelief on her face.

'Perhaps. But not for long. Because now we chant.'

'Chanting? You're definitely bonkers.'

Jeremy began moving their hands in time with their feet. 'Storm, storm, go away.'

'Come again another day?' Natalia's face lit up with a smile. 'Pretty sure that line's taken.'

'Which is why we don't bother with it. Besides, we don't want the storm to come back.'

Natalia nodded. 'Not while I'm still here.'

'So, chant.'

Together they chanted the line over and over. Their feet picking up in pace, their arms swinging higher and higher. As the momentum further grew, Jeremy lifted their arms up so the two of them twisted around back-to-back, before lifting their arms once more to face each other again.

'I think it's working.' Natalia's eyes gleamed and her skin glistened from the exertion of the dancing.

Jeremy cocked his head. She wasn't wrong. The thunder sounded further away. The rain had abated.

'We should keep going, though.' She dipped her chin. 'Just in case.'

'Just in case,' he echoed.

'Storm, storm, go away.'

Their arms lifted and they faced away from each other. Their backs so close, Jeremy could feel the heat radiating from Natalia.

'Storm, storm, go away.'

They twisted around to face each other, their bodies a little closer.

'Storm, storm, go away.'

Over they went.

'Storm, storm, go away.'

Over again, and once more, they met. Their toes all but touching. Their wrists grazing each other's as they swayed to the rhythm they'd created.

'Storm, storm,' Jeremy whispered, afraid of what was to come next. Knowing Natalia's lips were too close. Her eyes too wide, too hungry.

Her eyelashes fluttered shut as she rose the tiniest amount to equal his height. Her head angling just so.

It would be so easy to meet her lips with his own.

To feel her softness, to discover if the little lines that ran vertically down them could be sensed in a kiss. To wrap his arms around her waist, to reach up and stroke her hair, to open himself to her, to taste her. But to do so would be the beginning of the end. And the beginning had only just begun, and was so sweet he wasn't willing to sour the experience. Even if the darker side of him begged for him to do so.

'Go away.' Jeremy finished the chant, his tone barely there, then took a step back, stopping the moment in its tracks. 'Natalia. You're safe.'

And she was. From the storm. From her fears. From him.

A beetroot stain spread up her neck and over Natalia's cheeks. Abruptly, she dropped his hands and took a step back, turning away.

He'd embarrassed her by not reciprocating. Or embarrassed herself by thinking he would. Jeremy couldn't be sure which, but he knew that the sense of rejection would be intense, being that she'd experienced that exact feeling from a young age from the two people who ought to have embraced her. Loved her.

'You do a great storm dance, Natalia. You must be magic.' It wasn't the reaction he wanted to give her. That reaction would've involved bringing her close and soothing her pain away with a long hug, but Jeremy was sensible enough to know that was the last thing she wanted or needed from him. 'Did it help?'

Natalia's shoulders lifted, then fell. 'It did.' She

turned to face him. The high colour had abated to a rosy flush. 'Thank you.'

'Anytime.' Jeremy made a show of checking his watch. 'And as much fun as it's been, I should get going. Dawn's not far away and I need to get my beauty sleep.'

'There's not enough hours in the night for you to get that,' Natalia deadpanned.

Jeremy laughed, not remotely offended. If a gentle insult set things right between them, then so be it. 'You sound like one of my sisters.'

Natalia's lips further fell. Jeremy's heart twisted, and his gut grew heavy, like a boulder had rolled its way in and settled down for the night. Comparing Natalia to his sisters had been the right thing to do, had created further emotional – sensual – distance, but his body had spotted the lie, although said innocently, the second the words had left his mouth. But he couldn't take them back. To do so would leave a chance, and opening, a maybe, a possibility.

'Well, they're good women.' Natalia picked up the blanket and began folding it in half, then half again, before laying it over the back of the couch. 'So I'll take it as a compliment.'

'Good. Do.' Jeremy shoved his hands in his pockets, unsure what to do next.

'You were leaving, remember?' Natalia filled in the blank for him.

'Yes. Of course. Well. Good night. Or, good nearly morning.'

Natalia's thin smile was back, and stayed that way as she walked him to the front door, then shut it with the briefest of goodbyes.

Jeremy inhaled, taking in the fresh scent of rain mixed with the iron-esque aroma that came with the remnants of a storm. Cool and refreshing, it promised a new start. A chance of a better day.

After tonight's awkward ending with Natalia, he could only hope so.

NINE

Daft idiot. What the hell were you thinking all but throwing yourself at Jeremy like that? Are you that excited to be just another notch on his bedpost? Did you want to make the rest of your stay here awkward? And...

Natalia trudged up the lane, not seeing the bees bobbing about in the wild blooms that lined it, or the sparrow that appeared to be following her as she marched towards the pub where she was to meet said bedpost owner's sisters after being summoned by Gemma that morning.

AND... why the hell would you try to hook up with someone who would only reject you when the last thing you want is to be rejected? You are a ridiculous glutton for punishment and you need to get it together and figure your life out.

The inner voice had reached fever pitch, which Natalia took to mean it was done with berating her. Again.

Catching the sound of people chatting along with a hint of jazz music, Natalia felt the stress from the constant upbraiding abate. Spending an afternoon with Jeremy's sisters wasn't an ideal situation, given the way her night had ended, but at least it wasn't Jeremy himself, and she didn't believe him to be the kind to kiss and tell. Or to *not* kiss and tell, as was the case.

It would also provide further reprieve from the next round of undressing from her inner critic, which would no doubt include calling her a coward for hiding from Jeremy when he'd come by that morning to check on the vegetables and remove the tarps, before launching into how selfish she'd been for not helping him after he'd been so kind to her and helped her through her fear of thunderstorms.

Reaching the pub, Natalia took in the brick and tile building, with its doors thrown wide open, the entryway flanked by wine barrel planters that overflowed with chrysanthemums in pink, purple and red. Attached to the building's facade were more planters, these filled with herbs – chives, basil, rosemary, and a few other varieties Natalia wasn't familiar with. Overall, it had a welcoming vibe that enticed you to settle in for the afternoon and enjoy a few pints of cider over a bowl of chips. Or it would have if she wasn't about to face three women related to the man she'd nearly, almost – most definitely wanted to – kiss the night before.

Sucker for punishment, that's what you are. A hand-

some face paired with a moment of care and you're just begging to suffer fresh rejection.

'Natalia, I thought that was you. What are you waiting for?'

Make that all four of the women related to the man she'd all but thrown herself at.

Natalia closed her eyes and tried to pull herself together as Agnes Gordon swooped upon her, linked her arm through Natalia's, and all but dragged her into the pub.

'Girls, look who I found loitering outside,' she announced to her sisters, seated at a table in a corner of the pub.

Natalia took stock of her surroundings and noted the double doors that led to a garden bar. Strange that the family hadn't chosen to head outside with the rest of the patrons, who were taking advantage of the warm weather while huddling under the sun umbrellas, trying to avoid any chance of sunburn.

'She's wondering why we're the weirdos inside.' Gemma took a sip of her cider.

'Of course she is. Who wouldn't be?' Clare plucked a crisp from its bag and popped it in her mouth.

'Dare we show her?' Agnes arched her brows at her daughters, gesturing for Clare to shuffle over so she could sit next to her on the violet coloured cushioned banquette. 'Or do you think she'll think we're even odder than she already does?'

'I don't think you're odd,' Natalia protested. 'Yes, sitting indoors on a summer's day seems a little strange, but maybe you burn easily and don't want to deal with constantly sloshing sunscreen all over yourselves.'

'You're not wrong about that. The pale skin gene runs deep and burns easily in this family. Francesca looks like an astronaut in the getup she wears in order to tend the farm while avoiding the sun during the warmer months.' Agnes flicked her hand in Tilly's direction, then at the glass of wine sitting in front of Tilly.

Tilly nodded, got up and went to the bar, grabbing her mother's money card that appeared in Agnes' hand as if by magic as she passed by.

'Well, it does on the women's side. Dad and Jeremy tan up and rarely burn.' Gemma sat back with an irritated huff. 'Lucky buggers.'

'Well, they had to have something going for them, my darling.' Agnes reached into her emerald green cotton tote bag and pulled out a deck of cards. 'Because the real talent went to you girls, as is the way of the Gordon women.'

'Unlucky in love, but bursting with talent. Lucky us.' Tilly sighed, setting a glass of wine in front of her mother along with another packet of crisps. 'Which I guess makes Jeremy especially unlucky, no talent and no love.'

'For now,' Agnes replied, a knowing gleam in her eye. 'Natalia, grab yourself a drink and let's play cards.'

Knowing 'no' wasn't an option, Natalia obediently went to the bar.

'The Gordon girls taken you under their wing?' The barman, an older fellow with as much salt and pepper hair sprouting from his ears as he had above his eyes, enquired as he poured Natalia a pint of cider. 'Not often they take a shine to a random. You a bit like them?'

Natalia glanced over her shoulder at the four women, a good head shorter than she, their bodies more angular than voluptuous. There was no mistaking her as being one of them.

'Er, no. I'm just here working on their family farm for a month. They're just being hospitable.'

'Okay then.' Taking her card, the barman processed the order, then pushed the glass in her direction. 'I guess there's a first for everything. Good luck with that lot. They're a handful.'

Nodding her thanks, Natalia took the cider and walked back to the table, unsure what to make of the barman's comments. He almost made it sound like the Gordon women were usually unkind, giving people a wide berth, unlikely to let strangers close. The absolute opposite of what she'd encountered. Especially as the sisters were all dead keen to meet their matches – something you had to be open to. Cold shoulders did not rub warm hearts the right way.

'Did he tell you we're horrible?'

Natalia cringed at Gemma's voice, which was loud enough for the barman to hear.

'That we're a big old bunch of witches?' Tilly said every bit as loudly as her sister.

The women collapsed into a fit of laughter as the barman turned away, his red-veined cheeks turning a violent shade of scarlet.

'Don't mind him.' Agnes began shuffling the deck. 'The story of our family is a thing of legend around here. People don't know quite how to take us, so they tend to avoid us.'

She began dealing the cards, but not in a way that Natalia had ever seen before, nor were the cards familiar to her.

'What game are we playing?' she asked, taking in the three lines of three cards, each featuring roman numerals, strange pictures and the odd word or two.

'A game of seeing what might be.' Agnes' eyes narrowed as she focused on the spread before her. 'Some people like to keep their minds active by doing crosswords or number games. I like to encourage the girls to use their imagination to conjure up a possible future.'

'So, you tell fortunes?' No wonder the villagers thought the Gordon women were to be avoided. They weren't exactly indulging in run-of-the-mill hobbies. 'By looking at cards?'

'Tarot cards. It's been a family tradition since forever.' Clare picked up the deck and looked at the bottom. 'Two of cups.'

'Nice.' Gemma drummed her fingers on the table-top. 'Good omen for the festival.'

'At the age of ten, a deck is gifted to each Gordon girl. She then studies the meanings and learns to use her intuition to further find meanings in the cards.' Agnes took a sip of her wine. 'Have you never seen them before?'

Natalia shook her head. 'My mother and father weren't one for games. More likely to have their noses in some heavy tome, or using work as a way to relax.'

'Or escape.' Agnes' gaze was shrewd.

Natalia shivered, feeling picked over. Seen. Could Agnes see how her parents had chosen their work as doctors over their daughter? How they'd spent hours reading medical tomes and research papers rather than sit and read a frivolous work of fiction to her, other than the ones assigned by her school as compulsory homework. How Natalia, with her head in the clouds and her vivid imagination, had been a disappointment to the people who'd created her, who'd hoped for a child who would follow in their more scholarly footsteps?

'So,' Natalia searched for a way to divert the topic back to the Gordon family, not wanting to think about her own a second more than she had to. 'Why ten? Why not thirteen? Since you're all meant to be a bunch of witches, according to local legend.'

'Not a bunch, a coven. And we're not witches.' Tilly mumbled as she focused on the cards. 'And we don't know why ten's the age. It's just been that way since anyone can remember. A bit like the curse.'

'And what are you seeing in the cards?' Natalia noted the man juggling two discs, the heart through which three swords were pierced, and the two nude people with an angel of some sort presiding over them.

Gemma nudged Clare, her chin lifting ever so slightly, her gaze moving to a spot behind Natalia. 'Look what the cat dragged in.'

There was only one person in the village that the girls would address in such a way. The one person Natalia was avoiding. Instinctively, her shoulder muscles coiled tight and her spine straightened.

Smile. Her teeth gritted together. *Smile like a normal person.* She attempted to loosen her lips, managing to stretch them half a centimetre. *That'll have to do.*

Forcing herself to turn around, Natalia acknowledged Jeremy but didn't dare say a word of greeting, knowing her voice was likely to come out a high pitch squeak or crack mid-word in a way that would alert the women around her to the situation between them being not quite right.

'Breathe, girl,' Agnes whispered in her ear. 'Deep breath in, long breath out.'

So much for acting casual.

Doing as she was told, Natalia felt her shoulders ease, and her lips relax as Jeremy reached the table.

'Oh, god. I should just turn back and leave the way I came in.' He turned his attention to Natalia. 'Don't tell me they've roped you into one of their readings?'

'We were about to, if you hadn't interrupted.' Tilly shot her twin a look of irritation, then patted the seat beside her. 'Still, it's always fun to get your take on things. Sit. I'll shout you a beer for your troubles.'

Surprisingly, Jeremy did as he was told.

'Don't look so shocked.' He waggled his finger in Natalia's direction. 'If you'd known this lot as long as I have, you'd know there was no escaping their talon-like grips once they've sunk them into you.'

Given that she'd come to the pub on the understanding that they were meeting to finalise the girls' sunflower festival plans and found herself in the middle of her first ever tarot reading, Natalia found Jeremy's explanation all too easy to believe. And after the conversation with the barman, she was feeling like the Gordon women had somehow adopted her into the family without consulting her, and that the chances of leaving on her own terms were minimal. At least until her time at the farm was up; at that point, they'd have no choice but to let her go. Though to what or where, Natalia still had no idea.

'So, oh brother of mine.' Tilly tapped the cards. 'What do you see in the near future?'

'Near future?' Jeremy regarded his sister with surprise. 'You're not doing a love reading? Wonders never cease.'

'Oh, shush.' Tilly stuck her tongue out at him, then tapped the cards again. 'Less lip, more talk.'

'Sooner you do it, the sooner it's over, my love.' Agnes ruffled Jeremy's hair. 'Now tell your old mother what's popping into your head.'

Jeremy's shoulders rose, then fell, his gaze settling on the cards.

Natalia stilled, anticipation coiling in her chest, tightening it, as if some part of her was taking the reading seriously, even if the words to come were to be spoken by the one person in the family who had no interest in reading the future. Or perhaps that was why she cared, because despite the sting of rejection, she still had time for Jeremy. Wanted to know him, be around him, hear his thoughts.

'I see...' Jeremy stroked the shadow of stubble that grazed his jawline. 'A decision that needs to be made. A choice. One that could cause pain.'

'You're all but reading from the book,' Gemma groused. 'Use your intuition.'

'There's water there. Lots of it. And,' Jeremy placed his hand on a card with a woman that had a black cat sitting at her feet. 'Natalia with her sunflowers, looking happy with her lot in life.'

'God, you're basic.' Clare gave Jeremy a light shove. 'Water. Really? Got last night's bit of weather on the brain? Did the storm scare little whittle Jeremy like it used to when you were a boy? Honestly, Natalia, our brother is such a wimp. Who's scared of storms? They're great fun.'

Jeremy tensed, his nostril flaring with irritation. Because Clare had belittled him, or revealed a part that he'd not mentioned to Natalia and hadn't wanted her to know? Irritation flared in her gut. So, she could be vulnerable with him, but he refused to be vulnerable with her? Her secrets could be shared, but his had to be kept secret? His fear of storms? The possible ex who'd broken his heart? Was Jeremy even more closed off than anyone, even his own twin sister, realised? And if so, what other secrets was he keeping?

Jeremy met Natalia's gaze and moved his head back and forth so slightly no one else noticed. Was he telling her not to admit to her fear in order to protect her from his sisters' amusement at finding out that she, a full-grown woman, was terrified of storms? Or had been until Jeremy had distracted her from her fear with the storm dance, after making her feel okay, feel heard, feel like she was more than just a silly little girl for fearing the weather. Or was he asking her not to defend him, to just let his sisters have their fun so that the conversation would be over before it became an argument.

The ire that had flickered up sizzled out. She couldn't be angry with Jeremy for keeping his own fears close to his heart. Not when she'd never told a soul about her fear of storms or the reason for them. Perhaps he also had his reasons for not being open. Maybe his storms came in other forms. Perhaps emotional ones, ones that had stung his heart, like the swords in the heart on the card that lay between them.

'Just saying what I saw.' Jeremy pushed his chair back and stood up, leaving his beer undrunk. 'Like you asked me to.' He turned to his mother. 'By the way, I checked the vegetables this morning and they're fine.'

'They survived the storm? Without tarps?' Agnes

regarded her son. 'Or did you get up in the middle of the night and protect them?'

'The latter. Natalia, did I wake you? I tried to be quiet.'

Natalia found it odd that he'd keep their encounter entirely to himself, but perhaps that was what made him feel safe, the same way the blanket had kept her safe until the man before her had shown her there was nothing to fear.

'Slept as solidly as a standing stone.' She smiled up at him. 'I checked the sunflowers this morning, and they were somehow untouched.'

'Like a dome was keeping them safe.' Clare's eyes were wide and sparkling. 'A little bit of magic.'

'Or a freak occurrence.' Jeremy shook his head and gave an exasperated sigh. 'Honestly, no wonder half the village thinks this family's strange. You see rainbows and expect leprechauns, when anyone with half a rational brain in their head knows it's just light hitting water droplets.'

'Oh ho ho, so we're a science teacher now, are we?' Tilly mocked, one shoulder lifting as the other fell with each of the words.

'No, just sane.'

'That's enough of that.' Agnes brought the cards together, then added them to the deck. 'Jeremy, will we see you for dinner later?'

'I guess so.'

Jeremy's tone was flat, his lack of enthusiasm clear.

'Excellent.' Setting the deck down, Agnes clapped

her hands together. 'And Natalia will join us. Natalia, swing by Jeremy's and pick him up on the way so he can't try to get out of coming. That's an order, not a request.'

Natalia waited for Jeremy to protest, to tell his mother that Natalia didn't have to go, or to tell Natalia that she could say no, but his lips remained as flat as his disposition. An energy that was at odds with how he came across when it was just the two of them.

'Well, that's settled.' Standing, Agnes placed the tarot cards in her bag and took Jeremy by the arm. 'You can walk me home, son. And I'll see you girls at six. Don't get too tipsy or you won't enjoy dinner.'

The girls rolled their eyes at their mother's backs, then leaned in, indicating Natalia follow suit.

'Can't believe Jeremy couldn't see it.' Clare clucked her tongue in disappointment. 'It was so obvious.'

'What was obvious?' Natalia asked, as oblivious as Jeremy to the meaning of the cards.

'You mean you couldn't see it?' Tilly cocked her head to the side, her brows drawing together. 'What did you see?'

'Just cards. And two people who didn't know how to get it together, leaving them in pain and confusion. Like they were at odds with each other, but were right together.' Natalia tapped her chin in thought. 'Maybe it means one of you girls is going to meet someone at the festival, but they'll live somewhere else that makes it hard for you to be together, and you'll have to make a choice about where you'll live?'

Gemma face-palmed herself, crying out as she accidentally smacked her hand against her nose more forcefully than intended.

'That's Gemma's way of saying that you're as bad at this as Jeremy. Mostly.' Tilly passed Gemma a hanky to wipe the tears that were streaming down her cheeks.

'Mostly?' Natalia found it oddly exhilarating to think that she'd somehow read the cards correctly, even if she wasn't one hundred percent right. 'What did I get wrong?'

'That's for you to find out.' Tilly didn't elaborate further. 'And honestly, all that talk about water. Mum's wrong to say that the singing and sleepovers cured him of his fear. He's still clearly traumatised. Just being brave.'

Natalia hid a smile. It was becoming obvious why Jeremy liked to keep parts of his life separate from his family. To be a Gordon was to be loved in a way that could feel smothering. Cloistered. Where she was fiercely independent by necessity, Jeremy was as independent as he could be by choice. Though it didn't explain why he stayed close to home when he had a job that could see him live not just anywhere in England, but maybe even in other parts of the world.

'Don't feel sorry for him, Natalia. He's a big boy.' Gemma patted her hand. 'Now, how about we order some bowls of chips and get another round? I think Mum mentioned steak and kidney pie and I'm going to need a good excuse, like being too full on carbs and carbonated drinks, to not eat it.'

The girls gagged, then loudly agreed with Gemma's idea.

'Chips all round.'

'Two wines for me.'

'Grab another bag of crisps while you're at it.'

'Anything for you, Natalia?' Gemma pulled out her money card. 'My shout.'

'Actually,' Natalia stifled a yawn as the previous evening's lack of sleep made itself known. 'I could really do with a nap. This wine's gone to my head.'

'But you barely had any.' Tilly pulled Natalia's glass towards her. 'Ah well, I'll do the right and less wasteful thing and finish it, since you're not going to.'

'Just call me a lightweight. Drink away.' Grateful to not have had her tiredness, when she'd lied through her teeth and said she slept through the storm, called into question, Natalia picked up her bag. 'I'll see you all later.'

The girls waved her off, then leaned in, their furious whispers reaching Natalia's ears as she left.

'Those two.'

'Up and down.'

'Can't see the river for the bloody sunflowers.'

'This festival will be the making of them.'

Shaking her head as she stepped into the late afternoon air, perfumed by the herbs in the window boxes, tinged with the delicate scent of the chrysanthemums, Natalia couldn't help but smile. The Gordons may not be family, and Gordon Glen may not be home, but right then, between being instructed to attend dinner and being brought into family traditions, it felt a lot like she'd found a place that could become exactly that.

It was just a pity that in few weeks, she'd have to leave.

TEN

Jeremy stood to the side of his cottage's window and peered out at the lane, searching for any sign of Natalia. Seeing a flicker of movement, he bobbed back, then cursed himself, realising it was just a duck and its friend going on an early evening meander.

Why was he so nervous? This was Natalia. Someone he'd known for only a few days. Barely a colleague. Not yet a friend. Sure, he liked her – more and more as he got to know here – and there was that weird shock he experienced whenever they touched and that odd pull he felt towards her, but that wasn't cause to be metaphorically curtain twitching every few seconds like he was waiting to go on a date, while battling the uncomfortable feeling of having an army of ants trotting through his veins, making him skittish.

Forcing himself away from the window, Jeremy went to the kitchen, opened the fridge and pulled out the bottle of wine he kept in case – more like, when –

his sisters or mother popped in unannounced demanding a glass of something strong and a chinwag.

Grabbing a water glass from its place in the cupboard next to the fridge, he poured himself a little, then necked it back. Liquid courage wasn't usually his style, but if he didn't settle down soon, he would likely jump out of his skin the minute Natalia turned up on his doorstep and knocked at his door.

Shutting the fridge, Jeremy turned and leaned against it with a sigh. All these years, he'd kept himself out of emotional entanglements. Kept things simple with women. Had mutually enjoyable events that went no further than one time. And now? All it took was a funny, smart woman with lips that were made for kissing and eyes that he could spend hours looking into hoping to find the essence of her within them, to turn him into a blithering, lane-watching, long-tailed-cat-in-a-roomful-of-rocking-chairs idiot.

Clenching his jaw, he promised himself he'd get a grip. Natalia was just another woman. Attractive, yes. A good conversationalist, yes. Not afraid of hard work – even if it meant facing her fears in order to help him – yes. Vulnerable and tough and willing to be open if needed. Yes.

And that was the problem.

He'd seen her pain and listened. He'd acted. He'd cared. When he could've kept his heart and mind guarded, he'd allowed the drawbridge to fall, giving her access like the fool he was.

Three timid raps from the front of the cottage met

his ears. He checked his watch, already knowing it was Natalia and that she was right on time. Though the gentleness of the knocks surprised him. Perhaps she was as nervous as he was to be alone together after the previous night. Was worried that the intimacy of the situation had changed the tentative steps towards friendship that they'd forged. If his family got wind of their shared nerves, they'd wonder and nag and question why until someone spilled the beans, which would be awkward for the both of them. There was only one thing for it.

Hurrying to the front door, Jeremy swung it open.

'Natalia. Good to see you. Come on in.'

Looking a touch stunned at his exuberance, Natalia did as she was told, only to look beyond shocked when Jeremy gave her a hearty slap on the back.

If they were going to be friends, then he'd treat her like he treated his mates. One of the boys. One of the lads. No deep and meaningful chit chat. No talk about past traumas and the emotional responses they created. Just good old shallow puddle exchanges.

'Sorry about my mum forcing you to dinner. They're good like that. My mates get the same treatment all the time.'

Natalia glanced round the open plan living room, taking it all in. Jeremy felt his breath still as part of him wondered how she felt about how he lived. If she liked his simple style, or if she found him impossibly boring compared to the vibrant space the rest of his family inhabited.

'Do your friends ever say no?' She returned her attention to Jeremy. 'Do you?'

Jeremy's attempt at jocularity wavered for a split second. Was it so obvious how useless he was in the face of the women in his family? That despite having dreams of finding a place in the world outside of Gordon Glen, he'd never been able to cut the cords. Because they wouldn't let him. Or, if he were being honest with himself, he didn't know what life would look like without them in it, and didn't know that he wanted to find out. An inner truth that he was more ashamed of than he'd ever admit to anyone.

'Because I don't know that I could if I were you.' Natalia took another step inside, her hand running down the length of his buttery, caramel-coloured leather couch. 'They're so... strong. Forceful. They make last night's storm look like a puff of fresh air.'

Relaxing his smile, which he suspected had become more rictus than welcoming, Jeremy nodded his agreement. 'They're a handful. And no one ever goes against their requests. Even the people who aren't scared of them.'

Natalia perched on the sofa's arm. 'You mean people really are fearful of them? I noticed that the barman wasn't all that keen to serve them. Kind of felt like he wished they were anywhere but there, to be honest. But I just figured it was to do with him being religious or something and not liking fortune-telling cards being brought out in his presence.'

'Maybe it's too harsh to say people are scared of them.' Jeremy leaned against the wall and tried to explain his family's complicated relationship with the villagers who'd settled in Gordon Glen over the years. 'It's more that people don't know how to take them. It's like they're as intimidated by them as they are in awe of them. The fortune telling and mysterious proclamations of things to come can make people nervous, and yet they love living in a village with a history. You should see the place come Halloween, everyone gets into the spirit of it.'

'Or the ghost of it?' Natalia screwed up her nose. 'Sorry. Had to.'

Jeremy laughed. 'Nothing to be sorry for. You're right. They get into the ghost of it. And the vampire. And the werewolves.'

'And the witches.'

'No.' Jeremy shook his head. 'They leave that for our family. It's the one day of the year that my sisters and mother will read cards for those brave enough to sit before them, and I think people are afraid if they turn up dressed in a witches costume they'll offend them so much they'll stop doing it. Rumour has it they're pretty accurate. Not that I've ever seen anything they say come true.' Jeremy unhooked his sweater from the hat stand by the front door. 'Speaking of offending them, we better get a move on. Mum hates it when I'm late.'

Locking the door behind them, the walk to his

family home was uneventful. Jeremy ensuring the conversation didn't stray into territory that might see them open up, be vulnerable with each other. Not that he had to try hard, Natalia seemed as determined to keep things casual as he did, pointing out the behaviour of two birds that were sunbathing on a stone fence while a cat kept a close eye on them, or how the clouds that dotted the sky looked like dragons and puppies.

Soon enough, the sunshine yellow door greeted them, welcoming them in, even though it was shut. Even after all these years, the entryway to the home he'd grown up in could lighten his mood, to make him feel like whatever had happened that day, that week, that year, he would be okay once he was ensconced inside.

As if sensing their presence, the door flew wide open; his mother appearing in the space it created a second later.

'I thought I felt you two standing out here like a couple of gormless wonders.' She stepped to the side and waved them in. 'In you get. The cheeseboard's on the verge of being demolished by that father of yours. If you're lucky, you might get a little gouda or a bit of brie in you.'

'I'd started to wonder if your father was a figment of your combined imaginations,' Natalia murmured as they headed inside.

'The men in the family can feel a bit like that,' Jeremy replied with a shrug of his shoulders.

Natalia's brows drew together, her gaze curious,

then straightened up, a polite smile appearing on her face in readiness to meet the man who'd had fifty percent of something to do with the birth of he and his sisters, and yet – like all the Gordon men before him, both blood and those who'd married into the family – had been overshadowed by the women. Even men like his father, who in any other world would've been the main attraction, as Natalia was about to find out.

Acknowledging his dad with a nod, Jeremy positioned himself so he could get a look at Natalia's face when she met the man. Used to seeing people look dazed and not just a touch confused in the presence of his sisters and mothers, it was a secret joy for him to watch their reactions when they met Jim Grant.

'Hello, Natalia.' Jim stood, his height and broad shoulders almost filling the living room. 'The girls have spoken so much about you. You've made quite the impression.' He reached out and encased Natalia's hands in his own large ones. 'It's always nice to have fresh blood in the Glen. Keeps things interesting. And how have the sunflowers been treating you?'

Natalia's mouth morphed into a small, but very much there, o-shape. 'Er, fine. Survived the, er, storm.'

'Good, good. I know Francesca would hate for anything to happen to those flowers. She was most worried about leaving them, but she felt the time for a holiday had come, and who was she to ignore the winds of change?'

'Yes. Exactly.' Natalia's head cocked to the side. 'Um, you probably get this often but...'

His father's eyes narrowed. 'Let me guess... I look like a thriller writer who used to do the talk show circuit whenever he had a new book but then went into Hermitude, despite still releasing two books a year?'

Jeremy pressed his lips together and tried not to laugh at his father's usual spiel, the one he used whenever someone recognised him. Which wasn't often, because of the hermit part being correct. Between falling in love with Agnes, creating children with her, then sitting back and being happy with the ensuing mayhem that was their ways, he'd done his part well by the Gordon clan. And had done so happily. Something Jeremy still couldn't quite fathom. Even though his father loved his family, as he did, resentment at the situation he found himself in wound its way around his heart, making him wish he could've been born to almost anyone else, anywhere else.

'Um, yes. That.' Natalia's brows somehow further tightened. 'Must get tedious. People thinking that you're someone you're not.'

'Well, it's always nice to be compared to a man that once was described as...'

Jeremy prepared to silently say the words that were about to come from his father's mouth.

'..."the dashing darling of the thriller genre"'.

'Dad, how many more years are you going to dine out on that for?' Tilly let out an 'ugh' of embarrassment, then helped herself to a cube of feta. 'You've got to move on.'

Jim indicated Natalia take a seat, then poured her a

glass of rosé, before sitting back down in the mustard-coloured velvet wingback chair he favoured. 'Why should I? You lot just see me as wallpaper. Or a wardrobe hanger. Something to lean against or drape your woes and worries on. A man has to remember that at one point in time he was fawned over. Helps him get out of bed each day.'

His mother, glass of wine in hand, settled on his father's knee and ran her fingers through his lush, salt and pepper mop of hair. 'Poor darling, must be so hard to be so dashing but so overlooked. To have four women who adore you telling you they love you regularly. Tough life.' His mother planted a long kiss on Jim's lips, sending Tilly into a gagging fit, while Natalia looked away, her cheeks becoming rosy at such an obvious show of affection.

Jeremy stepped in, not wanting Natalia to feel any more uncomfortable than she already did. 'Mum, Dad, can we keep the teenage handsy-ness to a minimum while we have a guest?'

'Such a killjoy,' His mother grumped. 'But I'm sure we can manage it for one night.'

'Much appreciated.' Jeremy took the seat next to Natalia, then bent over and dragged the cheese platter closer to them. 'Hungry?'

'No.' Natalia shook her head.

'Those two launching themselves at each other has that effect on people.' Jeremy grimaced, then helped himself to a cracker, loading it with gouda and pickled onion.

'Ew, don't eat that. You might want to kiss someone later.' Tilly made to swipe the cracker from his hand, but Jeremy placed it in his mouth before she could.

'Don't talk with your mouthful,' Agnes ordered, just as he was about to tell Tilly he could do what he wanted.

'So, Natalia.' Tilly leaned in. 'We consulted Gemma's deck of cards after you left the pub this afternoon and we're holding the first of the sunflower festival events in a week's time.

'The, er, cards told you that the sunflowers would be in bloom by then?' Natalia took a sip of her rosé, followed by another. 'Do you think you can organise the festival in time?'

'It's a picnic amongst the plants.' Tilly shrugged her shoulders. 'It doesn't matter what state the sunflowers are in. It's the vibe, the ambience. The idea that romance can bloom with a simple meal between people. It's like...' Tilly glanced up at the ceiling, searching for an answer. 'A budding thing. Love doesn't just happen, it has to bud, like the sunflowers.'

Jeremy swallowed his mouthful of food, promising himself he'd stick to small bites only, lest his family try to railroad Natalia into more events, dinners or tarot card readings, and he needed to swoop in and save her.

'Okay, I see where you're going. However,' Natalia's lips quirked to the side. 'Just to be clear, there's only going to be three events, right? Three events, and that's it. Picnic, silent disco, then the opening day when people can pick their own sunflowers, take photos, and roam around.'

'Also known as the original and only idea that was meant to be happening.' Jeremy added, realising Natalia didn't need his help, but wanting her to know he had her back should they try to press her into a fresh idea that might pass through their whimsical minds.

'Nope. That's it. Three events are perfect. Any less and it's not a festival, any more and we'll be making a rod for Natalia's back.' Tilly waved at Gemma as she walked through the door, a bottle of fizz in one hand, a bucket of ice in the other.

'Why are we sitting in here? It's far nicer out in the garden.' Gemma waved at Jeremy to carry the cheese platter. 'Honestly, let's enjoy the lighter evenings while they're here.'

Doing as he was told, Jeremy picked up the platter and trailed after his family, Natalia at his side.

'I thought your family didn't do the sun?' she said in a hushed tone.

Jeremy didn't reply, once again wanting to see the look on Natalia's face when she discovered the answer for herself.

'Such a good idea, Gemma.' His mother rubbed Gemma's back as they trooped through the kitchen's back door. 'Now, where's Clare?'

'Upstairs reading some astrology book. She said she'll be down after she's boned up on the ins and outs of planets going retrograde, or some such thing.' The disdain in Gemma's voice was all too apparent, and for once, Jeremy found himself in agreement with her. 'Everyone knows the cards are the way to go. They see what we can't. Or tell us what we refuse to listen to. The stars just move around in the sky in such a predictable fashion. It's all a bit too basic.'

Almost in agreement.

As far as Jeremy was concerned, any form of fortune telling was a have. You made your own fate with every choice, every decision, every action. Fate wasn't a destination laid out for you that you had to stumble down until you reached the end of the path.

Approaching the backdoor, he stepped aside and gave a small flourish. 'After you.'

'Why thank you, kind Sir.' Natalia replied in a slightly off, but still charming attempt at a southern American accent.

Jeremy looked down at his feet in order to hide his smile as a soft 'oh' met his ears. The summer garden never failed to impress guests, and even in his mind's eye he could see why.

Gauzy shade sails in pastel colours of lilac, pink and mint criss-crossed their way over the patio. Surrounding the area was a garden that flourished in an uproar of colour with roses, geraniums, and hydrangeas jockeying for attention. Underneath the shade sails the outdoor furniture, handcrafted from foraged pallets by his father, then painted a pastel lemon and furnished with homemade cushions covered in a cantaloupe shade of fabric, invited people to settle in and get comfortable. And even though it was still light out, thousands of tiny fairy lights threaded through the plants and braided up the poles that held the shade sails, twinkled merrily, adding a touch of magic to the ambience.

'I feel like I've stepped into a fairy tale,' breathed Natalia. 'It's beautiful.'

'Thank you.' His mother settled into one of the two single outdoor chairs, with his father taking the seat opposite. 'We all worked hard on it.'

'All? Even you?' Natalia nudged Jeremy. 'This is the polar opposite of your home.'

'Isn't it just?' Clare stepped around Natalia and made herself at home on the three-seater couch. Gemma and Tilly planting themselves on either side of her soon after. 'Jeremy hasn't met a shade of beige that he doesn't love. How he came up with the colour scheme for the garden never ceases to amaze me. He even managed to make it beautiful in winter when everything else is half dead.'

Such was the backhandedness of the compliment, Jeremy didn't know whether to give his sister the two-finger salute or thank her for her kindness.

'I thought Jeremy's place was perfectly fine.' Natalia settled into the two-seater couch.

'"Perfectly fine"', Gemma mimicked Natalia. 'That means you think it's boring'

'It's functional.' Jeremy interrupted, wishing his sisters could leave his way of living alone, if only for one night. 'I know where everything is.'

'It's bland.' Clare screwed her nose up. 'Banal, even.'

'How's your place decorated?' Tilly leaned forward. 'I can't imagine you being bland, boring or banal.'

Natalia shrugged. 'Can't say I've an aesthetic worth mentioning. I've kept my life simplified down to everything you can carry in a suitcase and a couple of boxes for years.'

'No real home, then?' His mother's eyes gleamed, and Jeremy's stomach sank as he saw his sisters' nudge each other.

'Does that mean there's an opening for one?' Tilly brought her hands together. 'Gordon Glen is a great place to live. Good people.'

'Good people, like us.' Clare nodded enthusiastically. 'There are worse places to settle down.'

'Jeremy has an extra room. You could move in with him once Aunty Francesca gets back.' Gemma widened her eyes at Jeremy, and it was all he could do not to stick his tongue out at her. 'You could even decorate it any way you want. I'm sure he won't mind since he doesn't care about these things. So long as he can find everything.'

'Natalia,' Jeremy stood up, tired of his sisters' banter. 'Ignore them. They're being ridiculous. And if this level of behaviour is going to continue, then I'm going to need a beer. Anyone want one?'

'I'll take one, son.' Jim flashed him the thumbs up, as much of a sign that he wanted the beer as that even if it didn't always seem like it, he'd have Jeremy's back if the women got too wild with their words and ways.

Heading to the kitchen, Jeremy opened the fridge and paused, taking a moment to breathe away the irritation that had squirrelled its way from his gut to his heart. He loved his sisters, his mother too, but they had a way of making him feel like he'd never be good enough to be a Gordon. That all his ways were at odds with the family he was born into. That he wasn't a real Gordon because his ways were simple rather than outlandish, and his head wasn't up in the clouds but firmly planted on terra firma, where he didn't have to look for signs or hidden meanings, instead taking everything and everyone at face value. Which, on the whole, had worked out well for him.

'Need a hand with the beers?'

Natalia's scent reached him before she did, and he allowed himself to inhale, knowing she couldn't see how its musky, peachy aroma soothed him in a way regular deep breathing never could.

'I'm sorry about your sisters. They're being a touch out of line. At least, more so than I've seen to date.'

Jeremy took out two bottles, set them on the bench, then twisted off the caps. 'They're fine. You get used to it.'

'Perhaps.' Natalia blocked Jeremy from closing the fridge door. 'I've been instructed to bring more cheese.'

Jeremy pulled out a fresh round of brie and passed it to her. 'God forbid those three get up to get their own cheese.'

Natalia grinned. 'I think they're trying to set you and I up. All that talk of me staying here long term, of moving in with you. I just explained to them I'm only here until the end of the month, and that I have commitments made that prevent me from staying. That's not entirely true, by the way, but it should stop them giving you or me – us – further grief.'

Jeremy huffed out a sigh. 'That's what you think. They're probably plotting how to rid you of your pesky responsibilities while we're in here. Figuring out some sort of responsibility banishing spell.'

'If only it were that easy.' Natalia's lips turned down, her chest rising and falling. With a shake of her head, her smile reappeared. 'Anyway, the sooner we head out there, the sooner we can stop any potential plotting in its tracks.'

Jeremy looked on as Natalia headed back outside with the brie. He didn't need to be a so-called empath to notice that the idea of returning home disturbed Natalia. That she wasn't looking forward to it. Which begged not one, but two questions. Why would the idea of returning to a city she'd grown up in cause her so much pain? And why was he so tempted to fix things so that he never had to see her lips turn down ever again?

'Natalia, there you are,' Clare cried out. 'You were gone so long we thought you two had snuck away to get to know each other better.'

Letting out a groan, Jeremy hurried outside, ready to put a stop to any further insinuations that something romantic was happening between himself and Natalia. He opened his mouth to tell Clare to keep her comments to herself, but Gemma pointed at him, then brought her fingers to her lips and zipped them, leaving a smarmy smile that caused his gut to fall towards the patio floor.

'So, we've been talking.' Gemma took the brie from Natalia with a nod of thanks, then ripped into the packaging and set it on the platter.

'Told you so, Natalia.' Jeremy took a seat on the two-seater couch beside Natalia, keeping as far away from her as possible so as not to give his sisters any ideas.

'Told her what?' Tilly angled her head to the side.

'That you're full of bright ideas.' Natalia helped herself to more wine, then took a sip as long and glass-emptying as Jeremy's had been. 'So, what were you talking about?'

Clare's eyes narrowed, her lips pursing in a manner that Jeremy knew meant she had a plan in mind, one that he wouldn't like. 'We decided while you two were busy getting beer and cheese that you, darling brother, ought to take Natalia to the picnic.'

'Not going to happen.' Jeremy shook his head so quickly he saw stars for a second. 'I'll be busy on the farm.'

'It's on a Saturday. You never work on Saturdays. It's your day off.' Tilly grinned like the cat who'd got the cream, or the sister who'd put her brother in a position that would make him look like a right dickhead if he found any more excuses to not accompany the person sitting next to him to an event when she knew no one else in the village.

Except she did.

'Why don't you take her, Tilly? Or Gemma. Or Clare. You're more fun than I. I'm too boring, bland and banal, remember?'

'We were talking about your style, not your personality.' Gemma smirked. 'Though in saying that...'

'In saying that, your personality is great.' Clare elbowed Gemma, who oophed in pain. 'The thing is, we girls are going to be too busy getting to know potential love interests – or lust interests – to babysit her.'

'Um,' Natalia held up her hand. 'Can I just say that I don't need babysitting because I'm not going either. I'll happily hang out in the farmhouse and read a book, or go for a walk down to the river and take a swim, maybe stop in at the pub and enjoy a wine in the beer garden.'

Jeremy shot Natalia a grateful smile. As much for getting him out of going to his sisters' event as for not hating him for being so reticent to go with her.

'Well then, that's that sorted.' Agnes clapped her hands, signifying the decision was made. 'You two are going together. I'll make the picnic lunch, I'll even drop it off at Francesca's. And I will not accept no for an answer.'

'But I said n-' Natalia attempted to set his mother right.

Agnes' nose lengthened, her lips thinned, her

demeanour becoming as still as the shade sails on the breezeless evening. 'You're going to have a marvellous time. *Both* of you.'

Natalia's gaze met Jeremy's. The look in her eyes was as helpless as the one he imagined he was projecting. They'd been Agnesed. Ignored, overridden, forced to do what the matriarch of the Gordon family decided.

'It'll be great.' Tilly's head bobbed back and forth to a tune only she could hear. 'You can wingman for each other. And maybe, if we're lucky, Jeremy will finally fall in love and break this stupid family curse so that the rest of us can finally find love for both a good time and a long time.'

Dropping his head, seeing no way to get around his mother's decision, especially when Natalia's tongue seemed to be as glued to the top of her mouth as his was, Jeremy let out a sigh, reminding himself it was only a picnic lunch. Not a date. There was nothing romantic about it.

What was the worst that could happen?

ELEVEN

'I'm sorry.' Jeremy held out a posy of daisies.

Natalia took them for the conciliatory nature in which they'd been given, rather than seeing anything remotely romantic in the gesture. After the dinner at his family home, she knew there was nothing more to the flowers than a man who felt terrible that she'd been pushed into a picnic with him. Not that she'd have said no if he'd asked of his own accord. Spending time with Jeremy was in no way a hardship.

The past two weeks had seen their friendship blossom as they spent days out in the fields tending to the produce, stopping in the afternoon for a bite to eat and a dip in the river. The fact that a moment of weakness had seen her almost kiss him seemed ridiculous now. Sure, she'd caught the odd moment of speculation on his face, a lingering glance in her direction as she wallowed in the shallows of the river in nothing but her swimsuit, but that didn't mean he saw her in any other way than a friend. He was simply a man with a somewhat-naked woman in his presence. Keeping one's eyes above the chin wasn't easy. Lord knew she'd taken in his toned stomach and taut thighs more times than was necessary.

Taking the daisies, she indicated he follow her into the farmhouse. 'No, I'm the one who needs to be apologising.'

'You? Whatever for?'

'For letting this happen. For allowing your family to push you into a picnic with me. I'm sorry I didn't realise how forceful they were. How demanding they could be.' She pulled a mug out from the cupboard, filled it with water from the sink, and placed the daisies in it.

'And perhaps I shouldn't be such a pushover.' Jeremy reached over and tweaked a daisy so that it was pointing outwards.

Natalia caught the hint of self-disgust in Jeremy's words and her heart panged at the way he saw himself – as someone who was easily told what to do, manipulated by his family. Someone who allowed themselves to be trod all over by their whims and wants.

'You're not a pushover.' Natalia picked a daisy out from its makeshift vase and placed it behind Jeremy's ear.

'Yes, I am.' He removed the daisy and placed it back in the mug.

'If you were a pushover, you'd have kept the daisy tucked behind your ear in order to please me.'

'That's different. You're different.' Jeremy's gaze went to his shoes, his upper lip lifting in a sneer that could only have been directed at himself.

'Jeremy.' Natalia placed her hand over his, hoping to draw his attention away from his inner turmoil. '"No" is a full sentence and anyone is allowed to say it. Even you. Even to your family.'

'Even if said family created this for us to dine on?' Jeremy hefted up the wicker picnic basket. Any hint of self-disgust replaced by a smile that made Natalia's heart go strange and fluttery, like she'd disturbed a kaleidoscope of sleeping butterflies. 'There's even proper champagne. Which I'm pretty sure is my mother's way of not so much apologising as trying to make everything better.'

'That's her version of the icing on the cake?'

'More like the sugar on the snare.' Jeremy rolled his eyes. 'But at least it's something, I guess. So, shall we?'

Natalia nodded. 'We shall.'

Stepping out into the backyard, Natalia was struck by the sheer amount of people who'd arrived for the picnic. She'd heard the cars parking up in the last half an hour, caught the laughter and chatter of people passing by the cottage, but hadn't realised how popular the event was. And not just with singles. People had clearly ignored the social media posts and posters that Jeremy's sisters had put around the village and in those beyond saying it was a picnic in the sunflowers for singles to get to know each other and decided to make a day of it anyway, with families finding shady spots to sit in while the kids ran about. Folk in their later years meandered hand-in-hand, blankets over their arms and baskets of food at their sides, finding a place to sit back and relax.

'Outnumbered by the happily coupled.' Jeremy clucked his tongue. 'The girls will be devastated.'

'You sound so sad for them.' Natalia pressed her hand to her heart. 'Devastated at their potential loss of lust interests.'

Jeremy pointed to a spot just outside of the sunflower field, where a willow tree edged the river bank. 'It's what they get for being so meddlesome. And for thinking the world will bend to their will.'

'Do they really think that?' Natalia tried to imagine a world where people bent to her will. Not that she felt others walked all over her, but she certainly hadn't experienced a life where people did as she asked, wanted or needed. Everything she had, she'd had to work for. Her parents never giving her a dime, let alone a word of support. Her revelation to them, before she left London for Gordon Glen, that she was finally thinking of going to university, had even raised a 'hmm' of approval.

'I don't just think that, I've lived it. It's what happens when you're a Gordon man living in a Gordon woman's world. They're literally raised being told they're superior. That they're special. It doesn't exactly breed humility.'

'Ironic, since it's you who apparently holds the key to their happiness.' Natalia took the plaid picnic blanket from its spot over Jeremy's forearm and spread it out over the grass.

Jeremy set the basket down, then sat beside it. Stretching his legs out in front of him, he kicked off his leather sandals, then pointed his toes in a stretch. Natalia tried not to notice the way the movement emphasised the line that ran down his calf muscles, or the way his thighs tensed, teasing at the possibility of further muscles underneath his cargo shorts.

He's just a friend, she reminded herself. *One that has no interest in you.*

'That may be so, but being a Gordon man, I don't hold the power of,' he lifted his hands and waggled his fingers. 'Magic.'

With a derisive snort, Jeremy opened the basket and began pulling out all manner of treats, from cheeses, pickles and sliced deli meats to plump strawberries and ruby-coloured cherries, followed by a crusty loaf of bread and the aforementioned bottle of champagne.

'Looks amazing.' Natalia's stomach gurgled in appreciation at the spread before them. 'Your mum really pushed the boat out.'

Jeremy peered into the basket. 'Almost. She forgot wine glasses.'

'We could take sips from the bottle?' Natalia suggested, not wanting to forego the fizz simply because of a lack of glassware.

'Or I could head back to the farmhouse and grab a

couple of glasses.' Jeremy was up and off before she could say a word.

Reaching for a strawberry, Natalia placed it in her mouth, relishing the vibrancy of the juice, the sweetness of the fruit. Maybe coming to the picnic wasn't such a bad idea after all. If she'd remained at the farmhouse, she'd have had a peanut butter sandwich for lunch, and there wouldn't have been a lick of champagne, probably just a cup of tea. Then there was the company. Chatting with Jeremy was far more interesting than spending even more time in her own head. There were only so many times she could listen to herself ponder what her future looked like, what path of study her parents would consider amenable for their wayward daughter. Let alone how she was going to force herself back to the city after discovering how peaceful, how satisfying country life could be.

'You look deep in thought.'

An unfamiliar voice broke her reverie, and Natalia looked up to see a blond-haired man with a bakery bag in hand, making a move to sit beside her.

'Oh, that spot's-'

'Perfect,' he interrupted, giving her an overly white-toothed grin. 'Love that there's shade, the view of the river, and a pretty face to appreciate.'

Natalia cringed at the cheesiness of the line and went to move the man along, not wanting to encourage him to stay by saying or doing nothing. 'That's-'

The man face-palmed himself. 'A horrible, cheesy line. One I should've never used, but did because my brain went offline. I'm so sorry.' He offered his hand. 'I'm Michael, by the way. Recently single, very unused to talking to other women who aren't family members or friends of my wife, but doing my best because my friends said that after a year I should really stop wallowing in my grief and get out there and meet someone. Even if it's just as a friend.'

Natalia took in the barrage of words, then read between the lines: Michael was recently widowed and out of his depth but doing his best.

'I'm sorry about your wife.' She shook his hand. 'I'm Natalia.'

Michael let out an exaggerated breath. 'Phew. Introductions done. Not too difficult, despite the shocking start, and you didn't make me feel like a sad, lonely old man, or make me get more in depth about what brought me here. Thank you. You're a scholar and a saint.'

Natalia chuckled as Michael pressed his hands together and angled them in her direction. 'Not a scholar. Not much of a saint, either. I'll take the compliment, though. So, are you a local?'

'Which means you're not a local, because if you were, you'd know I'm not. I feel like this is a place where everyone knows everyone until they don't, then they make it their business to find out.' Michael pulled a pasty out of its bag and eyed it. 'Pasties are unsexy, aren't they? I should've gone the route you did and brought food that would make people want to sit with me.'

Natalia eyed the golden pastry and shrugged. 'I think there's always a place for comfort food.'

'Good point. Lord knows I need it here.' Michael set the pasty down. 'So, what brings you to Gordon Glen? Aside from the obvious.'

'Oh, I'm not here as a single looking to mingle, more of a wing woman to an unwilling participant.'

'It seems you attract them,' Michael grimaced. 'And where is said unwilling participant? Hiding amongst the sunflowers?'

'Probably.' Natalia giggled again, warming to Michael's easy manner. 'So what kind of person are you hoping to meet?'

'Someone who likes my terribly bland cooking, doesn't mind that I'm a bit of a neat freak, and won't be too upset if I talk about my wife now and then.' Michael's eyes went to the blanket, then he picked up his pasty and took a big bite.

Anything to hide his still very raw pain, Natalia surmised. Reaching out, she laid a hand on his knee, unsurprised when he jerked in fright at the foreign touch.

'Sorry,' he mumbled. 'Not used to...'

'I understand.' Natalia leaned in so she could say what she hoped would help Michael with no nearby picnickers overhearing. 'And I hope you don't mind my saying, but I want you to know you don't have to listen to your friends. Or do anything you don't feel ready to do. The right person will come along when you're ready.'

'Twice in one lifetime?' Michael shook his head and frowned. 'Could anyone be that lucky?'

'You strike me as a good person, and I'd like to think that good people attract good things. So, yes, I think you could be that lucky.'

Michael placed his hand over Natalia's and gave it a squeeze. 'I'm really glad I barged in on your doomed wing-woman picnic set up.'

'Same.' Natalia straightened up. 'Now how would you like a strawberry to go with that pasty?'

'Who am I to say no to something that looks so sweet?' Michael wrinkled his nose, then rolled his eyes at the double entendre that was anything but.

A shadow darkened the picnic blanket. Natalia looked up to see Jeremy towering over them, wine glasses in hand, with a look on his face that gave the impression he'd caught wind of an unpleasant bodily odour.

'Didn't take you long to find someone to chat to.' Jeremy made no move to take a seat. 'Would it be better if I left you two alone?'

Natalia caught the tension in his tone, which only added to the curiosity of his put out facial expression. If she didn't know better, she'd have thought he was jealous. Except it couldn't be that. He'd made it clear when he'd avoided her lips the night of the storm that he didn't see her that way. That she was a friend and nothing more. And only ever could be, since he had no interest in romantic relationships, and she had zero desire to be with anyone who could so easily reject her, who treated connections so lightly. One night she could've done, and – if she were honest with herself – would have done that night, seeking comfort over common sense. But in the harsh light of day, Jeremy wasn't for her. And never could be.

Michael raised his hand, then dropped it as Jeremy's hands remained at his side. 'I'm Michael. Forced here by friends. Managed to find the one other person who was in the same position.' He grinned at Natalia. 'Like attracts like, I guess.'

Natalia patted the ground. 'Jeremy, sit. You're blocking the view of the lovebirds being interrupted by the families who've turned up.'

'I know, right?' Tilly bowled up to them, the area between her brows lined with consternation. 'What part of "singles picnic" do these people not understand? And how do they think bringing those petri dishes they call children will foster interest between those who have yet to breed, and might not even want to?' Tilly heaved in a breath, then noticed Jeremy and Natalia weren't alone, her eyes softening at the sight of a good-looking man. 'Not that there's anything wrong with children. Lovely things that they are. Positively adorable.'

'But passion killers, all the same?' Michael grinned up at Tilly, seemingly charmed by her rant.

'Exactly.' Tilly nodded, then thrust her hand out. 'Hi. I'm Tilly. Single. It's nice to meet you.'

Michael shook her hand. 'And I'm Michael.

Widower. Here under duress. But it's still nice to meet you.'

'In that case.' Tilly pulled Michael up off the blanket with surprising ease considering he was taller and appeared heavier than she was by a considerable amount. 'You can come dine with me. I've yet to find another single amongst all these...' Tilly shuddered. 'Families.'

Waving goodbye, the two set off to find a spot amongst the sunflowers, leaving Natalia staring at a still glowering Jeremy.

'Now will you sit?' She patted the ground once again. 'And why do you look like you've got a poisonous spider in your pants? Anyone would think you just came across your girlfriend – or would be girlfriend – being chatted up by another man.'

It was only said as a joke, but Jeremy's eyes further narrowed and his nostrils flared.

'Jeremy, I'm joking. Now get those glasses down here and let's enjoy this picnic that your mother lovingly put together.'

His expression remained peeved, but Jeremy did as he was told.

Popping the cork, Natalia poured the champagne into the glasses, unable to enjoy the tiny beads threading their way up to the top before popping, because she couldn't help but feel she'd done something wrong.

'Cheers to a great day.' Jeremy lifted the glass, his voice as flat as the atmosphere between them.

'No.' Natalia kept her glass down. 'I'm not saying cheers when you're acting all odd and I don't know why.'

'Fine, I'll drink to a lovely summer's day without you.' Jeremy took a sip of his champagne, his gaze going to the river before them, its water meandering along in a way that could've lulled a person to sleep if they weren't so tense for a reason Natalia wasn't allowed to be privy to.

Losing her taste for the liquid in her hand, Natalia set in down on a flat spot of the grass. 'So, you're going to be churlish and remote on top of irritated, for no good reason that I can see? Well, this is going to be a marvellous time. Perhaps I should follow Tilly and Michael and see if they'll keep me company.'

Jeremy shrugged like Natalia's suggestion was no big deal, but his fulcrum tensed in a further show of displeasure.

Seeing being as reasonable as one could be in the face of someone being obstinate wasn't working, Natalia decided to bring out the big guns. It would either see Jeremy storm off or get him to open up. Which, at this point, would be fine. Anything had to be better than sitting opposite a man who was acting like you were as welcome as the plague.

'Is this what broke you up with the girl from university? You'd get all sullen and rude whenever something displeased you? Did she finally get sick of this...' She circled her finger in his direction. 'Shitty behaviour and send you on your way? Was that why you came home all heartbroken and mopey?'

Jeremy's head jerked back, his brows drawing together, any trace of annoyance replaced by confusion. Because she knew about the girl? Or that she'd pegged his behaviour so correctly? Both?

'And, while you might think you can treat someone you care about like that, maybe even someone you were in love with, you can't behave like that way with me.' Natalia brought her hand to her heart. 'I'm a friend, remember? Not someone to be toyed with. Not one of your one and done women. I don't expect red carpets to be rolled out for me, and for you to greet me like I'm the queen of the world, but I sure as hell don't expect you to give me the cold shoulder just because you come back to find me chatting with a man, when you and I are not together.'

Jeremy drew his legs up to his chest and wrapped his arms around his knees. 'Are you done?'

'Quite.' Natalia made to stand up. 'I no longer see the point in dealing with a person who can be as cold as my parents could be whenever I didn't meet their expectations. At least they had reason to do so. I was never academic enough to succeed at achieving their hoity toity ways and ambitions. You? You've known me all of five minutes in the grand scheme of things, so you haven't had time to come to expect anything of me.'

'This is true, but not quite true.' Jeremy's head angled to the side. 'We've not known each other long enough for me to decide I know exactly who you are, but I can tell you who I thought you weren't.'

Natalia's stomach tightened as the feeling crept over her that by staying she was walking into a trap. One that was too late to back out from. 'And who did you think I wasn't?'

'Someone who listened to my sister's madcap beliefs and presumed she was correct.'

'I've never once said I believe in the stupid curse,' Natalia retorted. 'And I don't know what that has to do with this. With us.' She pointed to Jeremy, then back to herself.

'I'm not talking about the bloody curse. I'm talking about Camille.'

'Camille?' Natalia feigned confusion, not wanting to give just how much she knew about Jeremy's ex-girlfriend.

'Blonde. Great smile. Went to university with me. If you dug into the internet long enough, you might've seen a picture of us with our arms wrapped around each other in the way that a couple might look. If they were a couple, that is.'

Natalia bit down on her lip and nodded. A boulder-sized sense of idiocy rolling into her gut as she realised that perhaps she'd gotten the wrong end of the stick that Tilly had given her – a stick that may well have been made of presumptions.

'Camille was my best friend.' Jeremy's face slackened, as if saying the words pained him.

'Was?' Natalia went to squash the urge to reach out

to Jeremy, to take his hand in hers and comfort him, then remembered how he'd done exactly that to her the night of the storm, and how good it had felt to have someone be there for her when she needed it most. One look at the lack of colour in his cheeks and the dullness in his eyes told her Jeremy needed a friend to be there at that moment.

Tentatively, Natalia reached out and placed her hand on top of his, feeling the roughness of his weathered hands, the strength that lay in them thanks to hours working the fields. He flipped his hand over and their fingers interlocked. A surge of energy pulsed in the hollow where their palms didn't meet, the power of it travelling up her arm, then through her body, causing a river of goose bumps in its wake. She glanced up at Jeremy and caught the flush of red high on his cheekbones, the look of consternation that flashed through his tiger's eye brown eyes.

Natalia waited for him to remove his hand, to back away from the odd sense of electricity that continued to move between them, but their fingers remained entwined.

Had he held hands like this with Camille? Did they have a similar energetic connection? Was it stronger? Deeper? Jealousy clawed at Natalia's heart. She did her best to beat it off, reminding herself that Camille was no longer in the picture, that Camille was just a friend to Jeremy, as she was just a friend to Jeremy. That it was daft to feel irritated by a relationship that hadn't existed for years, especially when she'd only known Jeremy for two weeks.

'Was.' Jeremy confirmed. 'We fell out when I left university after my second year. She thought I should've stayed, should've tried harder, shouldn't have given up so easily.' He shook his head, annoyance flashing in a curl of lip. 'She couldn't understand that I was needed at home.'

Natalia struggled to understand Jeremy's anger, his sadness. Or why his friend would give up on him so easily. 'So, you fell out because you came back to Gordon Glen?'

'We fell out because she believed I was ruining my potential.' Jeremy picked a cherry up by its stalk and twisted it back and forth. His chest lifted as if he had something else to say, but Jeremy remained silent.

'There's more?' Natalia enquired, knowing there had to be, but not wanting to push more than was fair. Or more than she'd want to be pushed if she were in Jeremy's shoes.

'It was just...' Jeremy's jaw clenched, the muscle beneath his ear bulging. 'It's hard to focus on doing what you want, becoming who you want to be, when you've got three sisters in your ear demanding to know when you would return home next. Who made light of your hopes of becoming an architect. Laughing that I'd undertaken that path because I clearly planned on building a big family home for when I finally fell in love, made lots of Gordon babies and broke the curse so they could live their lives and find love too.'

Natalia exhaled slowly, knowing what it was like to not meet expectations, but not understanding what it was like to give up a dream to please another. 'And Camille knew this? About your family?'

Jeremy set the cherry down with a sigh. 'She made the mistake of coming home during the holidays once.'

'Mistake? Your family are...' Natalia attempted to find a polite way to describe the chaotic nature of his family. The hustle. The bustle. The fierceness. The openness. 'They're a lot, but they've only ever been lovely to me.'

'To you, they're lovely. To Camille, they were not.' Jeremy's lips pursed in thought. 'I think they saw Camille as a threat. Someone who had sway over me, who could influence me to do what I wanted rather than what they wanted. And she was quick to interrupt them whenever they talked about me quitting university, reminding me I was so close to finishing my degree and to give up would be to fail myself. You can imagine how well that sat with my sisters.'

Natalia pressed her lips together, trying to make sense of the situation. Why would the Gordon women have been so hard on Camille when she could've been the key to breaking their family's love curse?

'You're wondering why my family didn't like her if they thought she was my girlfriend, even though I made it clear she was just a friend?' Jeremy's brows rose.

Natalia gave a sheepish shrug. 'Am I that obvious?'

'More like you're smart enough to know it made no

sense. As if my family ever does.' Jeremy rolled his eyes. 'At the end of the day... well, technically, right from the start... they didn't like her. More like they didn't think she was right for the family. That she didn't fit in. So, they gave her the cold shoulder, ignored her questions, forgot to offer her a drink or a snack. And I'm pretty sure one of my sisters put a prickle in her bed every night so that she never quite slept soundly. I've never seen anyone so glad to see the back of Gordon Glen.'

'Understandable.' Natalia tried to comprehend a welcome – or lack thereof – like that from the Gordon family. 'If they'd treated me like that, I'd never have stood in front of that yellow door again. Which I guess Camille didn't.'

Jeremy's shoulders drooped, along with his lips. 'Which is more my fault than my sisters'. When I dropped out of university, Camille tried to do her best to convince me to stay, but she couldn't understand that I didn't choose to leave. I *had* to leave. She blamed my sisters. Was angry at the way I let them railroad me into a different future than the one I dreamed of. Said things that...' Jeremy's Adam's apple bobbed in his throat, like the words were too hard to say and his body was protecting him by not letting them out. 'Things that weren't true and do not need to be repeated.'

Natalia wasn't so sure. There was a reason they said the truth hurt and, in this case, the truth might've been so painful that it ended a friendship. So painful that it could end her burgeoning friendship with

Jeremy if she pushed harder and tried to pry the entire story from him.

'It sounds like a horrible situation. Caught between your best friend and your family. Your dreams and the responsibilities of home. I wouldn't wish that on anyone.'

Jeremy squeezed her hand in silent thanks, sending another dizzying ripple of energy through her.

'But what I don't understand is that none of what you've just said explains why you were so awful to Michael, or why you became a Jeremy-shaped snowman when talking to me when you saw Michael sitting on our picnic blanket.'

Jeremy turned to face her, his eyes blazing with intensity. 'Because, contrary to what my sister thought, Camille really was only ever a friend. I know she's beautiful and funny and possibly one of the smartest people I've ever met, but I never saw her as anything else than as a great mate. You, though?'

Natalia's heart stilled as she glimpsed where the conversation was going. Or perhaps where she hoped it was going, but didn't dare to even consider until the words were out and the truth was known.

'You, Natalia, I see as more. Even though I don't want to. Even though I know it's a bad idea, because I'm not after anything more than one simple night with anyone, and you deserve so much more than that. You deserve the world. The universe. Universes within universes, if such a thing exists.'

Jeremy made to pull his hand from hers, stopping

as Natalia's hand involuntarily tightened around his. Her body betraying her thoughts; saying 'stay' when she knew it better that he break away. She didn't know whether to feel relief knowing that she could trust her feelings, her intuition that there was something between herself and Jeremy, or to let the rising anxiety take over knowing that they could never be what each other needed. Not when he couldn't commit to a relationship and, even if he changed his mind, she couldn't commit to staying in Gordon Glen.

'Your words just now might be the most beautiful thing anyone has ever said to me. Ever.'

Jeremy's chin dipped, hiding his eyes, making it impossible for Natalia to know what he was thinking.

'I sense a "but",' he whispered.

'Not a "but", more of a...' Natalia searched for a way to be honest without making herself feel weak for having the feelings she did. 'The truth is, I don't want to get hurt. And I don't want to risk rejection. I've felt it too long, too deeply, to have another layer added by a person I've come to...' Natalia bit her tongue as the word "love" threatened to escape. Love was too strong a word, an emotion. And her friendship with Jeremy was too new. 'A person I've come to care for.'

So much for being honest. It wasn't a lie that she cared for Jeremy, but her emotions for him ran deeper. No one before him had caused her to light up inside with a simple smile. Or made her want to overcome her fears in order to raise herself in their estimation. Or made her want to risk everything in order to feel something.

Then risk something, her inner voice goaded. *Accept that you can only give him a short amount of time. Prepare for the worst and hope for the best.*

The best being, what? For Jeremy to do a one-eighty on his feelings about long-term relationships? For him to choose her over his determination to remain single. For Natalia to find a home in Gordon Glen that she could never find with her parents, or by following a path that would please them?

'I know I'm not perfect, Natalia. I know you deserve more, but I can promise you I won't reject you. I won't make you feel uncared for, or unwanted. I just can't promise you forever.'

Jeremy's gaze met hers and she saw surrender in his eyes, and a firestorm of desire, of want, of need.

'I guess no one can promise "forever". Not really.' Natalia bit down on her lip as she summoned the courage to decide. To follow her heart over her head. 'I guess all we have...' She angled her head to the side as she leaned towards Jeremy. 'All we have is right now. And right now is the best we can give to anyone. To each other. So, no expectations. No rules. Let's just be us.'

'Us.' Jeremy repeated, inching closer. 'I'd like that. Very much.'

Natalia's breath caught in her throat as their lips touched, feather soft. The energy she'd felt pass between their hands transferred to their mouths. Every line on Jeremy's lip amplified, the pout of his lips plush, velvety, as the pressure of his lips upon hers increased. Jeremy's hand came to rest upon her cheek, as warm and tender as the kiss they shared.

For the briefest of moments, their lips parted and their tongues met for mere but the most delicious of seconds. An acknowledgement that now, with people all around, wasn't the time to deepen, to explore, but a silent promise that there would be time, later.

They broke apart, Natalia as breathless as Jeremy's eyes were wide, dilated and not just a touch dazed.

'That was...' Jeremy shook his head, like he was trying to wake from a dream.

Natalia brought her fingertips to her lips, half-surprised that Jeremy's lips were no longer there. As if his lips belonged with her, as her lips belonged with him. As if even if they were to be apart, they would carry a piece of that kiss forever.

'Agreed.' Natalia forced herself to sit back, to regain her equilibrium. 'That was...'

'That was an excellent reason to come to this event.' Jeremy picked up his glass. 'And to that I say "cheers".'

Natalia raised her glass, and they clinked, then took a sip of champagne.

Lost in each other's eyes, they missed the huddle of Gordon girls hiding behind the sunflowers. The knowing smiles. The gentle high-fives. The hope that they too might find love yet.

So long as their brother didn't bugger things up.

TWELVE

Pulling one last carrot from its earthy home, Jeremy placed it in the basket, then pushed himself up and leaned back, tipping his head to the sky as he stretched his aching back. Glancing at the farmhouse, he wondered if Natalia was in there, hiding from him, regretting the conversation she'd had with him, or the kiss that had sent his head spinning and his heart into a tizzy. Part of it yelling at him he was being foolish, that he was tripping down a path that would lead to falling on his face. The other part happy to go along with something that felt more right, more connected, than any other kiss he'd experienced before.

'Morning, son.'

Jeremy turned to see his father striding towards him, one of his mother's sun hats atop his head, its brim bouncing with every step his father took.

'Hey, Dad. Not like you to pay the farm a visit.'

'Struggling with a plot point and not in the mood to

go for a run, so I figured I could come give you a hand.' His father reached into the bum bag that Clare had bought for an eighties dress up party and brought out Tilly's pink-handled trowel 'Just tell me where to dig and I'll dig.'

Jeremy took the trowel from his father and ran the pad of his thumb over its edge. As he suspected, it was bought for looks rather than use. Squatting down, Jeremy picked up his own trowel and handed it to his father. 'Here. This one will actually make its way into the dirt.'

'Thanks. So, where's Natalia? I'd have thought she'd have been out here lending a hand.'

You and me both. Jeremy flicked the churlish thought away.

Despite the odd connection he felt towards Natalia, he'd made it clear to her he couldn't be anything more than a for now rather than forever, so he had no right to her time, her thoughts, *her*. If he wanted to keep things light, then he had to act like it.

'It's not in her job description to help me out, even though she does when she can. She's probably just gone to get something from the shop.'

'Probably.' His father's brows drew together. 'Didn't pass her on the way though, or see her in the village when I popped in to say hi to Tilly.'

'Then maybe she's having a sleep in. I imagine she was up late dealing to the mess left by the hoards yesterday.' Something he'd offered to help her with, but she'd waved him off saying she was in charge of the sunflower patch so it was her job to clean up along with his sisters', since the event was their idea and for their benefit.

'Sounds about right.' John put the pink trowel back in the bum bag. 'I heard the girls come in around ten last night. Amazingly high in spirit too, considering they'd had a long day and, according to Clare, "not a single peng lad to show for it".' "Peng".' He shook his head. 'Whatever happened to calling someone "fit". What even is peng?'

'No idea.' Jeremy went to glance over at the farmhouse again, then stopped himself. He was not about to lose his head over a woman, no matter how 'peng' she might be, assuming a woman could be peng. 'Probably some slang the youths say that the girls saw on some social media platform.'

'Probably. Stupid bloody word,' his father grumbled under his breath. 'Anyway, your mother said she was sick of the sight of me mooching around the house being all foul because I couldn't figure out how to make the murderer not so obvious to all and sundry, so I figured I'd wander out here and get some air, and maybe some inspiration. So, what's next on the list of things to do?'

'I was about to head over to the nursery and check on the seedlings for the winter crop.'

'Well, I'll come along too. If I dare pop my head through the front door of ours within the next couple of hours, I'm bound to lose it.'

Jeremy smiled to himself as the two walked

companionably towards the nursery. His father and mother really were as different as onions and cauliflower. His mum, despite her overbearing ways, being able to survive, if not thrive in most situations, whereas his father, who appeared solid and steadfast on the outside, needed just the right growing conditions, like a cauliflower, to flourish. Still, despite their differences, or perhaps because of them, the two were as in love as ever.

Entering the nursery, Jeremy pointed out a table at the far end. 'It's time to sow the kale. Aunty Francesca's got some Redbor, and Black Magic kale that she's keen to grow this year.'

'Oh, great. Let's get sewing.' His father nodded, his enthusiasm not reaching his eyes.

Jeremy grinned to himself. Five minutes in and his father had lost all interest in the reason for being there. The man was as much of a farmer as Jeremy was a writer. Pulling out a stool, he indicated for his father to sit.

'Dad, how about you keep me company while I prep the plug trays, and you can tell me what it was like joining our mad family back in the days before we kids were born.'

'Is it really that obvious that I'm not green thumbed?' His father grimaced. Plopping himself down, he anchored his elbows on the bench and interlaced his fingers. 'Don't answer that. I'm aware I'm the worst in the garden. Luckily, that wasn't a tick in the "against" box when your mother decided to keep me on.'

'Keep you on?' Jeremy rolled his eyes as he shovelled seed raising mix into the containers. 'You've met yourself, right? Without being weird, you're a bit of a catch, Dad. Successful. Well off. Kind. An all-round, good human being.'

His father shrugged the compliment off. 'Nice of you to say, but I was awkward as they come. You know the saying "wouldn't say boo to a ghost?".'

Jeremy nodded.

'Well, I wouldn't even say boo to a ghost in my head. My editor and agent learned quickly that if they wanted to have a conversation with me, it would have to be through email. Or regular mail at the beginning of my career, because I couldn't afford the internet and didn't want to leave the house to use the library's.'

'Oh wow.' Jeremy poked holes into the seed raising mix. 'No internet at home. I forgot how old you are.'

His father tutted. 'Keep that tongue in cheek, lad. I might not be able to help you with the farm, but if my temper was piqued, I could do a good job of temper tantrumming my way to destroying a goodly amount of it.'

'Noted.' Jeremy pressed his hands together in a show of apology, knowing his father didn't have an ounce of temper in him. If anything, he was so mellow there had been times Jeremy had thought he was too much of a pushover, especially when it came to the women in his household.

'If anything, it was your mother who showed me who I could be if I just got out of my own way.'

'Which was when you were here doing research for a book, right?' Jeremy set the tray aside and began prepping the next.

'Right.' His father's gaze grew distant as he took the trip down memory lane. 'She was so beautiful, so bright, so much bigger than anything in this village. You'd hear her laugh before you saw her – which gave me ample time to make my getaway. But it was like she could sense me before she saw me, because seconds later she'd be dancing around me, asking me questions, talking about her day, wondering how long I'd be staying and if I'd like to go around to hers for a drink.'

'It's hard to say no to her.' Jeremy tried not to squirm as his father's eyes met his, the softness disappearing, replaced by a sense of interrogation, as if he could see inside Jeremy's mind, where the anger at his family, at his heritage, at himself, resided.

'It's hard to say no to any of the women in that family.' His father acknowledged what he heard, what he saw within Jeremy, with a nod. 'They're a tough bunch to navigate once they get an idea into their heads. Especially when it's a collective whim.'

'Is this the bit where you say "that's why we lads have to stick together"?' Jeremy attempted to lighten the mood.

'Not at all. You and I don't stand a chance, by ourselves or together. I don't think any man in the

Gordon family ever has. May I?' His father pointed to a tray. 'I don't think that's something I can stuff up.'

Passing the tray, along with a bag of seeds in his direction, Jeremy returned to his work, while trying to understand his father's point of view. 'So if you were so shy and so awkward, what drew her to you? Was it because she knew she could browbeat you into staying here?' *Like my family did to me?*

'Actually, son, that's not quite the case. Your mother wanted out of Gordon Glen. Wanted to do what your uncle did and travel before settling down in a spot that caught her fancy. Over as many cups of tea or glasses of wine as she could set in front of me before I made my excuses, she would regale me at length with tales of how her life would look one day. Talk of skinny dipping off some nudist-friendly beach in Australia. Bungy jumping off the world's highest bungee in China. Experiencing twenty-four hours of sunshine in Iceland. "Anywhere but here", is what she'd tell me.'

Jeremy tried to reconcile the idea of this woman his father spoke of with his image of his mother, who had always seemed nothing but joyful living in her brightly painted home, filled with colours and textures and half-finished art projects she'd cast aside in favour of a new idea, and failed. The two didn't match. He'd never once heard her talk about leaving Gordon Glen.

'You look as confused as she made me feel. So much talk, so much hand movement, so much vibrancy. She was the opposite to anything I'd ever known, which is what I think drew her to me.'

Jeremy watched his father carefully place a seed in each of the holes he'd created, his brows drawn together as intensely as they did whilst he wrote his books. 'So she liked that you didn't tell her to go away? That you just did what she said?'

'I think what she liked was that I had a sense of stability. I'm boring. Raised in a happy family. Allowed to be who I was. To the point that I sometimes wonder if my sister, your aunty, and I are too independent. Unlike you lot, we only talk on days of significance. Birthdays, absolutely. Sometimes not even at Christmas.'

'Can there be such a thing as being too independent?' Jeremy asked, half envying his father and aunty for having that experience, while also unable to imagine how it would feel. Even during his time at university, he'd felt connected – too connected – to where he came from.

'I think so. Water?'

Jeremy passed the small watering can he kept on the counter over.

'Think about it. When was the last time your aunty visited? Or I visited her? We have love for each other, but we've never felt the need to co-exist. It's freeing, but it's also sad. Thankfully, once your mother dragged me under her wing, I was gifted an instant family and never had to feel alone ever again.'

Through the shade cloth, Jeremy caught movement by the farmhouse. Natalia was up, or back. His heart rate quickened at the thought of seeing her, touching her, knowing her. That's if common sense hadn't prevailed, and she still wanted to have anything to do with him.

'I look at Natalia and think she must feel a bit like I did.' His father picked up the tray and walked it over to the end of the bench and set it next to the seedlings Jeremy had potted the day before. 'Caught up in a whirlwind whenever she's around the girls or your mother. They've taken quite the shine to her. She's lucky to have you to shield her from their curiosity.'

'Which could also be called "intrusiveness".' Jeremy slid off the stool and followed his father to the nursery entrance, where he could see Natalia walking into the sunflower field, her hand trailing against the plants' leaves, her head tipped to the tightly budded flowers, her lips moving with words he could not hear.

'Anyway, I don't think she's lucky to have me.' Jeremy's stomach coiled tight at the admission. He wasn't used to being so honest with his father. With anyone. But maybe if he was ever going to become unstuck from his ways, he'd need to be. 'She's too good for me. I'm only going to end up hurting her if I let her get too close.'

'Because of your bachelor ways?' His father nudged him in the side.

Jeremy turned to see a twinkle in his father's eyes, a twitch of lips that appeared on the verge of smiling, if not outright laughing.

'I know I spend most of my time holed up in my office writing, but even I'm aware of your commitment-phobic nature. It's hard to miss the way the girls go on about it.'

'Yeah, well,' Jeremy kicked the dirt with the heel of his foot, uncomfortable with the idea that his ways had reached his gossip-hating father's ears. 'Is there anything wrong with not wanting to be harangued by yet another person for the rest of your life?'

'Is that how you see your mother and I? Am I harangued?'

'Well, no. She lets you do you. Most of the time. But then, you're also not a first-born Gordon male. I'm the key to this family's happiness. Apparently. Stupid fairy tale.'

'Perhaps. But it's not a fairy tale if there isn't a happy ending. Without a happy ending, all you've got is a tragedy.'

And letting Natalia go would be exactly that. Jeremy didn't contradict the voice in his head. If he was going to be truthful, he had to listen to his own truth, too.

'Look.' His father took hold of Jeremy's shoulder and gave it a squeeze. 'I don't know about this family curse situation, son. As far as I'm concerned, people make their own fate. But, perhaps in believing in its existence so desperately, your sisters, and those who went before them, made the curse become truth.'

'So, are you saying it's up to me to *not* do what they want me to do so they can find love on their own terms?'

His father released Jeremy's shoulder, then leaned

against the nursery's doorway, his arms crossing, his brows raising. 'Is that what you think you have to do? Isn't that what you've already been doing?'

'Well, no. Yes. Maybe unintentionally?' Jeremy exhaled and tried to get his thoughts in order. 'I will admit that when I'm prodded, I've been known to get mulish about things, but I've never set out to hurt my sisters in doing so.'

'You just don't want to be pushed around by them?' His father grinned. 'Harangued, even?'

Jeremy widened his eyes and nodded. 'Well, yes. That. Exactly.'

'Understandable. So, before I head off home and start tapping away at this story of mine, let me tell you this one last thing about how I met your mother. Walk with me?'

Jeremy didn't answer, just followed his father out into the fields, interested to learn a new piece of his family's history.

'I was never meant to be here in the first place. I was travelling through on the way down to the coast to do some research for my next book, and my car just stopped on the outskirts of the village. Completely cut out. Engine gave up the ghost. It was your grandmother, your mum's mum, who found me, took me under her wing, found me a place to stay and then organised for my car to get fixed. Which took a long time. Longer than I think it probably ought to have taken. But by the time it was done, I realised I didn't want to be anywhere else.'

'So, you're saying my grandmother orchestrated the whole thing?'

His father threw his head back and laughed. 'Oh, she wishes she had that much power. What I'm saying is that while I might think that people make their own fate, sometimes I think Fate-with-a-capital-F likes to lend a hand.'

Jeremy snorted. 'Yeah, well. I'll believe that when I see it. And by "it", I mean Fate walking up to me with a smirk on its face and telling me I've no choice but to do as I'm told.'

Natalia emerged from the sunflower patch, and Jeremy raised a hand, feeling his heart warm as he received a wave and a smile as sunny as the flowers she had been tending.

'Speaking of fate,' his father murmured, then slapped Jeremy on the back. 'That's enough father-son chat for the day. You go hang out with your friend. Who's a girl. Some might even say that makes her a girlfriend.' His father winked, then let out another short laugh when Jeremy let out an 'ugh' of disgust. 'Just stop worrying about hurting her. She's a grown woman. I'm sure she can take care of herself.'

After a quick greeting to Natalia, his father took off towards the lane, leaving Jeremy to wonder if Natalia could take care of herself. His father wasn't wrong. She was a grown woman, but Jeremy had seen the scared little girl hiding underneath the blanket the night of the storm, and he would never forgive himself if he hurt her. However unintentionally. Which meant he had to be intentional in his actions.

Jogging over to Natalia, he promised himself he was going to continue to be straight up, honest to a fault, and never give her the idea or belief that he could offer more than he could give.

'Natalia, how do you feel about lunch?'

Natalia smiled, the warmth in her eyes paling in comparison to the warmth her smile brought to his heart. 'I thought you'd never ask.'

THIRTEEN

Natalia raised her arms into a stretch and allowed the sun to caress her face. 'Oh, it's nice not to have to hang around inside the pub on a beautiful day. I feel for your mother and sisters being so prone to burning.'

'Don't worry about them.' Jeremy set the menu he'd been looking at down on the picnic table. 'Yes, they burn, but I'm pretty sure they get so much joy from terrorising the staff with their tarot talk that they're unbothered by the fact they can't hang out here amongst the sunbeams.'

'I still find it hard to believe people are really that antsy about your family.' Natalia released the stretch and picked up the menu, ready to let her stomach tell her what she was in the mood to eat.

Nachos? No.

Chicken noodle salad? Not today.

Steak with hand-cut fries and a side salad? A cow mooed in the distance. *Not anymore.*

'Believe it, because they really are.'

'Sad. They're missing out on a lot of fun. I'm going to have the gazpacho. You?'

'Steak for me.' Jeremy stood, pulling his wallet out of his shorts' pocket. 'And it's my shout.'

'How do you feel about chip stealing? Because I'm a bit of a thief.' Tugging her wallet out of her bag, Natalia rifled around for some money. 'And I'll pay my way. It's not like we're on a date. And I don't know many friends who shout each other pub lunches. Coffee, yes. A wine or beer, sure. So long as the other person gets the next round. But a proper meal complete with a pint of cider?'

'We're us, remember?' Jeremy shooed the money away. 'We do things our way. And I'm shouting.'

Natalia sensed Jeremy's stubbornness and nodded her assent. 'Well, next time it's my turn to buy. That's my way. I don't want you, me, *us*, to feel like we owe each other anything. I don't want things to end badly.'

Jeremy's lips twitched to the side, his brows drew together, creating a line between them.

Natalia waved her finger at him. 'If you're going to say that paying for me is the gentlemanly thing to do – the thing you always do with women you like – then I'm going to race inside, order and pay before you even get a foot in the pub door. I don't want to be like the others. This is different, remember?'

'Fine.' The crease disappeared, and Jeremy's lips and brows settled back into their usual spots. 'I guess I hadn't thought things through all that well.'

'Because some other part of you is doing all the thinking?' Natalia stashed her handbag under the table. 'Actually, don't answer that. Just go order.' Her stomach rumbled, loud enough for Jeremy to laugh on hearing it. 'My stomach demands it.'

Jeremy bowed. 'Well, your stomach's wish is my command.'

Natalia sank back in her chair and took a moment to appreciate the perfectly peachy roundness of Jeremy's bum. If it looked that good covered in the sturdy cotton fabric of his cargo shorts, how delightful would it be in the flesh? A shiver of delight ran over her. If things kept going the way they were between them, she'd likely find out.

From the depths of her bag, her mobile bleeped with a message notification, followed by the whoosh of an incoming email. Pulling the phone out, Natalia's heart sank as she took in the message from her mother.

Natalia, looking forward to discussing your future plans. Have emailed university prospectus. Talk soon, Mum.

No kiss as a sign off. No 'love'. No sign of affection. Part of Natalia wanted to take the 'looking forward' and believe it meant her mother was truly looking forward to having a chat with her, but Natalia knew her mother's style of messaging well enough to know that was how she framed all messages in which she had to have a conversation with someone sometime in the future. Natalia could just as easily be a client, an acquaintance or a complete stranger that her mother was forced to interact with.

'You okay?' Jeremy placed the order number down on the table and slid back into his seat. 'You've gone all gloomy. Are you really that annoyed about not paying?'

'No, of course not.' Natalia forced a smile. 'Just got a message from my mum.'

'Oh.' Jeremy picked the table number up and moved it to the side in better sight of the pub's back door. 'Was she checking in on you? Seeing how things were here?'

Natalia went to give Jeremy the 'are you on something' look of disdain, but pulled herself back. He didn't deserve to have her pain taken out on him, especially when he came from a family that was the exact opposite of hers.

'After what I talked about the night of the storm, do you think that's what she was messaging to say?'

Jeremy screwed his face up and shook his head. 'No, of course it wouldn't be that. I'm sorry. Insensitive of me.'

'You've nothing to be sorry about. It's hard to fathom growing up in a home like mine, unless you did the actual growing up there.' Natalia pulled her sunglasses down from her head, wanting to cover the tears that were threatening to make themselves known. 'She wants to talk about my future.'

'For when you go back.' Jeremy's chest deflated and his jaw tightened.

At the idea of her leaving? Or because he hated

seeing her hurt by her own family? The latter, Natalia decided. It had to be. He'd made his position on long-term relationships beyond clear. Hell, if she wasn't leaving in a couple of weeks, Natalia doubted they'd be an 'us' in that moment, that Jeremy would've even dared break his one night only rule.

'Exactly.' Natalia tried to relax into the chair, but found herself gripping its sides at the thought of packing her rucksack and leaving this beautiful, quirky and utterly delightful piece of the country. 'Apparently she's emailed through a university prospectus so that I can begin to plan my future career.'

'Let me guess. She wants it to be a job that's super serious? One that will make you more money in one year than I make in four once you've got your degree, or degrees, and ground your way up the ladder?'

'Probably.' Natalia felt a heavy sensation in her chest, as if a lead brick had been placed within it. 'No, there's no "probably" about it. Definitely. I don't see her approving of a job as a florist, or a makeup artist or, I don't know, a professional clown.'

'There's a degree for clowns?' Jeremy nudged her ankle with his foot under the table. 'Because if there is, I might send the prospectus my sisters' way. They'd make quite the troupe.'

'Funny.' Natalia knew Jeremy was attempting to lighten the atmosphere, to make her smile, but even the idea of the Gordon girls tripping over each other and hamming it up for an audience couldn't dispel the feeling in her heart that told her she was making a huge mistake by trying to please her parents, by not following her heart. 'It's stupid. All of it.' She lifted her hands in the air, an admission of truth that she was aware she'd walked herself into the corner, that she had no one to blame but herself for being in her current position. 'I guess with my last job winding up and with nothing new on the horizon, it felt like now was my last chance to impress them, to make them see me as worthy, as worthwhile.' She pressed her lips together, not wanting to say what she really felt. It was too embarrassing. Too pathetic.

'To make them love you.' Jeremy's tone was as gentle as the scent of jasmine that wafted from the boxed gardens bordering the pub's backyard. 'As you deserve to be loved.'

Their eyes locked. The air disappeared from Natalia's lungs, from the world itself. She'd never felt so seen, so known. This man sitting across from her, who'd known her all of a fortnight, could see who she was, what she needed, and wasn't afraid to verbalise it when she couldn't, even if he could not give her the exact thing that he said she deserved. But that didn't mean that whatever chemistry lay between them couldn't be treated with the respect and care that it deserved. That she couldn't open her own heart to him in the way she'd been fearful to, had run from, her whole life.

And that's how you set yourself up for failure, you idiot.

Natalia tore her gaze away from Jeremy. She'd

crossed from knowing where the boundaries lay between them to a fantasy land where Gordon women's lives were intertwined with a curse, where dances saw off storms, where men so easily spoke of love to her because they loved her rather than out of a need to comfort her, as Jeremy would've intended.

The voice that told the truth was right; she was an idiot. And she couldn't let Jeremy's innate goodness lead her on to think that because he understood her, he would or could love her.

'Gazpacho. Steak.' A harried waitress set Natalia's bowl of soup in front of her, followed by Jeremy's steak, salad, and chips.

'Thanks, Sylvie.' Jeremy flashed her the thumbs up. 'Looks delish. Extra chips too, I see. Thank Delia for me.'

'Yes, thank you.' Natalia smiled up at the waitress, noticing the woman's quick intake of breath as she took in Jeremy, the pinkening of her cheeks, and the sucking in of her bottom lip before releasing it, pinker and a touch plumper than before.

Natalia mentally rolled her eyes, grateful for the reminder of who she was dealing with – the village heartthrob. She and Jeremy were no big deal, as light and sweet as candy floss, not as dense and all-consuming as a black hole. If only she could have a Sylvie around all the time to keep her miscreant heart, which yearned to bend, break or completely ignore logic, in check.

Picking up her soup spoon, Natalia turned her

attention to Jeremy, whose brows were knitted together once more, his eyes narrowed in thought. 'Shall we?'

Jeremy shook himself, not unlike the way the local dogs did after a swim in the river, and picked up his knife and fork. 'We shall. It looks good.'

Taking a sip of her soup, Natalia closed her eyes. The rich, yet light and zesty flavours danced over her tongue.

'You're making me think I've made a mistake.'

Natalia opened her eyes, thinking Jeremy was talking about their easy-going entanglement, to see him pointing at her soup as he popped a chip into his mouth. His eyes bulged, and he began flapping his hand furiously while puffing.

'Hot. So hot. Too hot.'

'I don't know about that.' Natalia saw a chance to even the strange emotional landscape. 'Being flashed half-masticated food is anything but hot.' She wrinkled her nose and let out a light laugh. 'Do that to any would-be girlfriends and they'll be off running down the lane like they're hoping to win a gold medal.'

'Oh, shush.' Jeremy picked up a chip and threw it at Natalia. 'You know I've got no interest in girlfriends. Though thanks for the tip should I find myself in danger of getting one.'

'Five second rule.' Natalia picked the chip up off the table and ate it. Instantly regretting the decision as intense heat seared her tongue, the rest of her mouth following suit. 'Bloody hell, that *is* hot.'

'Karma.' Jeremy waggled his shoulders up and

down. 'And now we're even. I showed you a mouthful of food, and you just grossed me out by eating off the table. We're the only two people who can put up with each other.'

Tears watered in Natalia's eyes as she chewed the chip and swallowed it down, before washing the searing heat away with a big gulp of ice-cold cider. Free from pain, she tried not to read too much into Jeremy's throwaway comment. It would be so easy to take the idea of their being the only two people in the world who could put up with each other and believe it meant he saw her as more than just a short-term fling. That there was a chance they could make something more of their future together. But to do so, to let even a ray of hope in, would lead to being blinded by lies, and blindsided by inevitable rejection. Jeremy may be attracted to her, he may think and say all the nice things, but he'd also made his commitment-phobic ways clear. And she had to respect that.

'So, if we're the only two people who can put up with each other's disgusting ways, shall we go to this silent disco together?' Natalia caught the look of disquiet on Jeremy's face. Had he changed his mind about them being something more, something else, something ill-defined, but something that had seen her stomach turn into the world's busiest trampoline park whenever she thought of the kiss with its promise of more to come?

Sensing the rejection she was trying to avoid, she went into damage control.

'As friends, of course. I mean, if that's what you'd prefer.'

'No.' Jeremy's foot found Natalia's under the table and nudged it. 'I would not prefer. What I'd prefer is for us to go as us. You and me.'

'You and me.' Definitely ill-defined, but better than being just friends.

'Do we – you and me – need to set some rules here?' Natalia bit down on her bottom lip, trying not to make what they were talking about a big deal. Half-afraid that in creating guidelines, Jeremy would decide their unconventional relationship was too hard and skip out before it even properly started. 'So that we're both clear on each other's boundaries? So we can't somehow hurt each other? We've danced around the topic, but I think it's better that we set what this is down in concrete.'

Jeremy stilled for a moment, then took a long sip of his beer. 'Are you still leaving once Aunty Francesca gets back from her holiday?'

Natalia nodded. 'Obviously. If my parents had anything to do with it they'd have me home right now, no doubt bound to a chair while they lectured me about my lost years and how I'd have to study three times harder to catch up with the rest of the world. Why?'

'Well, if you're going and I'm staying, then why do we need rules? Why complicate things? It's just two people who get on having a good time.'

Natalia could almost imagine the same line being

used on the women Jeremy had seduced in the past. *'It's just two people who get on having a good time... for one night.'*

Except this was two weeks, not one night, and a lot could change in two weeks.

'Natalia, we both know the score. You have a life waiting for you outside of Gordon Glen, and I am bound to this place whether I like it or not. There's no chance things can get weird, or deep. Not when we both know the consequences of taking things too far. But that doesn't mean we can't get to know each other better. So long as we know that two weeks is all we have.'

Natalia stared at the streaks of red soup leftover in her bowl, regretting the decision to choose such an acidic lunch now that the contents were burning in her stomach, threatening to make their way back up. Jeremy made it sound so simple, but it wasn't. Two weeks from now, her life would change forever, and not in a good way. Buckling down, studying, pleasing her parents over pleasing herself. A bird trapped in a cage. A situation only made worse because she was voluntarily entering the cage, then padlocking the door behind her.

Which meant she had two weeks to be free, to do as she pleased, and the man sitting opposite pleased her very much. The only catch? She couldn't let the feelings she'd caught, the ones she was trying to ignore, deepen. *Easy,* she told herself. *Just pretend they're not there, like you're pretending returning to London is fine and dandy.*

Ignoring her inner-voice's acerbic tone, Natalia made her decision.

"You're right. We don't need rules. We know what this is. More importantly, we know what this can't be. We'll be fine. So, does that mean you'll come to the silent disco with me?'

Jeremy tapped his chin with his index finger. 'Depends. Can you dance? Because I'm amazing on the dance floor and need a partner who can keep up with me. If you've two left feet, tell me now.'

'I'm telling you nothing. You'll have to find out.' Snatching another chip from Jeremy's plate, Natalia threw it in his direction, chortling as it bounced off the finger that was still tapping his chin.

Jeremy gasped in mock-horror. 'I can't believe you wasted a chip like that.'

'And I can't believe how big your head is.' Natalia's laughter increased as Jeremy's face morphed from shocked to wounded, his eyes widening, his hands crossing over his heart.

Sitting back in her seat, her amusement subsiding to a chuckle, Natalia wondered when she'd last laughed so easily, so often. She searched her memories and found she couldn't remember. Two weeks in Gordon Glen had turned her humdrum life on its head, infusing it with humour, vibrancy and a joie de vivre she'd never experienced.

How much more would she love life here in two weeks' time?

Her heart sank as she realised it wasn't just Jeremy she had to keep at an emotional distance if she was to leave without hurting herself - it was Gordon Glen itself.

FOURTEEN

Tilly grooved by, her arms waving in the air, her shoulders bopping back and forth. 'Are you guys having the best time ever? Isn't this the best ever? I'm having the best time ever.' Closing her eyes, she began shuffling backwards to a beat that sounded nothing like the one in Jeremy's ears.

'Is she, er, on something, or has she been indulging in something a little, or a lot, illegal...' Natalia's hands bopped up and down like she was pegging laundry to a washing line. 'Because six in the morning seems a little early to be getting that kind of party started.'

'You'd think so, but that's not Tilly's style.' Jeremy gave the thumbs up to a couple who were break-dancing just outside of the sunflower field, sending a fluff of dust into the air. 'My sister is just one of those super annoying early morning types. Bounces out of bed with a smile. Chatters more than the birds during the dawn chorus. Doesn't even need coffee either.'

'Annoying.'

'Very. On the plus side, she crashes out by nine at night, so we owl-types in the family can enjoy a few hours of peace and quiet before we take ourselves off to bed.'

'Hoot, hoot.' Natalia wrinkled her nose in the way that drove Jeremy crazy with desire, then turned the sound up on her mobile phone, her arms switching to a pumping action, her hands closed into fists, as her body shimmied in time with the music, the hemline of her simple cotton shift dress riding up her thighs with each beat, giving glimpses of tanned, firm skin that he wanted nothing more to touch, to caress, to kiss.

The all too familiar pants twitch that made itself known whenever Natalia was near reared up.

Settle, petal, he commanded, tearing his gaze away from her dress and focusing on the convivial surrounds.

His sisters would be thrilled. Unlike the picnic, the sunflower field was bustling with people in their twenties and thirties, none of them wearing a ring on their left hand finger. The call for 'singles only' had been heard and answered. The results looking to be successful, when an earlier dance through to the riverbank had seen a fair few of them snuggled up on the picnic blankets Clare had begged and borrowed from those she knew, getting to know each other better – be it by talk or touch.

Natalia waved and smiled to someone over his shoulder. Turning around, Jeremy glimpsed Gemma dragging a blond-haired man with a dazed look upon his face towards the picnic blankets.

'Should we?' Natalia swooped her hand out toward the path Gemma had taken.

'No. Most definitely not.'

Natalia's face fell, and Jeremy kicked himself for making it sound like he didn't want to spend time with her in a more horizontal position.

'Would you want to watch your sister snog someone?'

Her lips curled up. 'Yeah. No. I don't even have to imagine what that would feel like to know I wouldn't want to experience it.'

In Jeremy's ears, the song faded out, and silence followed. Checking his watch, Jeremy saw the disco had ended. Three hours of dancing had blitzed by. Every second spent with Natalia was so enjoyable time had flown. More than enjoyable… easy. Their rhythm matching each other's perfectly. Their ability to read each other's tempo or direction change bordering on eerie. If he believed in his mother's woowoo ways, he'd almost think there was some kind of telepathy going on between them. Though not being one to fall for magical thinking, he could only conclude that his sisters had done a fantastic job curating the playlist, making it easy to see what a fellow dancer's next steps would be. Unless you were Tilly, who, for all her enthusiasm, had all the rhythm of a tipsy rooster.

Pulling out her earbuds, Natalia pocketed them in her dress' pocket. 'So, what do we do now?'

Jeremy glanced around at the departing crowd. Some hand-in-hand, others chatting amiably with a new friend, a few heading off alone, their steps bouncy as their heads nodded to whatever music was now playing in their ears.

'Do we go to the café? Get to work in the fields? It's just I've got so much...' Natalia wrung her hands, then shimmied her body. 'So much energy. You know what I mean?'

Jeremy caught her hand. 'I know what you mean. And I have an idea that might help burn all that energy off.'

'Oh.' Natalia's eyes widened. 'Are you suggesting...'

'We go for a swim in the river.' Jeremy dropped her hand. 'Last one in is a rotten potato.'

Taking off through the sunflowers, his arms pumping as fast as his legs, Jeremy began stripping off his clothing, then stopped, remembering people might still be down at the riverbank. Including Gemma. If there was one thing he did not need, it was Gemma seeing he and Natalia dressed only in their smalls. That piece of information would race through his family like wildfire, complete with talk of Jeremy falling in love, of the curse being lifted, of happiness and joy and wondrousness for the Gordon women once more. A pressure he did not need. Not when he was simply having fun with a woman he liked, and nothing more.

Natalia tapped his shoulder, her breath ragged. 'What's going on? Why'd you stop?'

'There might be people still down there and I'm dressed like this.' He swept his hand down the length of his body, then turned around to see Natalia wearing a simple black bra, with matching underwear. No lace, no trim, no diamantes or whatever other fancy adornments he'd seen on bras before. Just long, muscular, tanned limbs and scraps of simple fabric.

He'd never seen anything or anyone so attractive in his life.

Feeling that all too familiar tug in his smalls, he turned around, not wanting Natalia to see just how much her outfit, or lack thereof, had piqued his interest. 'Follow me.'

Not waiting for an answer, Jeremy took off through the sunflowers, trying not to damage their leaves or stems as he weaved his way towards the adjacent field, while hoping the farmer who owned that parcel of land wasn't around. He no more wanted Natalia to be embarrassed in public in her state of undress than he wanted to deal with Felix Thomas and his gun-happy ways.

Reaching the border, Jeremy poked his head out between the flowers. 'The coast is clear.'

Natalia tapped him on the shoulder. 'Why does the coast have to be clear?'

'Because this is the spot that borders the land of that farmer I told you about. The one who's prone to pointing guns at people who don't belong on his land. Which is everyone. Even kids at Halloween. And carollers at Christmas.'

'Kids? What kind of farmer points a gun at kids? Or carollers?'

'One who hates how much this village loves celebrating the holidays. He despises the level of decorating that's done almost as much as he hates unexpected visitors.' Double checking they were fine to head down to the river, Jeremy ducked down and indicated Natalia to do the same.

Soft steps close behind told Jeremy Natalia was following him as he scuttled along.

'I'm going to have to come back and visit during those holidays. Honestly, the more that's revealed about Gordon Glen, the more it sounds like a good time. Well, except for the gun-toting kid and caroller-threatening farmer thing.'

Jeremy's heart jumped at the thought of seeing Natalia again, of showing her how the village went all out for their events.

Stupid, he chastised himself. If Natalia was off studying and doing what she had to do to seek the approval of her family, there was no way she was going to come back to the middle of nowhere.

Out of the corner of his eye, he caught the glint of something metallic. 'Down. Now.'

He reached behind him to make sure Natalia had heard him and felt a soft piece of material upon his fingertips. Which meant he had laid hands on one of two clothed areas, both of which he had no place touching out of the blue. His cheeks flared hot, and he snatched his hand away.

'Shit. Sorry. Just thought I saw something glinting over that way.' Jeremy pointed towards the orchard.

'A CD on a tree.'

'Maybe.' Jeremy slowly blew out a breath, feeling the heat from his cheeks recede.

'That wasn't a question. I can see it from here. The farmer's got CDs hanging from his trees.'

'Of course. It helps keep the birds away from his plums when they're ripening.' Regaining his composure, Jeremy moved forward. 'Not far now.'

Sure enough, the ripple of water wandering over stones and brushing along banks met their ears.

Checking to see none of the early morning revellers had wandered upstream, Jeremy gave Natalia the thumbs up signal, then bolted towards the river and cannonballed in, wanting to give Natalia the chance to enter the water without feeling self-conscious about her state of undress. Not that she'd seemed all that worried before.

More like you're not wanting to find yourself with a tent in your pants the second you see her in such a state for longer than a few seconds.

Bubbles erupted from Jeremy's nose as he snorted underwater at the ridiculousness of the thought. The chilly temperature of the river would stop any such actions coming to fruition anytime soon.

Fresh bubbles erupted beside him as Natalia jumped in. Kicking up, he surfaced, only to be splashed in the face.

'I can't believe you were happy to risk us being shot

at by a holiday-hating gun-toting farmer in order to avoid your family.' Natalia rolled her eyes and let out a dramatic huff.

Jeremy laughed and splashed her back. 'What can I say? I would rather risk bodily injury than have my family gasbagging about us being in our smalls.'

Another wave of water hit him in the face. 'Well, a bit of consultation wouldn't have gone astray.'

'Consult with this.' Spreading his arm wide, Jeremy propelled it over the water, creating a small tsunami.

Squealing, Natalia ducked under and disappeared. Moments later, something latched onto Jeremy's leg, then dragged him under. Looking down, he saw a smiling Natalia kicking and paddling away from him.

She wanted to play? Game on.

AN HOUR LATER, Jeremy could safely say he'd never been dunked so much in his life. Or had so much fun having it done.

Half-climbing, half-dragging himself out of the river, he offered a hand to Natalia.

'Are you going to help me up and then let me go just as I've found my footing?' she asked, her eyes narrowing with suspicion. 'Because I don't think my arms or legs have it in me to try to get out a second time. You'll be leaving me for the eels. I'd be fish fodder.'

How she knew that was what he'd half-planned to

do as the ultimate revenge for his last dunking, which had seen him swallow half the river, Jeremy didn't know. But what he knew more was that he didn't want Natalia being fish fodder or an edible for an eel. What he wanted was to keep hanging out with her, keep laughing, keep bantering, keep being them.

'Promise I won't. Pinkie swear.'

Hooking pinkies, the zips and zaps of electricity that cascaded through his body whenever they touched, sparked into life. The first few times, Jeremy thought he'd been imagining it, but whenever it happened, Natalia's eyes would widen and she'd get the cutest look of astonishment on her face for a second before shaking it off. Whatever lay between them wasn't a figment of his imagination. It was real. And the energy seemed to grow stronger with each and every touch, no matter how seemingly insignificant.

Releasing pinkies, he took hold of her hand and was overwhelmed with dizziness as the energy surged. *Dehydration*, he told himself. Had to be. He'd need to up his water intake. Even if he'd just taken in half the river during their dunk-fest.

'You okay?' Natalia's head cocked to the side. 'You're looking a bit dazed.'

'Just hot and bothered.' Jeremy replied, then pulled her up onto the bank, before collapsing onto the grass, bringing Natalia down with him.

'Understandable.' Natalia fanned herself, despite a very obvious rash of goose bumps pimpling her droplet-beaded body.

Which he was very much not paying attention to. Especially making sure to ignore the curve of her thighs, the roundness of her belly, and the dip at her waist, which led to...

Nope. Jeremy tore his eyes away from and flopped onto his back and closed his eyes, bathing in the sun, enjoying the scratchy feeling of the river water drying on his skin. Beside him, he felt Natalia shift, then shivered as a shadow stole the sun from the right side of his body.

'Cold?' Natalia's hand trailed down his arm. 'I can warm you up if you'd like?'

Any other woman, any other time, Jeremy would've said 'yes' in a heartbeat, but this wasn't any other woman, or any other time. This was Natalia. And he had a feeling – no, a knowing – about what Natalia was hoping to happen next, but he didn't want to push things this far, this fast. Unlike with other women, with Natalia it felt... wrong.

'I'm fine.' He wriggled away from her back into full sunlight. 'The sun's warm enough.'

'Oh. Okay.'

Jeremy heard the disappointment in Natalia's voice, but refused to give in simply to make her happy. There was time for that. Two weeks. There was no need to hurry things along.

He jerked in surprise as a fresh shadow swamped his entire body, and cold water dripped upon his bare skin. Opening his eyes, he found Natalia hovering over him.

'Natalia. What are you doing?'

'Planking. What does it look like?'

'It looks like you're hovering over top of me while performing some bizarre water torture upon me.' Jeremy jerked as a fresh drop of river water fell from Natalia's hip onto his. 'Is there a point to this?'

'There is.' Natalia's lips quirked to the side for a moment, before settling back. Their natural plumpness further emphasised thanks to a combination of her pose and gravity.

How easy would it be to raise his head? To suck her bottom lip in? To tease her until she begged him to take her home? But he wouldn't. He couldn't.

'Jeremy Gordon, don't you want me? Is this you playing with me? First you kiss me, then you take me out to lunch, then you dance with me, and, well, you bang on about how straight up you are with the women you meet, but all I'm getting is blanked whenever I make any kind of move on you. Yet you say we're not just friends. We're us. But what even is us?'

Natalia's arms shook with the endurance of holding herself up.

'Natalia, you can relax.'

'Not until I get an answer.'

'Fine.' Jeremy glanced away, struggling to fully comprehend his feelings towards Natalia and his inability to take their relationship further.

Focusing on Natalia's face, terrified that if he glanced down and noticed, revelled, in the curve of her breast as it threatened to spill from her simple black, cotton bra, or the way her lush curves were centimetres away from bare skin, that all reason, all determination to do what was right would be lost.

'Will you hate me if I'm honest with you?'

Natalia shook her head. 'It's all I want from you.' Her nose wrinkled. 'Well, almost all I want.'

'Understandable. And relatable.' Jeremy reached up and ran his finger down the length of her nose, causing it to smooth out. 'The thing is, I know what this is to me. What we are. All that we can be. I didn't come down in the last rain shower. Or thunderstorm. And I'm old enough and ugly enough to know what I want. And what I want is you. I won't deny that.'

'Then, what's the hold up?' Natalia's eyes squinted with the effort of keeping herself up.

'The holdup is…' Jeremy took hold of her biceps in an effort to further support her, knowing if he attempted to move her to the ground, she'd be angry at him for scuppering her plan. 'I like you. Like, really like you.'

Natalia's eyes widened. 'As in you properly like me.'

'Yes.' Jeremy nodded. 'And the more I get to know you, the more time I spend with you, the more that feeling deepens. And it scares me.'

'Oh.' Her answer found, Natalia collapsed on to her side and faced Jeremy, using her arm as a pillow. 'Oh.'

'Exactly.' Jeremy rolled over, mirroring her position. 'Oh.'

'So, what do we do about it? Stop seeing each other? Go back to being friends? Friendly? Wind time back to the day we met, but act like none of this happened? Just be colleagues?'

With every suggestion, Jeremy's heart felt hollower. The idea of treating Natalia as a friend, a colleague, an almost-stranger created a chilly vacuum in his chest.

'Do you think you could do that?' he asked, needing to see how the idea of rewinding their relationship affected Natalia. Not wanting her to feel like she didn't have a say in what happened next.

Her lashes lowered, hiding her feelings, and her chest hitched as she thought his question through.

'I think...' she met his gaze, her eyes burning with intensity. 'That going backward, that choosing to go backward, would feel like the greatest rejection of all. Not you rejecting me, but me rejecting the truth.'

'And that is?'

'That I like you too much to ignore this feeling I get whenever you're around me. All jittery and bubbly. Also, settling and cosy. Like we could do anything together and it would be fun, but we'd be fine. I'd be fine. I'd be safe. With you.'

Jeremy took Natalia's hand, touched by her words. 'Which, considering my reputation, is quite the thing to say.'

'Except if your reputation was as solid as you and those around you think it is, you'd have had your wicked way with me when I went to kiss you the night of the storm. Except you didn't. You chose not to.'

'Couldn't.' The word came out in a whisper. 'I didn't want to hurt you. It's the last thing I want. It's what's held me back this whole time. Knowing that exploring what's between us, deepening it further, could cause you – us – pain.'

'Us.' Natalia leaned in and placed a feather-light kiss upon his lips. 'Not just any old "us", but big, scary "us".'

'Very big. Very scary.' Jeremy's stomach knotted as he thought about his family's reaction if they overheard this conversation. Discovered the depths of his feelings for Natalia. How happy they'd be. How they'd feel like they'd won.

'I guess you're worried about the pressure your family will put on you, on us, when – if – we take things further?'

Jeremy placed a hand on Natalia's soft cheek. 'You know me too well. And in so little time, too.'

'And you don't know me?' She turned her head and kissed his palm.

Jeremy couldn't deny her words. In one fortnight he had come to know Natalia Hawthorne. Daughter to two people who didn't treat her with the care parents ought to. Two doctors who wanted their daughter to go into their field. Who'd shown no interest in her once they realised she wouldn't. Leaving her to figure life out alone. To roam from job to job. Keeping her life in a rucksack and a couple of boxes. Never truly settling anywhere. Always afraid of the rejection that deep roots, deeper bonds invited. Yet, even with that cold, unfeeling start to life, Natalia was warm, caring, brave. Unafraid of the new. Unafraid to try. Even if it meant putting her heart on the line for someone who'd never been able to do it himself.

Yes, he knew her. Which is why he was terrified to hurt her.

Natalia traced a pattern over the back of his hand, letting it trail down his forearm, reaching his elbow, where she diverted to the line that ran the length of his waist, down towards the area that had fully woken, giving Natalia a physical answer, when what she deserved was the emotional one.

'I know you.' Jeremy stopped her hand as it moved towards the area, then brought it up to his lips and placed a kiss up on. A promise. 'Which is why I won't hurt you.'

'Good.' Natalia rolled back on top of him, pressing the length of her sun-warmed body against his. 'Because I won't let myself be hurt.'

Cupping her face with his hands, Jeremy stared into Natalia's eyes, which glinted with joy. 'My beautiful Natalia.'

And he knew she was his. At least she was for the next two weeks.

FIFTEEN

'This is stupid. I feel nervous when I shouldn't feel nervous at all. It's not like I've never met your family or spent time with them. I know what I'm getting into.' Natalia ran her hand through her hair as they walked down the lane to Jeremy's family home, hoping she didn't look like she'd just rolled out of bed. Which she had.

Jeremy's bed, to be exact.

The white cotton-sheeted rectangle becoming her second home over the last week. A sacred space where they'd had conversations ranging from childhood hopes and dreams to the little questions people asked each other: favourite colour – Jeremy's was navy blue. Food you couldn't live without – potatoes, for both of them. Favourite time of year – anytime that included Natalia in it, according to Jeremy. An answer that had caused her heart to go gooey and briefly imagine them together forever until she reminded herself that she could only be in Jeremy's life for a little longer. That forever wasn't the deal; for now was their reality. That hadn't stopped her from daydreaming of another way things could go, though…

'You're nervous too?' Jeremy turned to her, his face pale. 'Because I feel like they're going to have kittens once they figure things out.'

'But we're not going to let that happen, right?' Natalia attempted to flatten a crease out of her linen shirt. 'We're going to act the same as always. Just a couple of friends who work at the farm coming to dinner together after a day hard at work. We won't give them any reason to create unnecessary pressure and ruin everything for us.'

Us. The word still caused happiness to spill through her whenever she thought about it. Whenever Jeremy used it. Which was often. So much so that whenever she went on her morning stroll through the sunflower field, checking in on the blooms and welcoming them to a new day, she'd found herself fantasising about a future in Gordon Glen. So much so, she'd even dared to look at local job listings, hoping she could find a way to stay. Yes, she would disappoint her parents. Again. But, at this point, they had to be used to her being their biggest disappointment, just as she was used to being a disappointment. Staying in Gordon Glen, being with Jeremy, exploring who they could be with time on their side, would be worth their coldness, their sharpness, their indifference.

'Act cool. Act calm. Act casual.' Jeremy shook his

head and exhaled in exasperation. 'Who am I kidding? They're going to know the moment they see us.'

Natalia grinned and hip-bumped Jeremy. 'Because they've spent the afternoon in the pub reading the cards and seeing what was next for the Gordon family's love life?'

'They wish.' Jeremy rolled his eyes. 'More like because it's really bloody hard to stop smiling when you're around me. As hard as it is for me to take my eyes off you. They'll know something's up the second they try to wind me up about being a single man who hates love and is going to doom the family to being a bunch of spinsters and, instead of retaliating, I let their comments flow over me like water off a duck's back. They'll see that I've changed, and that the reason I've changed is you.'

Natalia stopped, her heart blossoming so large she was sure it was about to burst. 'That might just be the most wonderful thing anyone has ever said about me.'

Jeremy bent over and picked a dandelion from the grass verge that ran the length of the lane, then tucked it behind Natalia's ear. 'I'm just being honest. This last week has been...'

'Magical? Just what your sisters and mother hoped for?' Natalia teased, bringing her hand up to the flower, ensuring it wouldn't fall out.

'Better than magical. It's been perfect.' Jeremy wrapped an arm around her waist and brought him to her, his lips brushing against hers in the way that made

Natalia's toes curl and her heart beat faster. 'You are perfect. You make my life better.'

Then ask me to stay. Natalia pushed the thought out, hoping the strange energy that saw her and Jeremy click, that saw them act in sync so often, would go so far as to their thoughts. Despite knowing it was whimsical thinking, her heart sank as his lips remained still. Was Jeremy really going to give up on them one week from now? Would he simply let her go?

'I wish I could ask you to stay for another week or two, but it wouldn't be fair. Not when you've a future to think about. What with the study and your family expecting you home.' Jeremy turned away and began the trek to his parents' place. 'Maybe I could visit you once you've settled in?'

'Yeah. Maybe.' Natalia's cheekbones ached with the effort of keeping her smile plastered on her face. Did Jeremy want a long-distance relationship? Or was he hoping to keep her on as some kind of port in a storm? A booty call? She tamped down the anger that flared hot and fierce in her stomach. She knew what she'd signed up for when they'd agreed to be together for the last couple of weeks of her stay. To feel furious at Jeremy was unfair. The only thing to be furious at was the situation, which wasn't changing. Or wouldn't change, unless someone attempted to make a change. 'Or maybe...' Natalia licked her lips, preparing for the worst, but hoping for the best. 'Perhaps I could stay.'

Jeremy's feet stilled once more. 'Stay? Here? In Gordon Glen?'

Natalia kept her hands relaxed as she faced him, not wanting to appear antagonistic, or to give him a reason to say 'no' by getting into a fight. 'Is it that bad of an idea? I mean, I could get a job. I could find a place to live. I wouldn't be expecting us to move in together. Not so soon. Maybe not ever, if that works for us. But I think it would be wrong to not give this, give *us* a fair shot. Tell me if I'm wrong, but I get the feeling I'm not the only one who feels that we've something special going on here.' *You have my heart in my hands. Please don't break your promise to not hurt me. Please don't break my heart.*

Jeremy stroked his chin, his lips pursing in thought.

Was he looking for a way to let her down nicely, or for a way to make it work? Natalia crossed her fingers and hoped for the latter.

'You know, I could have a chat with some of the local farmers to see if they need a farmhand. There's not a lot of work around these parts, but I think a person could cobble together a few jobs and earn enough to get by. And since you've all but lived at mine this past week, you could continue doing so until a place that suited you became available.'

Natalia couldn't believe her ears. This was happening. Jeremy wanted her to stay. He saw a future with her. Natalia's feet itched to do a happy dance, but she kept them firmly on the ground, afraid if she moved she'd go stratospheric with happiness and never come back down to earth.

'And maybe I could eventually save enough to open up my own flower farm?' Natalia took Jeremy's hands in hers. 'I've enjoyed babysitting sunflowers. I can imagine babysitting roses and tulips and dahlias and, I don't know, anything that blooms and grows in this area.'

'Most things, if you ask my aunty. Gordon magic at work, she says.' Jeremy went to roll his eyes, then stopped. 'And maybe there's something in that.'

'You believe in magic now? What's made you change your mind?' Natalia knew the answer, but wanted to hear it from Jeremy's lips.

Jeremy leaned in, a smile brightening his eyes. 'It feels a little like magic brought me you.'

'Or maybe it brought you to me.' Sliding her hand around his neck, Natalia brought Jeremy in for a long kiss. Tasting the wholesome meal of porridge they'd scoffed down at lunch, the slight sourness of wine they'd enjoyed in his backyard earlier that afternoon after finishing up at the farm, and the sweetness of a man who was open with her. Who made her feel wanted. Special. Worthy.

She broke the kiss, but didn't lean away. 'You've just made me the happiest woman in the world. I didn't believe anyone could ever feel this way about me. That anyone could want me for me. Would be willing to change, for me.'

Jeremy placed a soft kiss on her lips. 'You made it easy. The moment I met you, I knew there was something special about you. About us. And to deny that would be foolish. You make me want to be the best that I can be, and letting you go, not fighting for us, would mean I wasn't being my best. It would make me a coward, a stubborn one, allowing a once in a lifetime feeling to leave in order to prove my sisters wrong. That's not just cowardice, it's stupidity.'

'And you're not stupid. Not remotely.' Natalia tipped her head to the sky, half-expecting to find a winged angel, bow and arrow in hand, smiling with glee at a job well done.

'Looking for something?' Jeremy took Natalia's hand in his.

Natalia shook her head. 'No, I've everything I need right here.'

Facing Jeremy, she revelled in the glow that emanated from his face. The look of a man who was sure of his decisions, who would not change his mind, who would not hurt her. She touched the dandelion once more, making sure it was there, ensuring this entire sequence wasn't some mad dream. That she would not wake up and discover she'd deluded herself into creating a world that couldn't be. The flower was still tucked behind her ear, its petals as soft as ever, as was the expression on Jeremy's face.

'So, does this mean we should ditch that idea of hiding us from your family?' She held her breath, knowing being honest with the Gordon clan was the last hurdle for Jeremy. Knowing that their reaction, while not cruel, wasn't likely to be kind, or sweet, or gently understanding.

'Absolutely.' Jeremy tugged Natalia's hand, and they began heading toward his family home. 'Let's get a move on. The sooner we get there, the sooner we can tell them, the sooner we can get over my sisters cawing and cackling over how their mighty brother has fallen.'

SIXTEEN

You've got this. You're fine. You've got this. You're fine, Jeremy silently chanted. The words whirring through his head faster and faster the closer they got to the bright yellow door, which he knew would lead to all manner of grief once his sisters discovered that their dedicated bachelor of a brother had fallen head over heels.

Every few steps he sneaked a look at Natalia, hoping the confidence, the joy she radiated would seep into him. For a split second, it would, before rushing away as the image of Gemma, Clare and Tilly crowding around him, their excitement at the family curse being broken, their delight in having Jeremy renege on his ways swamping him.

Natalia squeezed his hand as they reached the door. 'I don't think I've ever been this happy in my entire life.'

The orange and pink violas that lined the brick

garden path bobbed in the breeze, as if nodding their agreement. His sisters would say that was a positive sign, yet Jeremy's gloomy outlook failed to lift.

'You'll be fine.' Natalia kissed his hand, then dropped it. 'I promise. If they give you grief, if they tease you, remember it's coming from a place of love.'

She wasn't wrong, but neither did the rightness of Natalia's comment settle Jeremy's nerves. Nor did the so-called calming inhalation then exhalation he took as he opened the door and stepped over its threshold.

'Mum, Dad, we're here.'

Following the sound of laughter, Jeremy found his family out on the patio, a cheese and fruit platter on the table, glasses of wine and beer in hand or sitting in front of them. Business as usual. A good sign? Or a sign that what he expected to happen would happen, and that he'd have to be the one to act business as *un*usual. In other words, he wasn't allowed to become irritated, defensive, or twist what was an amazing turn of events in his personal life into a sour one.

'My baby first-and-only born boy.' His mother angled her cheek for a kiss. 'So good of you and Natalia to join us. We'd begun to think you'd changed your mind.'

'And settle for tinned soup for dinner instead of a barbecue?' Natalia came to stand beside him. 'Never.'

'And that would be my signal to get the thing fired up.' His father stood, picked up his beer and wandered over to the barbecue, which was set deeper in the garden where it couldn't accidentally set fire to the gauze sunshades.

'Where have you been? In the fields? Are things looking good for this weekend's opening? Your father mentioned he potted up seeds. Any signs of life? Or have his deadly thumbs killed off the poor wee things before they've had a chance to become who they are meant to be?' His mother flipped open the cool box placed at her feet. 'Beer for you, my love. Natalia, would you like wine, beer or one of those god awful alco-pop things that Tilly's so fond of.'

'Wine for me. Whatever you're having.' Natalia pulled a double bean bag over and collapsed into it, patting the area beside it for Jeremy to sit on.

Jeremy debated sitting next to her, his desire to do so warring with his unwillingness to spend the whole evening being given grief by his sisters for doing the one thing he said he'd never do.

Taking the beer, he waved his hand at Clare and Gemma. 'Scoot over.'

Clare didn't budge. 'There's room next to Natalia. Go sit with her.'

Jeremy refused to let Clare's reticence dissuade him. 'Or I could sit between my second and third favourite sisters.'

'Which one's the second favourite?' Gemma asked, crossing her arms and raising her brows.

'You, of course. The other one just put up a fight. Immediately went down in my estimation.'

'So I was third favourite before that moment?'

Seeing a petty scrap in the making, Jeremy turned around and made to sit down, betting on his sisters moving rather than having him sit on their knees. Sure enough, his bottom met cushion and his ears met his siblings' grumbles of annoyance. And his eyes? Guilt curled tight in his stomach as he caught the confusion in Natalia's eyes. The rejection.

She'd understand once he explained his thinking, he told himself. She was reasonable. She got him. She knew how worried – afraid – he was about his sisters' reaction to his finding someone special, and that the timing had to be right when telling them.

'You say you want to be single, but if that's how you treat any other woman in your vicinity, then no wonder you've stayed that way for so long. Nobody wants your stinky arse in their immediate space.' Clare made a show of waving her hand in front of her nose. 'Smelly boy.'

'Oh, for goodness' sakes.' His mother finished pouring Natalia a wine, then topped up her own glass. 'Anyone would think you were children, not full-grown adults. Now, Jeremy, where are the answers to my questions?'

'As you surmised, Natalia and I have been working in the fields. I checked on the seeds and they don't look to be dead yet, but I can't be too sure. I've yet to see any signs of life. I, however, have faith in my father's ability to only kill most things rather than all.'

'I heard that,' his father chuntered from behind him. 'You kill a couple of house plants and forget to water the herb garden once or twice and suddenly you're tarred for life as a plant pest.'

'The entire herb garden died, Dad.' Tilly tsked her disgust. 'And you forgot to water them for an entire two weeks.'

'And that's my cue to go get the steaks, which will be cooked to medium-rare perfection, not left to go rubbery and grey, as you've all been known to do on occasion.' With a half bow, his father headed inside.

'And the sunflower field?' His mother turned to Natalia. 'Are the flowers feeling good? Are they excited about showing themselves off? I know Francesca was hoping it could become a regular thing if it all goes to plan, and she's rarely wrong about these things.'

Natalia stretched her legs out and took a sip of wine, her expression no longer radiating the joy it had on the way over. 'They've begun to bloom. They're looking happy. I had a chat with them the other day and they promised me everything would be right as rain.'

His mother's brows rose. 'You were actually chatting with them?'

'Of course she was.' Gemma smiled approvingly. 'Natalia understands how the world works.'

'That's why she feels like one of us.' Tilly turned her gaze on Jeremy. 'You know, a smart person would snap her up before someone else does.'

Tell them now, his heart urged.

His heart wasn't wrong. This was the perfect opportunity to make his sisters' day. To see his mother's face light up in a smile, but his tongue refused to cooperate.

Daring to glance at Natalia, Jeremy noted her stillness, her blank face, like she was waiting for him to make a move before she dared to react.

'A smarter person would know not to treat Natalia like a piece of meat you picked up at the shop.' Jeremy leaned over and helped himself to a wedge of brie and a rice cracker, even though his stomach was tense with self-disgust and his appetite zero. Why was he doing this to Natalia? Why was he doing this to himself? All he had to do was be honest about his feelings, and yet he couldn't. The words were trapped in a steel cage that was wrapped in a thousand chains and padlocked for extra security. 'I'm going to check on dad. It doesn't take this long to pull steaks from the fridge.'

Keeping his gaze firmly on his destination, afraid of what else he'd see on Natalia's face if he dared look her way, Jeremy strode to the kitchen to find his father leaning against the bench, looking like the cat that got the cream.

'So, you and Natalia got together, hey? Good for you, son.' His father clapped him on the back. 'She seems like a great woman. Hardworking, not a pushover, fits in with the family, which isn't the easiest of asks.'

Jeremy didn't bother to hide his surprise. 'You could tell? How'd you know? More to the point, how did *you* know and the rest of them are oblivious?'

His father half-snorted. 'I'm a writer. It's literally

my job to observe people and see what lies beneath their interactions. And what I saw out there was a young man keeping his distance from a woman he's attached to and a young woman in complete confusion about why he wouldn't want to sit next to her when all that mirrored body language would suggest an intimacy that wasn't quite there before when you two were indulging in lingering glances when you thought the other wasn't looking.'

'Mirrored body language?' Jeremy hadn't been aware that he and Natalia were so obvious. 'Really?'

'Shoulders and leg positions and the way two people lean forward and backward says a lot. You two are almost drinking in unison as well. Someone starts and the other finishes microseconds later. It's very cute.'

'Cute? Really, Dad?'

His father shrugged. 'Well, it is. And since you didn't give me a whole lot of cuteness as a teen when it came to dating, I'm making sure to revel in the joy of watching my son fall for someone.'

'Jeremy's fallen for someone? Oh my god.'

Tilly's high-pitched tone sent a shudder down Jeremy's spine.

'Girls.' Tilly ran to the door. 'Did you hear that? Jeremy's in loooooove.'

'Tilly, shut up.' Jeremy glared at his sister, who was too busy dancing a jig to notice.

'Sorry, son.' His father bit his lip. 'I didn't see her

come in. And I know how private you are about these things.'

'It's fine.' Jeremy didn't want his father to feel bad. He'd done nothing wrong. It wasn't his father's fault his sisters were nosey parkers who didn't know when to butt out or keep quiet in the face of family news. 'It's just not quite how I wanted them to find out.'

'Dare I say it, but rarely do things turn out the way we expect them to.' His father picked up the plate of steaks. 'Well, except for in love. So long as you don't let others – or yourself – get in your way. If you can manage that, then everything tends to turn out pretty well. In my experience, anyway.'

Jeremy followed his father out to find Tilly bouncing on the balls of her feet in front of Natalia, clapping her hands and chanting, 'I knew it. I knew it. I knew it!'

'Tilly, calm your farm.' Jeremy placed his hands on Tilly's shoulders. 'Natalia doesn't need to be accosted by an overenthusiastic puppy. No one needs that kind of pressure. Besides, it's early days yet. There's no need to make a big deal about it.' Jeremy regretted the words the moment they left his mouth. They negated everything he'd told Natalia. He'd minimised what was between them. And for what? To feel like he had the upper hand over his sisters? Over the stupid, bloody family curse that only existed in their minds? But he couldn't take the words back. It was too late. They were out there.

'So, you're saying you're together, but not quite?'

Tilly's eyes narrowed. 'God, you're such a selfish twat. We've spent years unable to find happiness because you've been so busy refusing to meet anyone or take anyone seriously after that girl broke your heart in university, and now that love is clearly here and we finally have a chance to be happy you're pumping the breaks? Taking things slow? Giving yourself room to back out?'

Jeremy didn't know what to say, not when his foot was firmly lodged in his mouth.

'Oh, early days, schmurly days.' Gemma raised her glass in Natalia's direction. 'Welcome to the family. I hate to say "I told you so", but we saw this in the cards the moment you set foot in town. We've all just been waiting for you two to get your acts together.'

'Wait, what?' Clare piped up. 'What's this about Jeremy having been in love before? Since when? And if that's the case, why were we single? Surely when he was happy we might've been happy.'

'If what Tilly says is true, then the reason nothing happened was because Jeremy hadn't experienced true love, my darling girl. It's got to be the real deal.' His mother sat back in her seat, her lips lifted in the smuggest of smiles.

'Your mother's right, Tilly.' Natalia spoke up, her eyes hard. 'The girl at university. She really was just a friend. Jeremy told me himself. So, there wasn't any heartbreak because there wasn't any love.'

'Thank you, Natalia.' Jeremy went to sit beside her, hoping by doing so she'd see he hadn't meant the words. That he'd felt trapped, accosted, unprepared to say the right thing. But now he was prepared to do the right thing, to be with her, to be beside her.

Natalia stretched her arm out, her hand in the place where his bottom ought to be stopping him from sitting down, then gave a small shake of her head, emphasising her point.

The churning in Jeremy's gut intensified. He didn't need tarot cards or even the ability to read body language to know things were about to go from bad to worse.

'The problem with your brother isn't that he's simply not wanted to fall in love, so hasn't. It's that he refuses to let himself be happy because it's the only control he has in this family. So long as you all believe in this curse, then he holds a small amount of power.'

'What the hell? Jeremy took a step backward, unable to believe what he was hearing. This was how Natalia saw him? This is what she felt about him deep down? 'What are you on about?'

Natalia raised her brows, her head cocked to the side. 'Tell me I'm wrong. Tell me that despite having the best intentions to come in here and declare us a couple, that the moment you saw the one little piece of power you have in this family flit away you didn't panic.'

'You don't know what you're talking about.' Jeremy sucked in a shuddering breath as he fought to keep calm, to not retaliate out of hurt. Or shame.

Natalia set her glass down to the side, then pushed

herself up. 'Oh, I think I do. I may have only been here for a few weeks, but I can see what's in front of me.'

'Oh, yeah? And what's that?' Jeremy braced himself, knowing what was to come next wouldn't be pretty, but he would handle it. He'd get over it. He was used to being told who he was or what he was by the women around him. Another woman doing exactly that was par for the course.

'A coward.' Natalia's eyes were flinty. 'Nothing more. Nothing less.'

'I don't need to hear this.' Jeremy turned away, only to see his sisters and mother had gathered around in a semi-circle. A coven of witches enjoying the bubble, bubble toil and trouble unfolding before them. He swallowed the laugh that rose at the absurdity of it all.

'Sure. Walk away. I don't blame you. You've made your feelings for me clear. Shown me you were all talk. You got what you wanted. The only thing you want from women, or so you've repeatedly told me. And for that, I can only be angry at myself. You told me who you were almost from the very beginning. It was me who chose not to believe you. Chose to believe that we were different, something more. Us.'

Jeremy caught the cracking of Natalia's voice. Heard her hurt, her pain; followed by footsteps as she walked away. For good? His heart ached at the thought.

'What the hell are you doing dilly-dallying?' Gemma flapped her hands in his direction. 'Fix this you idiot.'

Jeremy waited for them to say 'for us', 'you're

stealing our happiness', 'you owe us this', but no words came.

'Gemma's not talking about fixing this argument for them, my love.' His mother's tone was soft, her eyes gentle. Sad, almost. 'For you.'

SEVENTEEN

Natalia picked up her pace as the sound of the Gordon's front door slamming met her ears. With her cheeks aflame with anger and embarrassment, her heart aching from being so blatantly rejected, her head full of admonishment for what she'd said about Jeremy in front of his family, there was no way she wanted to speak to the man himself. Not right now. Perhaps never again.

'Natalia. Stop.'

She sped up as Jeremy called after her and debated whether it was worth breaking out into a trot to get away with him. Yes, it would look childish. It would also save her further pain.

'Seriously. Stop. Please. You can't just walk away from me. From us. Not like that. Not like it, we, us, meant nothing.'

Natalia whirled around, any hint of flight overtaken by fight. Jeremy was going to blame her for what happened at his family's home? After the way he'd treated her? Humiliated her? Worse. He would dare still call them 'us'?

She raised a finger in his direction. 'Don't you dare make this about something I've done wrong. I've done nothing wrong. I entered that house believing we were a couple, that we'd decided to build a future together, that we were going to be open about our relationship. Within minutes you changed your mind and made out we were nothing. Or next to nothing. That we were "early days".'

Jeremy's hands went to his hips, his chest heaving with exertion. 'And the minute you felt slighted, you went on the attack, calling me a coward. Which isn't true. Not in the slightest. I wasn't the one who ran away just now, was I? That's on you. The moment things got uncomfortable, you got out. Which shouldn't be a surprise considering that's your way of dealing with things.'

Natalia dropped her hand to her side, where it fisted along with the other. 'What's that supposed to mean?'

'When have you ever faced things that went wrong? When was the last time you stood up to your parents and told them they'd hurt you? That they ought to love you for who you are, not who they want you to be?'

Natalia's heart stilled. Every cell in her body vibrated with fury. Was Jeremy really going to turn his failings around on her? Trying to make this about her wounded heart, not his stubborn desire to be separate from his family, even if it meant hurting them by hurting himself, by keeping any chance of love at bay?

'Do not go there.' Natalia took a step forward. 'If you turn this around on me, there's no going back. That's my family, not yours. They're different. And you couldn't possibly understand what it was like to grow up in a home with them.'

'And yet you think you have the right to judge me? To judge how I felt growing up in a home where you're constantly harassed. Where every step, every move, is monitored. Where you're considered important because the future lies with you, but with that comes feeling nothing short of bullied by those who are meant to love you as they try to get you to do what they want before you're ready? Assuming that you're ever going to be ready, especially when love feels like it comes with strings attached.'

Natalia tried to see Jeremy's point of view, but failed. 'What strings attached come with being part of your family? I'd have given anything to be seen by those around me. Your family see you. They know how capable of love you are, how giving and caring you are. That's why they want to see you happy. Yes, there's the whole curse thing going on in the background, and I get the pressure it puts on you, but in doing so you've let it define you, you've let your family define you, when you don't have to. You can be your own person. And if you had, if you'd just been brave enough to show them how you felt about me rather than trying to control the situation, we wouldn't be here right now.'

Natalia drew in a shuddering breath and prayed Jeremy could see she was right. That he'd grown so used to feeling controlled that the only way he felt in control was to withhold the one thing his sisters believed they needed to be truly happy – love.

Jeremy began nodding, slowly at first, then increased in speed. 'Oh, that's rich coming from you. The very person who let her family define her, almost from the start.'

Natalia fought the urge to cover her ears, sensing Jeremy's words were going to be aimed straight at her heart. A place she'd shielded so well for so long. Until now. Until him.

'Every single thing you've done in life is because of your family's expectations. You felt unseen, so you made yourself that way. Never trying to do better, never reaching your potential because you didn't want to feel seen in trying. You felt unwanted. So, you kept your distance, furthered the emotional disconnect, made it so that even if they wanted to, they wouldn't find it easy to invite you over for morning tea, or dinner, or – I don't know – simply just a chat. You felt unloved. So, you chose never to love. You built up a wall around that heart of yours so strong and so high and so damn impenetrable all because you were once a little girl who was turned away when she was scared, and you took it to mean you had to stand on your own two feet, that you couldn't trust another human being to show you the care you deserved. And the moment I faltered, the moment I didn't do what you wanted, you chose to reject me rather than giving me a chance to work through my feelings with you in private.'

'That's not true.' Natalia felt her lower lip tremble at the truth of Jeremy's words. 'I'm not that hard. Not that harsh. Not that distant. I'm not like them.'

'You're exactly like them. You might show up with smiles and laughter. You might act carefree. But you're trapped in your own story. And I think you know it.'

'And you're not?' Natalia crossed her arms over her chest and straightened up, refusing to be spoken to like she was the worst person in the world, like she was a failure simply for doing the best she could to survive in a world where she'd felt unwanted. 'You refuse to leave Gordon Glen. You couldn't even stick it out at university for the full time. You chose to leave even when you had the support of your friend to keep you there. You refuse to do anything you love. You refuse to love full stop. All because you're so determined to do the opposite of what your family needs you to do in order for them to find happiness, to find love.'

'You cannot be serious?' Jeremy's words dripped with derision. 'For all the flippancy in which you spoke of that stupid bloody curse, you actually believe in it? They've got you thinking that their ridiculous belief that they need me to be in love, to be the person who bends to yet another woman's will, will make their lives whole?'

'It's got nothing to do with my belief in anything.

What it's got to do with is that you are willing to cut off your nose in order to spite your family's face.' Natalia caught the tremulous tone in her voice. She would not lose control in front of Jeremy. Would not show him how much his rejection hurt. Taking a deep breath in and out, easing the burn that had stung her nostrils, the telltale sign tears weren't far behind, she re-centred her thoughts, her emotions. 'Or should I say you're willing to cut off – or out – your heart rather than feel even less of a man than you already do for caring so much about how the women in your life treat you, and what they think of you.'

She searched Jeremy's face for signs that she'd got to him, hurt him, slashed through his stubbornness to the heart of the matter, but he remained as stoic as ever. His face granite, not a twitch or a hint of slackening of his features to be seen.

'Well, if that's the way you see me – as less of a man – then perhaps it's good I know that now before I allowed myself to fall any more for you than I already have.' His lips pressed together, flattening out. 'Or should I say, *had*.'

Natalia willed herself to remain as calm as Jeremy. As hard. As unbothered. But his admission stole the air from her lungs, the bravado from her heart. He'd fallen for her. Despite his talk of early days, he really had seen her in his world in a permanent way. Had seen a future together. And in one foul argument, his feelings had disappeared.

Which went to show how deep his feelings had

been. The deeper the emotion, the stronger the reaction. The bigger the attachment, the greater the need to detach when everything goes wrong.

'Well, I guess it's good that I'm leaving in a few days' time.' Natalia got the words out, despite the boulder in her throat. Jeremy blurred before her as tears welled. She dropped her arms to her side, knowing she needed to get away from him before he could see just which one of them was truly weak. 'Good luck with life, Jeremy. I hope being on your own makes you happy.'

Jeremy's face remained expressionless. Unmoved. Unbothered. 'It always has.'

Swivelling on his heel, he took off in the direction of his home.

Turn back, turn back, turn back, Natalia's heart whispered, but his steps continued, proving how easy it was for people to walk away from her, to see her as not worth investing time or effort in.

And it all started with the people she was running back to.

Pulling out her mobile she pulled up her mother's contact details.

Mum, we need to talk.

Three dots appeared, then stopped, then appeared again.

I'm at work.

No 'I'll talk to you later'. No 'hey, sweetheart'. No, at the very least, 'I'm at work, can I call later?'. No care. No interest. No love.

Turning away, refusing to let her shoulders hitch or her head hang as she fought the feeling of being not just alone but lonely in the world, Natalia made for the one place that felt safe, that felt like home – the sunflower field.

EIGHTEEN

The moment he'd entered the pub, Jeremy knew he ought to have turned around, but he hadn't. Because he was an idiot. That was the only answer for it. Anyone who was anything less than an idiot would've seen the huddle of Gordon women in their usual spot peering at their latest tarot reading, and immediately turned tail and scarpered before they harangued him into their madness. But here he was, seated across from his mother, harangued.

'What do you see, Jeremy?' His mother's eyes narrowed in concentration. 'I think I know what I'm seeing, but things are looking foggy.'

'Feeling foggy too.' Clare shivered involuntarily. 'Like there's been a damp shade cloth thrown over everything.'

'I'm getting that as well.' Tilly glanced up at her brother. 'I suppose you're feeling fancy free and full of joy? Not sensing this disturbance. Too busy being in lusty love with our lovely Natalia after dealing with your lover's spat?'

Jeremy's stomach turned and his heart twisted at Tilly's words, but he refused to show how they affected him. If it hadn't been for the women around him, he'd not be feeling this way. Lost. Confused. Bereft. And more determined than ever to keep love well out of his way.

His mother sat back in her seat, her eyes narrowed in speculation. 'I thought she went home because of a headache after you two sorted things out? That's what you told us, was it not?'

Jeremy remained still, unmoved, unwilling to give the truth away.

'I'm now thinking "not" might have been a tall tale. That, the truth is you've fallen out and there was no kissing and making up.'

'If that were true, wouldn't you have seen it in the cards? Is that not what all that doom and gloom is telling you? But you were all too busy thinking you'd won, celebrating that you'd finally gotten your way to notice.' Jeremy sunk his teeth into his tongue, shocked at talking back to his mother. In all his years, he'd never done it once, holding her in such high regard that the idea of being rude to her was beyond imagination.

'Girls.' His mother nodded at Tilly, Gemma and Clare. 'Leave me and your brother alone for a bit, okay?'

Three sets of eyes went from their mother to

Jeremy, assessing the situation. Jeremy straightened up, refusing to squirm under their curious gazes.

'Can I just say something?' Gemma's tone was quiet, not holding its usual imperiousness. 'If you don't mind?'

'When's that ever stopped you before?' Jeremy retorted.

'Never.' Gemma acknowledged his point with a nod. 'And that's part of the problem. I can see that. But I think you need to see that we haven't won a thing. This was never a competition. Or a race. Maybe consider that for a minute or two before shooting your mouth off again.' Her piece done, Gemma stood. 'Mum, how about we meet you back at the house? It's never too early to plan for Halloween, and that spread's put me in a dark mood.'

'If that would make you happy, my dear, of course. See you soon, my loves.'

Jeremy waited until his sisters had left, then, with three quarters of the reason he felt so tense gone, sank down into his chair.

'Oh no. You don't stay there. Not opposite me. We're not in opposition to each other. Come,' his mother patted the seat beside her. 'Sit next to me.'

Jeremy remained in place, pride keeping him glued to his spot, along with the fear that if he did as he was told, his mother would believe he'd always do as he was told.

'Oh, stop being a mule. Come.' She patted the seat with more force. 'I'm not going to cast some magical spell over you to make you do as I say, or force you to read the cards so you can make sense of your situation. I just want to chat, mother to son, son to mother.'

Not entirely believing her, but also not wanting to be called out for being stubborn again, Jeremy moved around to the other side of the table and sat in the chair previously taken up by Tilly. 'There. Does that make you happy?'

His mother remained facing forward. 'It does. Now, how are you feeling? In general. It doesn't have to be about a girl, or work, or us. How are you feeling within yourself?'

Like the damp shade cloth Clare spoke of has enshrouded my soul.

'I'm fine. Great. Dandy, even.'

He'd expected his mother to turn to him, a look of exasperation on her face at his lie, but she remained still, her gaze focused on something out the window. Jeremy followed it, and noticed the shop Tilly worked at, a single car parked out the front. A couple of bored teens hanging out to the right of it, sucking on ice lollies. The café's window was empty, being that it had shut a good hour ago. Nothing to see, as far as he could gather. Which could only mean one thing.

'Mum, if you're going into some weird trance right now with the intention of predicting my future, I'm out of here.'

Her hand landed on his knee and waggled it back and forth before returning to her lap. 'Hardly. The only trance I'm ever put in is when your father reads some of his work to me. I know he does very well for himself, but oh how I wish he'd turn his prose to romance. I find those books far more interesting. The emotional rollercoasters the characters go on, the intrigue, the breakups, the make ups, the sex – even if it's only inferred.' She flapped her hand in front of her face. 'It gets the old heart racing and the engine revving.'

'Oh my god, I'm leaving if you infer anything like that again.' Jeremy pushed his chair back a little to prove his point.

A faint smile danced upon his mother's lips. 'Nothing wrong with intrigue, my boy.'

He rolled his eyes. 'You're being obtuse.'

'Must run in the family,' she murmured. 'Some might say you get it from me.'

'I'm not obtuse,' Jeremy huffed. 'I say and do exactly as I mean.'

'Is that so?' His mother's eyebrow rose in silent disbelief. 'So, tell me how you are again?'

'I'm fine.'

'You're being obtuse.'

'And you're talking in circles.' Jeremy reached forward and grabbed Tilly's half-drunk glass of lemonade and took a sip. 'Everything here is fine. The farm's doing well. Aunty Francesca will be pleased. It's been a good summer. I can't complain.'

'And yet you did complain, in your own way, when you informed your sisters and I that we had won, that we'd gotten our own way when you'd fallen for our Natalia.'

Jeremy rankled at the use of 'our'. Natalia didn't belong to his mother, his sisters, or his father. She certainly didn't belong to him. She'd made certain of that when she'd called him out for letting his family define him.

'The thing is, and I want you to think seriously about this before answering... Did we really win? Because if we had, it would indicate that we had some influence over your coupling. That we'd manipulated the situation, so you'd be forced to feel something for her. Forced,' his mother repeated, gently bringing home her point.

Jeremy shifted in his seat, seeing her point, even though he'd rather not have. 'Maybe I wasn't "forced", but it wasn't like you were innocent. Any of you. You made sure Natalia and I would be together more times than I can count. At drinks. At dinner. In the pub. At the picnic. You did everything you could to make sure we had face time.'

'That may be so...'

Jeremy could feel the 'but' coming.

'But I have face time with people regularly – people at the shop, at the pub. When you were younger, I saw a fair bit of your teachers due to your inability to hand in homework on time – yet I never once developed feelings for any of those people. Things remained cordial. And we weren't the ones to invite her around to our home the first night she arrived.'

Every ounce of Jeremy resisted what his mother was saying. It made too much sense. And he was too angry to think sense, let alone feel it. 'That's because you love Dad. You'd never do anything to hurt him.'

His mother dipped her chin in agreement. 'This is true, but before your father came along, I spent time with other men regularly, but remained steadfastly single.'

Jeremy's shoulders tightened with irritation. His mother was being so reasonable, but she knew as well as he did that there was a very good reason for why she'd managed to stay single before, and not fall for anyone after meeting his father.

'That's because of the curse. Until Uncle Jack fell in love, you couldn't. At least that's what you told yourself so often you turned that fallacy into truth.' He necked the rest of the lemonade and pushed his chair back. 'Unless there's something to add to that story, which has been told so often that it's got its own track marks, then I don't want to hear it. It's old. It's boring. It's ruining my bloody life.'

His mother turned to face him, pinning him with a seriousness he rarely saw. 'Or maybe you are the one ruining your own life simply because you believe in that story as much as anyone else in the family, and you hate that you do.'

'You're wrong.' Jeremy crossed his arms and shook

his head. 'It's a load of bollocks, and the fact that people I love believe we're cursed astounds me.'

'Okay, then riddle me this, Jeremy Archer Gordon. If you don't believe in the curse, then why do you hold it over your sisters? Why have you actively chosen to not fall in love? Why is it the one time you fell in love you cut it off before it could properly bloom?'

'What are you even on about?' Jeremy tightened his grip on himself, refusing to admit the truth. 'I've never fallen in love. Not once.'

'So what was Natalia? Another passing fling? Someone you saw as a friend with benefits? No one special? Because I saw the way you looked at her, the way you would beam the moment she entered the room, the respect you gave her, the care you showed, and if that's not love then I apparently don't know what love is.'

The fight left Jeremy in one all-consuming exhale that saw his body go limp, right down to his arms, which fell to his side. He angled his head and searched the ceiling for answers. 'You can't fall in love with someone when you've known them all of three weeks.'

'Well, if that's the case, then why did I fall in love with your father the moment I laid eyes on him?'

Jeremy let out a 'pff' of annoyance at his mother's hyperbole. 'You're being fanciful.'

'No. I'm being real. I know there's the story of how we met when he got stuck in the village that we like to tell people, but there's more to it.' His mother's lips curled up in a small smile, her gaze growing softer.

'What your father doesn't know is that I saw him once. At a book signing. Well before we met here.'

Jeremy turned to his mother, unable to believe what he was hearing. 'Are you saying that you stalked Dad?'

She waved the comment away. 'Oh, don't be silly. I was on holiday in London, in desperate need of getting all this country air out of my lungs, and I saw that my favourite romance author was having a wee soiree at a bookstore to celebrate her new book, so I went, and your father was there.'

'Dad doesn't read romance. He'd rather spend a day on the farm pulling weeds.'

His mother's laughter filled the room, causing the few punters who'd chosen to stay out of the sun to look up from their beers.

'You're right. He wasn't there for the author, he was there with his agent, who happened to be the agent of the romance writer. She'd dragged him along on the pretence that it would help him get over his fear of book signings if he saw one in action.' His mother's lips pursed together disapprovingly. 'Although it was as clear as the coral lipstick on her lips and the way her ruby talons clung to his arm that she was hoping it might turn into something more than a little exercise of fear-facing.'

Jeremy tried to repress a grin, but couldn't. 'Jealous, Mum?'

'Oh, piffle. More irritated that people can't see what's right in front of their eyes, which in some cases is love and, in other cases, complete disinterest.'

'So, you were jealous.'

His mother lifted her index finger and brought it to his lips. 'Shush now, or your open invitation to come for breakfast, lunch or dinner at your leisure will be revoked.'

Jeremy mimed zipping his lips, quietly tickled to see his confident, self-assured mother in the throes of an emotion that, until a few seconds ago, he'd have sworn she was incapable of feeling.

'So, I saw your father, and there was something about him that drew me in. Yes, he was as dishy as they come, yes, he dressed well, in a bookish way, and yes, he was very kind to his agent, but I felt a connection between us. Like I'd been walking around my whole life with half a magnet inside me that was looking for its other half and, in that busy bookstore, I found it.'

Something in his mother's story tugged at Jeremy. He closed his eyes and found himself in the main lane of Gordon Glen, Natalia standing on the side with her bag, staring intently at her phone. A thrill had run through him – not the basic thrill of seeing a pretty new face, something he'd experienced plenty of times before, but something different... deeper. As if part of him had known that Natalia was meant to be in his life, even though no words had yet been spoken between them, and he had no idea of who she was or why she was there. And then there was the odd fizzing and zapping that happened when they touched...

Ever since that moment, he'd felt like he'd been

strapped into the seat of a rollercoaster that he couldn't stop, that he had no control over. Making him feel as if there was no other option but to know Natalia, to like Natalia. Maybe, if you believed his mother, to even love her.

He opened his eyes and faced his mother. 'So, what stopped you going up to dad right then and there? Wouldn't you have been happily loved up for even longer than you already are if you had?'

'It wasn't the right time.' His mother shrugged. 'Pure and simple. Had I tried to pry him away from that agent, we'd have ended up going nowhere. Wouldn't have been able to make it work.'

'Because of the curse? Because Uncle Jack hadn't met anyone, so you couldn't? Or wouldn't?' Jeremy didn't hide his disdain. The idea of his mother putting her love life on hold while waiting for her brother to find love was ridiculous.

'Because he lived in London and I lived in Gordon Glen.' His mother spoke to him like he was a simple child asking a simple question.

'So, you're saying the curse isn't real after all? That you think it's a load of hogwash? That all this talk of it is just a way to keep the air of mystery about the Gordon family that makes us famous – or infamous – around these parts?'

'No, dear. I'm saying that everything happens for a reason, and in our family that reason seems to keep repeating itself. Why that is? I have no idea. Maybe it simply comes down to timing. Maybe we're ready when we're ready. And maybe, just maybe, you weren't ready until Natalia made her way to the Glen. Or perhaps, in this case, she's the one who's not ready.' His mother patted his hand. 'And that's okay. If you two are anything like your father and I – and I'm inclined to think you are – your time will come when you can both make it work.' Scooping up her tarot cards, his mother shuffled them into a rectangle, then wrapped them in a paisley silk scarf. 'So, will we see you for dinner tonight?'

'Thanks for the offer, Mum, but I don't think so. I need some time to myself.' *More like some time to count the many ways you're an idiot.* After treating Natalia the way he had, after being so rude to her, there was no chance of her giving him the time of day ever again.

'Understandable. A little hanged man time would do you good.'

Jeremy rolled his eyes at his mother, knowing she was referencing a card in which a halo-headed man was hung upside down by one ankle. It had something to do with new ideas, or enlightenment, none of which Jeremy possessed. Some arguments – like the one he'd had with Natalia – were too hard to come back from.

NINETEEN

Natalia checked the sky for the umpteenth time. Still blue. Still cloudless. Still looking like a sign that the sunflower festival would go ahead the next day as planned without a hitch.

Relief flowed through her. The sooner the event was done and dusted, the sooner she could leave Gordon Glen, and all that had gone on, behind and get back to the business of trying to be someone she wasn't. The perfect daughter.

Her heart didn't so much sink but plummet at the thought. Seeing no other option but to follow her original plan, Natalia had called her parents at a time she knew they'd be home and given them the news that she'd be heading back to London to do an access to nursing course in the hopes of one day becoming an actual nurse.

Nursing? Had been her father's reply. A single word, said not with interest or pride, but as a question, with a hint of disdain tucked behind it, letting her know he felt it was beneath her. Beneath them. It had taken all her will not to hang up the phone then and there. At least her mother had made murmurings of approval, which had helped until she'd mentioned that Natalia could do further study in the future to become an independent prescriber, then perhaps in time she could look at going back to university to become a doctor.

That's if the career path sticks, Natalia. Which I hope, this time, it will. You're not getting any younger.

Though said with care, Natalia could read between the lines: her parents didn't believe she had it in her to be anything more than a failure.

If only they could see the field in front of her. The sunflowers' heads, now in full, fluttery bloom, turned towards the sun, bright and beautiful because they'd been tended with love.

'How can a person look so gloomy in the face of such happiness?'

Natalia looked over her shoulder to see Tilly making her way towards her, a purposeful look in her eyes.

'How can you say what I looked like when you couldn't even see my face?' Natalia offered up a smile to Tilly, not wanting her to think she was angry with the whole family – only one of them.

'Slumped shoulders, arms hanging limply at your side. And your hips look...' Tilly did the tiniest of squats before straightening up again. 'If hips could have a hangdog expression, then yours would. They look like if they could lie down and become one with the ground, let the dirt swallow them – and the rest of you – whole, then they'd do exactly that.'

Natalia dragged a hand over her eyes, which were heavy and grainy with lack of sleep. 'Sleeping for a long time does sound good.'

'But not forever good, right?' Tilly reached out and touched Natalia's forearm. 'Because that dickhead brother of mine's not worth doing anything that dramatic.'

'Of course not. I just...' *didn't know things could go so wrong so quickly when everything felt so right.*

Tilly's eyes narrowed, shrewdness darkening them. 'You just thought everything was perfect and then somehow it wasn't and you don't know why?'

'Look, you mind reader.' Natalia waggled her finger. 'Get out of that brain of mine.'

'Come.' Tilly took Natalia by the hand and dragged her in the direction of the river. 'All this standing's hurting my legs, which already hurt from standing at the shop all hours of the day.'

Seeing no point in putting up a fight, not even having the energy to do so, Natalia allowed herself to be pulled along, and was as grateful as Tilly to sit down at the river's edge.

'Maybe it's the noise of the water or the way the light plays off of it, but sitting here helps me focus, calms me, sorts the wheat from chaff that are my thoughts.' Tilly brought her knees up to her chest and wrapped her arms around her legs, then laid her head on her knees, her focus on Natalia. 'You know it's not your fault, right? The fight?'

Natalia shook her head. 'I don't see how it's not. I over-reacted. I attacked. I should've held my tongue.'

'Oh shush, you wouldn't be one of us if you were the type to hold your tongue.'

Natalia shook her head, not understanding where Tilly was coming from. 'But I'm not one of you. I'm not family. If I was, it would make what your brother and I have been up to this last week well and truly disgusting.'

'You're not wrong there.' Tilly mock gagged. 'But family doesn't have to involve blood. Surely you've met people during your life that got you, that you felt immediately comfortable with, bonded to?'

Natalia thought of all the jobs she'd held, all the flats she'd lived in, and all the connections she'd made during that time. They could be described as loose at best. Yes, she'd made friends, had acquaintances she'd hung out with, but she'd never felt bonded to them. They'd certainly never felt like family.

'No.' She shook her head. 'Not really. I mean, I've had people I enjoyed spending time with, but we've never.' She lifted her hands and interlaced the fingers. 'Connected. You know what I mean?'

'Not really.' Tilly wrinkled her nose in thought. 'I mean, there've been people who weren't fond of me, or when around me acted a bit like a cat in a paddock full of skittish steers and did their best to avoid me – part of being a girl of the Gordon clan – but I've always had my family. I don't think I could get away from them if I tried. I don't think I'd want to. But I guess all families are a bit like that.'

'I guess.' Natalia turned her attention to the river. Today it had its pace turned down, not so much rippling as rolling its way down stream, barely making a sound.

'Natalia, is that your way of saying you and your family aren't close? That you've literally never felt connected to anyone in your entire life? Until now. Because we're totally connected.' Tilly waggled her brows up and down and then nudged Natalia with her elbow. 'Even if you and Jeremy can't sort things out you know that me and my sisters are going to hound you for the rest of ever, right?'

Natalia found the tiniest of chuckles for Tilly. Barely a laugh. But a way to show that she appreciated their fondness for her. 'Good to know. Remind me to change my mobile number when I leave, okay?'

'Cheeky.' Tilly shook her head, her eyes wide with faux-offense. 'So how have you gone through life feeling the way you have?'

Natalia shrugged. 'Dunno. Just have. I guess it's been hard for me to feel comfortable with people.'

'You felt comfortable with us, didn't you?'

The first genuine smile since her fight with Jeremy made its way to Natalia's face. Tilly was right. She had. Almost from the very beginning. Being with the Gordon family had felt like slipping into a pair of well worn, soft denim jeans that clung to all the right places without feeling squeezed, uncomfortable or like you wanted to rip them off right then and there.

'I'm taking that smile as a yes.' Tilly tipped her head to the sun. 'So what's stopped you feeling that way before?'

Natalia closed her eyes and followed suit, relishing its warmth, the way the heat loosened her muscles. Her mind too. 'I guess with other people I always waited for the penny to drop, for them to realise I wasn't smart enough or funny enough or talented enough to spend time with. It was easier to keep them at arm's length than to give them the chance to tell me how they felt or what they didn't feel.'

Even as the words left her mouth, Natalia realised how daft she sounded. Not because her feelings weren't valid, but that she'd taken the way she believed her parents felt about her and projected them onto other people without giving them a chance.

'Do you think you're *not* smart, funny or talented? In other words, do you think you're dumb, boring and useless?' Tilly's tone was conversational, easy, but it held an edge of surprise, as if she couldn't believe Natalia would think such things about herself. 'Wherever did you get those ideas from? Because they're wrong. You really need to rewrite the script that's running through your head.'

Natalia lay down, then rolled over so she was facing the sunflower field. Anchoring her elbows to the grass, she cupped her chin in her hands and pondered

Tilly's question. Where had she got that idea from? Who'd specifically told her she wasn't smart, talented or funny? It was easy to blame her parents, but they'd never said as such. She'd just taken their lack of enthusiasm, their reticence, their coldness to mean they thought she wasn't worth caring about. But did that mean they didn't care? Was there a chance that they were simply unable to express feelings? That their own upbringings had created people who were incapable of wearing their hearts on their sleeves? Of being bright and vivacious and open with their feelings like the Gordon family? The *girls* of the family, she amended.

She thought back to her visits to her grandparents. On both sides, she'd witnessed stilted conversations that never went deeper than the weather and how work was going. Hugs were non-existent. Dinners quiet, breakfasts even quieter. It had been like visiting strangers.

'Do you think that a person born of two similar people can end up being entirely different?'

'You've met Jeremy, haven't you?' Tilly held up her hand, upon which an ant was traversing the valleys and cliffs of her knuckles. 'He's not much like us.'

Natalia turned to Tilly, surprised she'd say such a thing. 'And what makes you say that?'

'He hates anything to do with our family. Thinks we're stupid for believing in a curse that's plagued our family for generations. Hates the attention that comes with being us. I don't even know why he came back from university. I mean, if he was failing, he could've gone anywhere for work. He didn't need to return to Gordon Glen.'

Natalia nodded, not wanting to divulge Jeremy's reasons for returning: that he felt he had to, that he'd been bullied into coming home.

But had he? If Natalia could be wrong about her parents, if they loved her but didn't know how to show that love, then was there a chance that Jeremy had come back to the Glen not just to appease his family but because he secretly had wanted to? Because he'd missed the place? Had his sisters' behaviour been a convenient excuse to get him to return home, in the same way that Natalia's parents' behaviour had been a convenient excuse for her to keep people at bay? Because, despite her outward demeanour, she didn't know how to be open with people, because her feelings were in arrested development?

Or had been.

The Gordon family had changed that. They'd triggered something within her that made her want to reach out, to be there, to be part of something. To be more.

'Hey, Tilly.' Natalia nudged the person who was more than a friend, only she hadn't realised it until now.

Tilly glanced over. 'You don't have to say it. I know.'

'You know what?' Natalia challenged her.

'You love me. You love us. How could you not?'

Natalia grinned. 'With great difficulty.' Rolling

back over, she pushed herself into a sitting position. 'One more question, and you might think it's a weird one.'

Tilly's laughter was light and low. 'I read tarot cards on the daily and spend my spare time reading books on palm reading and, more recently, how to work with runes. Weird doesn't bother me. What's the question?'

Natalia squeezed her eyes shut, afraid of seeing Tilly fall apart with loud, booming laughter when she finally got the words out. 'What do you like about me? What makes me likeable? Why do you see me as family?'

'I see.' Tilly's tone was kind, understanding. So much so, Natalia felt so seen she wanted nothing more than to scurry over to the sunflower field and bury her head amongst their leaves out of embarrassment. 'You don't see yourself as others do. Oh, Natalia.'

A hand fell on Natalia's mid-back and began to circle it. Feeling safe, secure, no longer afraid of being humiliated or embarrassed, Natalia opened her eyes to see Tilly's eyes were as sad as her smile.

'You're a brilliant person, Natalia. You're hard-working, smart, funny. All those good things. But more than that, you're the most non-judgemental person I've ever met. You take people as they are and you let them be. Take my family, for example. Half the village ignore us because they think we're strange. The other half are nice to us because they're afraid of what they think we might be able to do. You've just gone with it.

Gone with us. We were safe to love you because you allowed us to be who we are. And if no one's ever told you how brilliant you are or allowed you to simply be who you are, that's on them. Also, maybe just because they didn't say it, it doesn't mean they didn't think it.'

Natalia nodded, thinking back to her relationship with her parents. For so long she'd believed she'd known the truth about their feelings for her, but that was based on assumption, not reality. If she wanted to know the truth, she'd have to ask, then be okay with the answer, whatever it was. Even then, it didn't have to affect her. Didn't have to make her morph into their version of Natalia. She could stand on her own two feet and be the person she was destined to be, be it smart or silly, funny or serious, zany or thoughtful, loving or… loving. Because unloving was not an option, not when she was surrounded by people she'd come to love. Even if one member of that family was angry with her at that moment.

'Thank you, Tilly. You're wise beyond your years.'

'Don't tell my sisters that. They'll start coming to me for advice, and there aren't enough hours in the day to deal with all their issues, whether real or made up in their heads. Anyway, I didn't want you to leave thinking that we didn't want you here. We'd miss you. Which brings me to why I really came.' Tilly broke the hug, her cheeks suffused with pink. 'Don't tell Jeremy I told you this…'

'Need I remind you that Jeremy's not talking to me, so there's no chance of me spilling any truths.'

'Perhaps not right now, but there's always one day, especially for you two.' Tilly brought her two index fingers together and made a kissy noise, then cracked up. 'God, I'm a nine-year-old. Ignore me. Except don't. Not about this. What I want to say when I'm not being ridiculous is... Don't be hard on Jeremy. He's had it tougher than it looks.'

Natalia dipped her chin and raised her brows. 'Tougher than it looks in that he's had three love-obsessed siblings constantly on his case to find someone to fall in love with? That it's been his life since the moment he was old enough to say "I do". That sometimes being part of a family so all-encompassing can feel claustrophobic and you're torn between wanting to escape but not being able to because secretly you adore each and every one of them?'

'Look who's the wise one now?' Tilly shook her head in admiration. 'You get him in a way no one else ever has or ever could. That's why you two are meant to be.' Tilly shrugged as if it was a fait accompli.

Natalia wasn't so sure. In all her years of imagining meeting someone who might love her, she'd thought it would be easy. You'd meet, get to know each other, work out the niggles, then live happily ever after, dealing with the odd issue as it came up like a team. As her parents had – but with more physical affection and kind words for each other. A lot more.

'And if we're not? Does that mean you're done for? That the curse will stay in effect? And,' Natalia bit down on her lip, hoping she wouldn't offend Tilly with her next question. 'Do you actually, truly, really believe in the curse?'

'Because we're mad if we do?' Tilly snorted. 'I mean, you wouldn't be wrong.' Her expression grew serious. 'If I were to be honest, when I really think long and hard about it in my cold, lonely bed in the middle of the night, I believe that in believing in the curse we've cursed ourselves. But since it's told to us from such a young age, it's really hard to find a way to not believe in it, if that makes sense.'

'So you're stuck in an infinite loop of your own making.'

'Unfortunately.' Tilly's lips turned down into a frown. 'And, to put it as ineloquently as possible, it sucks. If Jeremy doesn't sort himself out, I worry that we'll find ways to block love from entering our life. Or be too afraid to try in case the person we like rejects us. But if that does happen, at least we can blame it on the curse and Jeremy being single. So there's that at least.' Tilly attempted a brave smile, but it didn't reach her eyes.

Forgetting her own woes, and knowing all too well what it was like not to try for fear of rejection, Natalia leaned over and shoulder bumped Tilly. 'Don't be so hard on yourself. You're amazing. I bet if you were to turn all that amazingness you have on that guy you like, he won't just come around, he'll run around, grateful that you've finally given him the green light.'

Tilly's lower lip pushed out and shook her head. Somehow, I don't think so. I don't think a famous, worldly man like Benjamin would see much worth in a village-loving girl like me.'

'Well, at one point I bet you thought your brother would never like any girl enough to break up with her. Or kind of break up with her, since we were still so new.' *'Early days'*, as Jeremy had put it, even though it felt like they'd been together for far longer.

'So what you're saying is that the unthinkable can become thinkable?' Tilly pushed herself up and reached a hand out for Natalia.

Natalia took it and allowed herself to be pulled up. 'I'm saying exactly that. He's back at Christmas, right?'

'That's the word on the street. Or the lane.' Tilly waggled her brows up and down.

'Well, instead of magic, maybe it's time for a little Christmas miracle to happen in Gordon Glen.'

'Don't tell my mother that.' Tilly grimaced. 'She'd be horrified to think there was a festive deity out there who had the upper hand when it came to love in these parts.'

'Mad, you all are.' Natalia brought Tilly in for a brief hug. 'Thanks for being a friend. It's been nice getting to know you and your family. You're a special bunch.'

'Does that mean you're leaving?' Tilly's brows furrowed. 'For good? You're not going to take my advice and give Jeremy a chance to sort himself out?'

Natalia pursed her lips in thought as she took in the sparkling river for one of the last times. 'I don't think I can. Not after the way we left things. And seeing your brother regularly will only hurt me here...' She touched the spot where her heart lay beneath. 'While being another reminder of yet another failure.' With a long exhale, Natalia shook her head. 'It's time for me to be a grownup. To do the grownup thing. I can't keep swanning around from flat to flat, job to job the rest of my life. It's time to settle down and get serious. No more babysitting pets or plants, or flowers on picturesque farms for me, I'm afraid.' Natalia ignored the clanging in her chest.

Her heart could be alarmed by the path she was about to take, could rail against it, but her heart had only ever hurt her, while her head had served her well enough.

'Well, if that's your decision, then that's your decision, but make sure you stop in and say goodbye, because we'll all miss you. And that includes that daft brother of mine. In fact, he'll miss you most of all.'

'Did you see that in the cards?'

'No. I saw it in the way he looks at you – like you're the brightest sunflower in the field.'

Natalia pressed her lips together tight enough to hurt, trying to stem the prickling that stung her eyes. 'I promise I'll stop in,' she whispered, then turned away before Tilly could see the tears fall.

Just one more day, she repeated as she made her way to the farmhouse. *One more day and you can pretend you never fell in love with Gordon Glen, the family it was named after, or the son of said family, for the rest of your life.*

TWENTY

A low, angry rumble caused Jeremy to stir from his sleep.

A motorcycle, he decided. Someone passing through Gordon Glen late at night.

He pulled his pillow over his head and snuggled back down again, annoyed to have been woken after having taken so long to get to sleep. His mind full of thoughts of Natalia, of finding a way to apologise. Not in the hopes of getting back together, but in the hope that they could go back to being, if not friends, then civil with each other. She'd gone through so much, endured rejection after rejection at the hands of people who loved her. He didn't want the cycle to repeat because of his behaviour. She needed to know it wasn't her that had caused the issue. It was – well and truly – him.

His mind alert once again, Jeremy began acknowledging the parts of his body, starting with the toes on his right foot; a basic meditation his mother had taught him when he was a boy and struggling with heading to the Land of Nod.

Big right toe, the toe next to that, middle right toe, the toe next to th-

The rumble came again. Closer. Louder. Definitely not a motorcycle.

Jeremy rolled onto his back and picked up his mobile. It sounded like thunder, but surely it wasn't. Not again. Lightning didn't strike twice. Or, in this case, unexpected, unreported thunderstorms. Bringing up the radar, he took in the small blob on the screen. Just a passing storm. It'd last five minutes, if that. Nothing to worry about. The vegetables would survive it well enough, and there was always the chance it would break up or pass around Gordon Glen...

NATALIA AWOKE WITH A JOLT, her heart pounding in her chest, every fibre of her body feeling as if it had been electrocuted. Pushing herself up onto her elbows, she turned on the bedside lamp, then glanced around the room, half-wondering if there'd been an earthquake. Noticing that nothing had toppled and everything was where it should be, she leaned back in relief.

Just a bad dream, she reassured her body, which was still humming with low-level anxiety at the rude awakening.

Placing her hands on her stomach, Natalia attempted to inhale and exhale slowly, counting to four on one breath, then to six on the next.

Her body jerked involuntarily as a flash lit up the bedroom.

Just a car going by. Nothing more.

She closed her eyes again with the plan to restart her breathing, but found the air catch in her throat as a rumble roared from somewhere in the distance.

Too angry to be terrified, an internal scream rose from deep down in her gut. Really? A storm? Out of nowhere? She'd checked the weather report just before bedtime and there'd been no mention of it. She'd gone to sleep safe in the knowledge that her last duty in Gordon Glen was going to go off without a hitch. Yes, her love life might be in tatters, but the sunflowers were going to be in full bloom and as beautiful and in perfect condition as possible for the residents of the area to enjoy.

Another flash illuminated the room, and Natalia began counting the seconds, waiting for the thunder to follow.

One. Two. Three. Four. Five...

She reached twenty-five and sighed in relief as the grumble followed. The storm was ages away. Probably wouldn't even reach Gordon Glen. Natalia inched back down under the covers, drawing them up around her. The storm could make itself known all it wanted from far away. She had to get some shuteye if she was going to be peppy and personable to all who visited

Francesca's farm, rather than a bloodshot-eyed, bleary monster.

Resuming her breathing, she felt the delightful wooziness that came with dropping back into sleep, then froze as from above came the unmistakeable sound of juicy drops of rain hitting the roof. Followed by lightning. Followed by thunder. Seven seconds away.

This storm wasn't going anywhere.

Pushing back the covers, Natalia forced herself out of the safety of her shorty pyjamas and into a pair of denim shorts and a simple grey tank top. No point wearing too much clothing if she was just going to get soaked saving the sunflowers. How? She had no idea. But she owed it to Francesca, to the people of Gordon Glen, to the Gordons themselves to do her best to protect them.

DESPITE IT ONLY HAVING JUST GONE THREE in the morning, Jeremy had shaved his face. He'd done the washing up. Folded the pile of laundry sitting beside his bed, even his socks. And swept the kitchen floor. Unfortunately, distraction wasn't doing its job, and his mind kept betraying him by wandering to Natalia. Hoping she was okay, that she wasn't too scared by the storm. That she'd remember to dance it away, whooping and hollering with all her might, rather than hide from it.

Twice he'd picked up his mobile to text her, just to check in, to let her know she'd get through it, but pride as much as believing that she didn't want to hear from him had kept his fingers from prodding the surface of its screen.

Beyond the sitting room window, the storm raged. Rose bushes scratched the glass, their leaves whipping the panes, the thorns creating eerie screeches as they dragged across the smooth surface. Every few seconds, lightning flashed and thunder roared. The storm wasn't on top of them, but it was close, and it showed no signs of abating.

Jeremy refreshed the web browser, hoping the weather radar would show a cheerier picture just as a message notification pinged onto the laptop's screen. The momentary hope that it would be from Natalia fell away as he noticed Gemma's name at the top.

Jeremy. River's going to flood. Flash flooding alert, too. Stay home.

He rolled his eyes. Stay home? It wasn't even light yet. Where was he going to go? Where would anyone go in this weather? You'd have to be out of your mind to leave your house.

Continuing to the weather radar's page, he checked out the rain radar, instantly regretting his decision. This wasn't just a passing storm, it was a long line of turmoil that could cause more than just a bit of flash flooding. If the river rose high enough to flood, it would destroy the sunflowers, drown the fields, ruin his auntie's livelihood. It'd take months to come back from a storm like this. An entire season would be all but lost.

There was only one other person who knew this as well as he, and he feared they'd try to help.

Bypassing his car keys, Jeremy grabbed his raincoat and bolted out the door, arms and legs pumping, one word driving every move: Natalia.

Above him, lightning flashed every few seconds, the thunder growling so continuously he could no longer tell when an old rumble ended and a fresh rumble began.

Please stay inside. Please stay inside.

If she became caught in flood waters, they might sweep her away. The worst could happen. And the worst he couldn't bear to think about. If he were to lose her like that, for her to no longer exist on this earth, in this universe, his heart would never recover.

Anger at his pride, at his stupidity, spurred Jeremy on. Not even the wind whipping around him or the rain pummelling his skin slowed him down.

I'm coming, Natalia. Don't do anything brave.

FEAR THRUMMED THROUGH HER, but Natalia refused to let it win. In the seconds she'd taken to assess the situation, she'd understood there wasn't much she could do about the sunflowers. She wasn't strong enough to drive stakes that deep into the ground, let alone tall enough to create covers, but she could still protect the farm's vegetables.

The rain pelted down, hitting her skin like millions of tiny needles. Natalia scurried inside to grab the raincoat that hung on a hook just inside the kitchen door. Already soaked, she knew it wouldn't protect her from getting wetter, but it'd help her stop feeling like a human voodoo doll placed in the hands of a vengeful weather god.

Shrugging it on, Natalia raced out to the shed and began gathering as many stakes and as much tarpaulin as she could carry. Stopping to grab a mallet on the way out, she jumped in fright as another flash lit up the sky, followed by a boom of thunder.

You've got this. It'll be okay. You'll be okay.

Despite all the confidence in her mind's voice, her body refused to believe it and began shaking uncontrollably as she rushed to the fields, trying to remember which vegetables were the most profitable and therefore worth saving first. With fear blocking rational thought, Natalia gave up and focused on the courgettes. Dropping her tools, she sank to the sodden ground, feeling it squish beneath her weight, then took a stake, one edge of shade cloth and the mallet and got to work banging the stake into the ground.

Refusing to look up, keeping her gaze to the ground, ignoring the raging wind and rain, the almost constant lightning and the continual thunder, Natalia worked her way down the row, securing stake after stake, praying the effort would be worth it. That she wasn't risking her life and sanity for nothing. Every few minutes, against her will, she found herself looking for Jeremy, hoping he'd turn up. Hoping his work on the farm was worth more to him than his hatred of her. Her heart sinking when no call of her name was to be heard, when no face that she'd come to love came into view. Saving the farm's crops was all on her. Perhaps it was the universe's way of making her pay for thinking she could get out of her destiny, that there was another option that didn't involve returning to her family home and following the route expected of her.

Clenching her teeth, as much in determination as to stop them chittering, Natalia shuffled along the increasingly muddy ground, keeping low, and drove another stake into the sloppy dirt.

ROUNDING THE FARMHOUSE, his chest heaving, the blood pumping in his ears causing them to roar as loudly as the thunder, Jeremy came to a halt as he caught sight of something huddled over by the courgettes. No animal in its right mind would be out in this weather – unless that animal was of the human variety and named Jeremy. Or Natalia.

Begging his legs to not give up, he bolted in her direction, calling her name, despite knowing it was useless, a waste of energy. The wind and thunder so intense his words were whipped away into the ether.

Reaching her side, Jeremy collapsed onto the

ground and reached out. Natalia startled at his touch and let out a terrified scream.

'Natalia. It's me. I'm sorry. I should've come earlier. I'm the worst.'

Her face was as stark as the full moon that had hung in the sky when Jeremy had gone to bed. Her eyes as wide.

'It's fine.' She dipped her head, picked up a fresh stake and began hammering.

'Leave it.' He rested his hand on her forearm. 'It's not worth it.'

She shrugged him off. 'Of course it is. We saved the vegetables once. We can do it again.'

'Not if the river floods.'

Natalia paused, her head turning to look at him, her gaze panic stricken. 'Flood? As in the farm?'

'All of it.' Jeremy confirmed with a nod. His heart sinking at the loss, the devastation, the rebuilding that was to come. 'We've got to go. It's not safe.'

Lightning flashed and thunder crashed; the storm now on top of them.

Natalia's nostrils flared. 'We're not going anywhere. We can pile sandbags up along the riverbank. There's time. There has to be.'

Jeremy shook his head. 'There are no sandbags. Aunty Francesca only has them delivered if the weather report deems it necessary.'

'Then why were they delivered yesterday?' Natalia's brows drew together in consternation.

Aunty Francesca planned for this to happen. All of it. Natalia. The sunflowers. The weather. Us.

Jeremy pushed the absurd thought out of his head. There was no way his aunt had that kind of power, or that she could've known she'd need to get a load of sandbags in because an unexpected thunderstorm was on the horizon.

'I don't know.' Jeremy raised his hands, feeling more helpless than ever. He didn't get this world he lived in. Didn't understand the women around him. Or their ways. But that didn't mean he had to rail against them, create blockades to keep them at a distance. Or build walls of emotionless sandbags so they couldn't needle him with their ever-present, all-giving kind of love.

'Well, it doesn't matter.' Natalia pushed herself up and wiped her muddied hands on her jacket. 'We're going to save the farm.'

Turning on her heel, she strode towards the farmhouse, giving Jeremy no option other than to obey and follow. As he'd always ended up doing for the women he loved.

'I HAVE NO ARMS.' Natalia heaved the second to last sandbag onto the barrier she and Jeremy had built over the last two hours. 'My legs are dead. I don't even know if I'm alive anymore.'

Above her, lightning slashed the sky as if to remind her she was very much there and in the presence of her greatest fear. Except she didn't feel scared. She scanned her body, looking for goose bumps, or a jittery feeling in her chest, or the urge to run and hide in the darkest, quietest place possible. All was silent. If you ignored the agonised screaming of her muscles and the painful thudding of her heart as it whomped against her chest.

'I. Feel. You.' Jeremy dumped the last sandbag down. 'I don't think I even have the energy to get back to the farmhouse, let alone my own home.'

'Then don't.' Climbing atop their newly created boundary, Natalia patted the spot next to her. 'Maybe I'm courting certain doom, but I feel obliged to sit and wait and pray to the weather gods that the storm will move on before the river gets any higher.'

'Maybe we ought to try the infamous storm dance to get it to stop?' Jeremy heaved himself up with a soft groan, then swivelled around and let his legs dangle towards the river that raged below them.

'I don't know if my legs have it in them, but if you think it'll work, I could beg them to go the extra mile.'

Jeremy sighed. 'Honestly, I don't think there's magic enough in this world to stop that water rising if it wants to.'

'You don't think there's magic in this world full stop.' Weariness overcame Natalia and her whole body slumped, devoid of energy.

'Well, I've yet to see proof of it.'

Lightning brightened the world around them,

revealing the swirling water that grew higher by the minute.

Natalia stifled a yawn. 'And I think you're not wrong. I guess if there was magic in the world, I wouldn't have to be someone else for people to love me.'

JEREMY WAS unsure if the comment was directed at Natalia's relationship with her parents, at him, or the way she felt about herself. Whether it was one of or all three, the idea that she didn't believe she was good enough as she was to be loved by those around her pained him. If only she could see herself the way he saw her, maybe then she'd give up caring about what others thought. And maybe the only way that could happen was if he stopped trying to control the world around him, when it seemed the inevitable was to happen – that fate was always going to have the last say.

Inhaling, Jeremy held his breath and, in the dark, searched out Natalia's hand. Finding it hanging limply at her side, he wrapped his hand around it, gave it a squeeze and exhaled, preparing himself for rejection, for pain, for everything he deserved for being so stubborn, so horrible to the one woman in his life who'd never once tried to push him in any direction. Who'd never tried to tell him what to do or who to be. Who'd not let her own experiences and beliefs in life taint how she saw others. Even if it had changed how she saw herself.

'Natalia, you don't have to change, because you're perfect as you are.'

Natalia remained silent, her hand still in his, showing no signs of reaction, of even hearing his words.

'Anyone who tries to tell you who to be, or makes you feel less for being who you are, is an idiot. And I'm sorry if that means I'm saying your parents are idiots, even though for people who are meant to be super intelligent, they're acting super stupidly.'

Lightning flashed, briefly illuminating Natalia's face. Taut with unshed emotion. Trailed with moisture, which could be rain or tears, Jeremy didn't know. Perhaps would never know if he didn't get this moment right.

'If that's the case, then why is it so easy for people to let me go? I work hard, I do my best, I only say what needs to be said when pushed to my limit.' She nudged his shoulder. 'And, while we have this moment, I'm sorry for saying you were defined by your family. It was rude. Inexcusable. I was out of line.'

Jeremy returned the nudge. 'Or perfectly in line, because you weren't wrong. My family has defined me. How could they not have? Every interaction, every second spent with them, shaped me. All these years, I've been told I'm the key to their happiness, and that kind of pressure can make a person run the other way.'

'I get that,' Natalia yawned. 'I felt pressure to be a certain way, and I actually ran.'

'And I'm glad you eventually ran here.' Jeremy counted the seconds between the lightning and the thunder. Seven. The storm was moving away. Finally. 'You managed to do the unthinkable and get me to pull my head out of my arse.'

'Charming,' Natalia murmured. 'Couldn't you have said I made you see things in a different light?'

'A better light.'

Against him, Natalia shivered. Releasing her hand, Jeremy curled his arm around her shoulders, bringing her closer.

'Better. Brighter. You've given me clarity. I understand now that I'm not under my family's thumb any more than their happiness depends on me. We choose our paths. We choose our happiness.'

Natalia lay her head against his shoulder. 'So, what do we do next with all this clarity? Can we start again?'

'I'd like that.' Jeremy's heart swelled with happiness and he felt the now-familiar tug at his solar plexus. 'Hi Natalia, I'm Jeremy.'

'Hi Jeremy.' A yawn followed. 'I'm Natalia. Pleased to meet you.'

They shook hands, and, as damp as they were, Jeremy sensed the spark reignite.

Romantic love may not be on the cards – or in the cards, as his sisters would say – but he'd found steady ground with the woman he loved. Whatever happened next… Well, for all he knew, that was written in the stars. He just had to relinquish control and see what the new day would bring.

TWENTY-ONE

In the distance, a cow bellowed. Closer by, a morning chorus of early risers twittered hello to the world. In front of them, the river rippled, glistening in the morning sun.

Natalia went to stretch her arms, but found them pinned to her side. Panic thrummed through her at being unable to move. Had the river risen and whisked her off the mortal coil? Was this death? Being in the place where you met your end, able to hear, to feel, but physically stuck?

She attempted to lift her arms once more and felt a little give. Not stuck. Just trapped. By what? Forcing her exhausted eyes open, she glanced down to see a bigger pair of arms wrapped around her. Further down, a long leg was hooked over her own, keeping her in place.

Jeremy. Her Jeremy. The man who saw her, who understood her, who accepted her for who she was.

More than that, he relished it. Treasured her. And they'd agreed to start again.

Twisting around as much as she could, she took in the state of the sunflowers. Her moment of joy fizzling as she noted the raggedy leaves, the battered petals. Still beautiful, but not what they once were. A bit like her relationship with Jeremy. But if he could see the beauty in her, even after their ups and downs, then perhaps the crowds would see the beauty in the flowers. Either way, the farm was safe. The sunflowers would see another season.

Natalia giggled as Jeremy nuzzled her nape in his sleep, the way he had in the before times.

'What did I do?' The words were soft, slurred as he struggled to wake up.

'Just nuzzled me like a cat hoping for some attention.'

'Oh. Shit. Sorry.' Jeremy broke his hold on Natalia and scooted backwards. 'I'm not, you know, trying to push things.'

Natalia went to run her hand through her hair, grimacing as it got stuck. 'And who'd want to when the woman you were nuzzling has a rat's nest for a hairdo?' She rolled her eyes at herself.

Jeremy reached out and tucked a clump of damp, raggedy hair behind her ear. 'Can't say I noticed. You always look perfect to me.'

'"Perfect".' Natalia's heart glowed at the word. 'You said I was perfect last night. You said I gave you clarity.'

'Because you did. Because you have.' Jeremy climbed off the sandbags and held his hand out to Natalia.

Gratefully, she took it, her muscles protesting with every movement after the previous night's exertion.

'And now? Do you still have clarity?'

Jeremy's thumb caressed the back of her hand. 'More than ever. The storm washed away my stupidity. The sun's illuminated everything more than lightning ever could.'

'And what do you think?' *Think that you want me.*

'I think I need to get you to the farmhouse and cook you a hearty breakfast while you shower and get out of those damp, muddy clothes. I think after breakfast, we need to go for a walk and spend time together. Proper time. Not the kind of time where we're yelling at each other or traipsing sandbags over muddy fields. Then, I think we should set the sunflower festival up and greet those who come.' He looked over at the sunflowers and grimaced. 'Maybe offer a discount for buying them. Then, I think we should cook dinner together. After that-'

Tiring of Jeremy's plans to dip their way back into a relationship, Natalia reached up on her tiptoes, placed her hands on either side of his cheeks and sealed his lips with a kiss.

As soft as it was long, as sweet as it was filled with promise.

Jeremy broke away first, his lips curling into a smile that saw his eyes sparkle. 'Or we could do that.'

'A lot.'

'More than a lot.'

'A lot, a lot, then.' Natalia took his hand.

'How about forever?' Jeremy wrapped his arm around her waist and brought her to him. 'Would that work?'

'I think we'd make it work.'

Tilting her head once more, more than happy to keep the kisses coming, Natalia startled as a loud rustling came from the sunflowers.

'Oh my god, you're okay. Both of you. Thank the goddess.'

Natalia grinned as the Gordon women, led by Agnes, traipsed towards them, their faces four almost identical pictures of relief.

Agnes raised her arms and brought Natalia and Jeremy into a hug. 'You have no idea how worried we were when the storm went and went and went. We did our best to dance it away, but it was determined to settle in. Like it had its own agenda and refused to be swayed.'

Gemma crossed her arms, her gaze going from the tops of Natalia and Jeremy's heads to the tips of their feet. 'Why are you so damp? Don't tell me you were out in this all night?'

Natalia shrugged. 'We were afraid the crops would be ruined if we didn't sandbag the riverbank.'

'You what?' Clare ducked past them and ran the few steps to the river. 'You did too. You're bloody mad. It would've taken you an age to build this up. You could've been struck by lightning. Killed. All for a few fancy types of tomatoes and beans.'

'Well,' Jeremy lifted Natalia's and his entwined hands. 'It was worth it.'

'Bloody hell.' Tilly's eyes were wide with wonder. 'You two are steaming.'

Jeremy rolled his eyes. 'I mean, we're a good-looking couple, but I wouldn't say we're about to end up in the pages of a fashion magazine or star in some X-rated movie.'

'No, I mean you're actually steaming.' Tilly flicked her hand in their direction. 'There's steam coming off your heads and shoulders.'

'And what's with the hand holding?' Clare bounced up and down on her feet. 'Are you saying what I think you're saying? Are your hands saying what I think they're saying?'

'That we got out of our own way and decided not to listen to the people around us?' Natalia did her best to give the four a stern look but, on seeing the happiness in their eyes, gave up. 'Or we simply decided to stop ignoring what was staring us in the face?'

'Love,' Tilly breathed. 'True love. The kind that comes once in a lifetime.'

'The kind that breaks curses.' Gemma nodded sagely.

'The type that means we're finally going to get our own happily ever afters.' Clare resumed her bouncing, this time with added clapping. 'I can't believe this is finally happening.'

'And I can't believe I didn't realise our magic wasn't working for a reason.' Agnes wrapped herself in a happy hug. 'The best reason. It just needed time. Time and a good storm to be weathered to make you see how right you are for each other. You two are going to be so happy together.'

'Did you see this in the cards?' Jeremy replied, his tone tinged with sarcasm.

'No, my beautiful boy. I can see it in your eyes. Both pairs of eyes.' Her gaze dropped to their chests. 'And in your hearts. And in your auras.'

'Oh, so you read auras now?' Tilly pahed. 'Of course you do.'

'Mum,' Clare clucked her tongue. 'Stop being a show-off.'

'Reads auras, my arse.' Gemma rolled her eyes. 'She reads auras as well as Jeremy reads cards.'

Natalia grinned. She'd never thought she'd see the day that a Gordon girl would be sceptical about anything esoteric.

Agnes' left brow rose. 'Unbelievers remain unbeloved, my dear.'

'Oh, whatever.' Gemma waved her mother's comment away.

Tilly sucked in a breath, her eyes widening. 'But Jeremy does read cards. Remember what he said at the pub when Natalia first came? Something about a decision that needed to be made. A choice. Pain being caused...'

'And a whole lot of water.' Clare shook her head. 'Jeremy, there's hope for you yet.'

'I don't think so.' Jeremy tightened his grip on Natalia. 'I'm happy as I am, thank you very much. The only future I need to think about is the one standing beside me.'

'Good to hear.' Clare clapped her hands together. 'Well, now that these two have finally sorted themselves out, let's head into town. Who knows who might've turned up now that Jeremy's hooked up good and proper.' Linking arms with her sisters, the girls set off through the sunflowers, chatting with excitement.

'Those daughters of mine.' Agnes shook her head, her lips curved upwards, her cheeks high with the fondness, the love she held for her family. 'And that includes you, Natalia.'

Natalia pressed her lips together as her heart grew in her chest and hot tears prickled the back of her eyes.

'Welcome to the family.'

Leaning in, Agnes pressed a kiss to Natalia's cheeks, bathing Natalia in her earthy, patchouli scent.

Natalia brought an arm around Agnes' shoulders. 'Thank you for having me,' she whispered in her ear.

'Thank you for having *us*,' Agnes replied. 'We're so grateful for you.'

The bank broke, sending tears down Natalia's cheeks. Never in her life had she imagined a family being grateful for her, for a mother to see her as special, as someone to be embraced rather than tolerated.

Agnes broke the hug and looked over at her son. 'See you two for dinner tonight?'

'Will you hunt us down if we decide to do dinner alone?'

Agnes' nose narrowed, her lips compressed.

'That's a yes.' Jeremy sighed. 'Lucky Natalia and I have the rest of ever to find moments to spend alone time together.'

'Exactly.' With a nod, Agnes turned around, her kaftan billowing out as she followed the path her daughters had walked.

'"The rest of ever"?' Natalia wrapped her arms around Jeremy, bringing him close, feeling the heat of his body radiate against her, despite the damp clothing. 'You really, truly mean it?'

'I've never meant anything more.' Jeremy pressed a kiss to her forehead. 'You are smart.' He kissed her cheek. 'You are thoughtful.' Her temple. 'You are fierce.' The tip of her nose. 'You are gorgeous.' His lips touched hers for the briefest of moments, but held an eternity of promises. 'Inside and out.'

Natalia returned the kiss, feeling the spark between them flare and take flight as the kiss deepened, their mouths opening to each other, their tongues saying what their hearts had not been able to.

Until now.

A rustle beside them broke the kiss.

Following the sound of the noise, Natalia opened her eyes and gasped. 'Jeremy, look.'

Following suit, Jeremy's eyes widened at the scene

before them. 'That's not how sunflowers are meant to work.'

Around them the sunflowers, beaten and bruised by the storm, but as beautiful as ever, bobbed their heads in their direction, their leaves waving despite the lack of breeze, as if silently applauding their getting together. Their choosing each other. Their choosing love.

'Maybe I was wrong.' Jeremy cupped Natalia's cheek. 'Maybe magic is real.'

'Maybe magic is made of love.' Natalia's heart stilled as she prepared to put it on the line. 'And the sunflowers feel just how much I love you.'

'And how much I love you.'

Natalia gasped as she felt a tug in the centre of her chest, pulling her closer to Jeremy. If she half-closed her eyes, she could almost see a glimmering cord connecting them.

'You feel it, too?'

She looked up to see Jeremy shaking his head, his eyes luminous with wonder.

'I thought I was going crazy.'

Natalia checked to see if the cord was still visible, but it had disappeared, yet the energy pulsating between them remained. 'You've felt it before?'

'Only since the second I laid eyes on you.'

'Wow.' Natalia had no words to express what she'd seen, what she'd felt, what she believed. Perhaps it was better to accept that some things in life simply were magical, and to let them be rather than finding ways to disprove them. 'Well, it is what it is, and I'm glad that it is.'

'Me too.' Jeremy dropped a kiss on the top of her mussed hair. 'So,' he linked his arm through hers. 'Which of my sisters is next in the firing line of Cupid's arrow, do you think?'

'Well,' Natalia reached out and caressed the sunflowers as they made their way through the sodden field. 'I heard a certain television host is heading home...'

Jeremy groaned. 'I already feel sorry for the man. He doesn't know what's about to hit him.'

'Only the best family in the world.' Natalia nodded at the sunflowers, their leaves continuing to brush each other, their heads bobbing, congratulating the happy couple on a union that would last through ups and downs, times of drought and times of abundance, and, perhaps most importantly, storms and sunshine.

ACKNOWLEDGMENTS

I'm going to keep acknowledgements short, sweet and starting with... You.

A massive thank you to you, lovely reader, for taking the time to read my book. I truly appreciate your support, and hope that the first book in the Gordon Glen series brought you joy.

To my wonderful editor, Natalie Pole. Your support has helped me overcome all the fear, all the worry, all the imposter syndrome that comes with writing a book. You're amazing.

Finally, and as always, to my number one supporter, my husband. Thank you for believing in me, even when I don't believe in myself.

ABOUT THE AUTHOR

When she was little, Kellie Hailes declared she was going to write books when she grew up. It took a while for her to get there, with a career as a radio copywriter, freelance copywriter and beauty editor filling the dream-hole, until now. When the characters in her head aren't dictating their story to her, she can be found taking short walks, slow runs, eating good cheese and hanging out for her next coffee fix.

ALSO BY KELLIE HAILES

The Cosy Coffee Shop of Promises

The Big Little Festival

Christmas at the Second Chance Chocolate Shop

The Little Unicorn Gift Shop

The Little Bookshop at Herring Cove

The Little Bakery of Hopes and Dreams

Finding Home in Dolphin's Cove

Printed in Great Britain
by Amazon